SAVING SARAH

NAN REINHARDT

Saving Sarah

Copyright © 2017 Nan Reinhardt

Published by Fine Wine Romances

ISBN-13: 978-1-7336913-1-4

ISBN-10: 1733691316

Cover art by Chipperish Media

Cover art and logos Copyright © 2013 Chipperish Media

For Jim, who shows me every day what it means to be cherished.
Thank you, my love.

CHAPTER 1

A Lake Michigan breeze tugged Sarah Bennett's auburn tresses from the tight clip at her neck as she stood on the ferry next to her friend Julie Miles. They had been more than halfway across before Sarah worked up the courage to leave the car that was parked in the belly of the huge vessel. Julie had brought her coffee and a muffin that Sarah had only nibbled on. The women sat together quietly until Sarah opened the car door and stepped out. Even now she couldn't help scanning the area, peering into the tinted windows of the ferry cabin, searching…praying.

"He's not here, you know," Julie said, almost as if she could read Sarah's thoughts.

"In the clear-thinking part of my brain, I know that." Sarah stared out across the water, watching the breeze whip up tiny whitecaps on the surface. "But he's still out there and he won't give up."

"You don't know that." Julie sipped her coffee. "You hit the son of a bitch on the head with a skillet, baby. If he's smart, he'll stay away from you."

Sarah shivered in spite of the early May sunshine warming her bare arms. That awful night replayed in her head in an endless terrifying loop. After she'd bashed her ex-husband, she'd grabbed her emergency pack, shoved her laptop and wallet into it, and run down to check on Mack. The night watchman was groggy from being punched out and his lip was bleeding, but he was alive, thank God. Paul wasn't stupid; he hadn't hit Mack hard enough to really hurt him.

She turned to Julie. "I should've told the police about Paul when I used Mack's phone to call the ambulance." The horror of skulking around the alley behind the shelter, casting around for the long black Lincoln, and praying desperately that she wouldn't be stopped by Paul's driver sent another agonizing shiver through her.

"Sarah, come on, drink your coffee," Julie urged. "You need the caffeine and the sugar."

Sarah tried a small sip, but her heart rose to her throat as she remembered the scene she'd left behind three nights earlier. Maybe she should've stayed with Mack, but he was conscious and fully aware that she'd called for help. When he saw her backpack, he'd encouraged her to just go, so with a reassuring hug, she'd fled—straight to Julie and Will. And now she'd brought her dearest friend into this horrible mess.

Sarah pulled the clip out of her hair, raking shaky fingers through her unruly curls. "Jesus, Julie, what if I'd killed him? What if he'd died? How could I have lived with being a murderer?" She swallowed a sob, but gave it up and put her head down on the rail and wept.

Julie drew closer and wrapped her arms around Sarah, turning to allow her to rest her cheek against her friend's strong shoulder. She patted her gently, whispering wordless comforts and finally reached in her pocket for a tissue. "Here, dry your eyes. That's not what happened. When Will got there, Paul was gone and Mack was doing fine. We've got this. It's going to be okay."

Sarah pressed the tissue to her eyes, then she blew her nose and took a deep breath. She twisted the wet paper in her hand, searching for the words to describe the scene with Paul, still needing to process it. "So fucking typical of him to show up in a limo and lurk outside the shop."

"I still don't quite get why you didn't just call the police when you saw the car?" Julie crossed her arms, her head tilted in a question, not a judgment.

Sarah drank the coffee, letting it warm her all the way down to her belly. "Really, Jules? Parking on the street isn't a crime. What would I have said to the cops?"

"They could've at least checked it out, don't you think?"

"You sound like Mack." Sarah shook her head before she handed Julie her cup, gathered the tangled curls into a knot again, and clipped it in place.

"Mack's a smart man." Julie handed her coffee back before resting her elbows on the stainless steel railing. "Honey, you'll be safe in Willow Bay. I rented the apartment in my name and Noah Dixon is the soul of discretion. Carrie and Sophie will take you in and nobody wants to cross those two anyway. We take care of our own in the village. So it's going to be fine. Trust me."

"I trust you." Sarah met Julie's steady blue gaze. And she did trust her…mostly.

Sarah latched the deadbolt after Julie and Will left. No sooner had she walked away than she hurried back and double-checked it and the chain on the door of the apartment above the old boathouse at Dixon's Marina. It was a charming place with deep-cushioned denim sofas facing each other in front of a huge picture window that overlooked Willow Bay. Julie's friends, Carrie Reilly and Sophie Dugan, had cleaned thoroughly and the scent of lemon furniture polish blended with the fragrant piney air coming in through the open windows. Instinctively, Sarah hurried to the back of the apartment to shut the windows before reminding herself that someone would have to have a damn tall ladder to get to them.

She shook her head, left them open, but turned back and closed them part way, checking the screens to make sure they were securely latched, before she explored further. A small bedroom with a desk and a daybed under the loft stairs was decorated with amazing photos of the lake, vineyards, and a red-roofed lighthouse. An en-suite bathroom had a frosted window that she assured herself was latched tight and too small for an adult to get through anyway. The kitchen was sparkling white-painted cabinets and granite countertops with what appeared to be new stainless steel appliances.

She pulled open a cabinet and found cheerful flowered dishes, while another held glasses and stemware, and a bottom cupboard contained a set of high-end stainless steel pots and pans. Apparently, this kitchen was fully stocked. She could cook. She loved to cook and she'd done damn little of it in Chicago. There was always too much to be done at the shelter and in the shop. What a pleasure it would be to play with new recipes in this kitchen. A window above the stainless steel sink overlooked tall pines and a gravel parking area behind the boathouse. She reached up and checked the lock.

All good.

Open steps led to a huge master bedroom with a bathroom at least four times the size of her entire studio apartment in Chicago. And it had a big delicious shower with multiple showerheads. *Nice.* No window in that bathroom, thank God, and the bedroom windows looked out over the docks and the bay. They were cranked open and with an effort, Sarah left them that way. A ceiling fan circled lazily above a king-sized bed covered in a lovely pink-and-green quilt. Nothing here to be afraid of.

She was safe.

Back downstairs, she set her backpack on the white wicker desk at the bottom of the stairs, where she found a note from her landlord, Noah Dixon, welcoming her and giving her the Wi-Fi password and other incidentals about the apartment. When she went to the refrigerator for a drink of water, she found a casserole, a pie, fresh vegetables and fruit, eggs, milk, and a bottle of white wine. A note on the casserole let her know that Carrie and Sophie were only a phone call away.

Already, she was finding a small sense of safety here in this little town on the lake. Pulling out the casserole, she cut a serving, and discovered to her delight that it was chicken—her favorite. She put the square on a plate, covered it with a paper towel, and placed it in the microwave to reheat. Suddenly, she was famished, so she whipped up a salad with the veggies in the fridge. Someone, no doubt Carrie or Sophie, had even thoughtfully provided three different kinds of salad dressing. She chose the balsamic vinaigrette and even opened the wine—a crisp summer Riesling from a winery right there in Willow Bay—and poured a glass.

She sat on the high stool at the countertop, eating her lunch and watching the sailboats on the bay out the front window. After lunch, she would call Julie and talk to her about buying an inexpensive used car. She'd left hers in Chicago—abandoned it really. Maybe Will could go to the parking lot behind the shelter and get it and sell it for her.

No... Too dangerous. Paul probably had someone watching her car. It would just have to sit there until they towed it. It would go in the police impound auction, which was okay. That money went to a good cause.

She rinsed her dishes, stuck them in the dishwasher, and emptied her pack to take inventory—cell phone, wallet with a

Michigan driver's license, her passport, and a birth certificate. Everything made out in her new name.

"Sarah Jane Bennett." She said the name out loud, trying it on for size. Miraculously, the shelter's director had managed to get her new identity set up in just a matter of a few hours. Well, maybe not so miraculously—money talked even in these kinds of situations and Sarah had paid a pretty penny for the paperwork to escape.

She placed her laptop on the desk by the stairs and since the battery was low on her cell phone, she plugged it into the outlet by the kitchen bar. The rest of the things she packed carefully back into the pack, except for a framed picture that she set on the desk by her laptop. "Hey, baby," she whispered to the photo of the young girl in the simple wood frame, "here we are, in a new place again." She kissed her fingertips and touched the photo, tears welling up in her eyes.

Swallowing hard, she set the pack against the wall next to the front door before scooping up her purse and the suitcase that Will had packed for her when he went back to her apartment that night... That terrible night. Was it really only three days ago? A shudder wavered through her as she headed for the stairs.

At the bottom step, she paused, set the suitcase down, and went back to recheck the lock on the front door. It was bolted. She walked to the small mud room off the kitchen and verified the back door was locked, too, although she was dismayed to discover that it was a simple knob lock—no deadbolt. A trip to the hardware store in town just became the first item on her to-do list. For a moment, she debated wedging a chair under the knob, but with a deep breath, let it go. The door was locked, the window was too high to reach the lock from, so for now, it was okay.

The master bedroom welcomed her warmly with a shaft of afternoon light streaming in the windows opposite the French doors that opened off the loft. She dug into her purse and found her trusty old iPod, plugged it into the clock radio by the bed, and relaxed to Norah Jones as she emptied her suitcase onto the bed.

Bless Will's heart. He had literally *stuffed* all her clothes into the big case. It was clear he'd scooped her few belongings out of the beat-up dresser and closet in the tiny apartment, because the zipper was straining and it weighed a ton. Shoes, tops, underwear, skirts, and jeans nearly burst out when she unzipped the bag. Her cosmetics and toothbrush were tucked into the pocket in the front, along with everything from her shower, which he'd thoughtfully wrapped in a towel so nothing had soaked through the canvas of the suitcase. With everything laid out on the bed, she scanned the room for a dresser, but didn't see one.

She carried her toiletries into the bathroom and spotted two doors across from the shower. One revealed a fully stocked linen closet filled with towels, sheets, and everything she'd need in bathroom supplies for the next six months at least. She chuckled. "Thank you, Carrie and Sophie."

The other door led into the most amazing walk-in closet she'd ever seen—even more elegant than the one she'd left behind in Atlanta so many years ago. All white-stained wood, one side was drawers, baskets, and shoe racks that her meager wardrobe wouldn't begin to fill. A mirror on the back wall opened into a three-way and lighted up when she pressed the switch by the door to turn on the overhead lights. Sarah couldn't help laughing out loud thinking about how her few articles of clothing would look hanging in this closet. Somebody, probably Noah Dixon, sure knew how to appeal to female renters, because this closet was great, and clearly it had been done recently, because it still smelled of fresh paint and there wasn't a mark on any of the shoe racks.

Grinning for the first time in three days, she collected her shoes—all three pairs—and set them in the rack. Just as she placed her worn leather sandals, she heard a noise downstairs. She stood stock-still, listening. Yes. Someone had opened the back door and was clomping through the kitchen.

Oh holy shit!

Whoever it was hadn't even bothered to knock. Her heart leaped to her throat as she tiptoed into the bedroom and rummaged among the clothes piled on the bed for her purse.

The footsteps were getting closer, so she dug in the purse for the little .22 pistol she'd acquired just the night before. Who knew she'd ever have need of it in this sleepy little town? But what if Paul had her followed? The tread was too heavy to be Paul's, but maybe one of his gorillas…

She stepped to the French doors and peeked out, but wasn't close enough to the loft rail to see over. She was going to know soon enough, because from the sound of it, the intruder was headed right for the stairs.

Sarah tucked in as close to the wall as she could, peering out through the crack by the door hinges. A huge man clambered up the stairs, whistling as if he didn't have a care in the world.

What nerve! He'd broken into her apartment, but was acting as if he belonged here.

She squinted. Burly as a lumberjack, the guy's salt-and-pepper hair was longish and curled over his collar, and he wore trendy dark-framed glasses. In one hand, he carried several wooden poles that he'd probably used to break into the back door and in the other, a shopping bag.

Pure red rage surged through her and she stepped into the opening with both arms raised, the pistol aimed directly at the bastard's heart. "Stop right there!"

CHAPTER 2

It never occurred to Tony Reynard that someone would be in
the apartment over Noah's old boathouse because no one was
supposed to be there. Carrie had told him yesterday that Julie's
friend wasn't due until the weekend. He'd been patting himself on
the back for the last two days for getting the closet build-out done
so quickly. All he had left to do was install the poles for the
hanging clothes, which was where he was headed when a little
redheaded spitfire stepped out of the bedroom with a damned gun
in her hands. And, *oh shit,* those hands were shaking.

It took about ten seconds for him to assess the situation,
slowly step down one step from the top, and hold his hands, full
of closet poles and a shopping bag, up in the air.

"Hello," he said, keeping his tone as even and measured as he
could.

"Who are you?" Her voice trembled. Clearly, she was terrified, even though her crystal blue eyes were shooting angry
sparks. She was tiny—not much over five feet—and if she
weighed a hundred pounds soaking wet, he'd eat his favorite
Chicago Cubs hat.

"I'm Tony Reynard." He glanced over his shoulder and backed down another step.

"Don't move." She shook the gun at him and he realized it was a .22 semiautomatic, which could certainly be deadly, although by now he was fairly sure she wasn't going to shoot him.

"What are you doing here?" she asked.

"I'm going to put my hands down now, okay?"

"I wouldn't," she advised, sounding a little bit braver. "Unless you want a bullet through your heart."

"Hey, I'm just the local handyman." Tony kept his hands up and moved down one more step so they were more eye-to-eye. He'd reached his full height by the age of sixteen, so he'd learned not to tower over people. He didn't mean to be intimidating, but six feet three and two hundred and thirty pounds of bulky male tended to be daunting. "I'm here to install the poles in the new closet." He peered around her. "Looks like you could use them."

She eyed him suspiciously. "What's in the bag?" She jerked the gun toward the sack in his right hand.

From his vantage point, Tony could see that the safety was off and her finger was inside the trigger guard.

Shit.

He was fairly sure the damn thing was loaded—she seemed too serious to be trying to frighten him with an unloaded weapon. She was afraid, but she meant business. He wasn't interested in getting shot by a crazy-scared female, so he gave her his best charming smile even though sweat ran down his sides.

Just act calm. Show her you mean her no harm. That was the key.

"Hangers. I bought some of those velvet hanger things at the Target in Traverse City. Julie said you were arriving with only your clothes and nothing else from your place in Chicago, so I thought you might be able to use some hangers. I've also got some drawer liner here. Package says it smells like lavender."

She stared at him for what seemed like an eternity, but he didn't let his gaze waver...or his smile. Finally, she took a deep, shaky breath and slowly dropped her arms, still holding the gun in both hands.

"Maybe you could, um, take your finger out of the trigger guard and put the safety on before you shoot yourself in the foot," Tony suggested. "And I'm going to lower my arms now." When she didn't object and did as he recommended, he sagged against the stairwell wall for a moment before he said, "You must be Sarah, Julie's friend from Chicago."

Sarah's heart wouldn't stop pounding, even though she'd mostly figured out that this guy wasn't going to hurt her. However, now she was pissed. He stood on the stairs, clearly waiting for an invitation to come up, but somehow she couldn't say those words. Instead, anger won out and she lashed out, in spite of herself. "What the hell is the matter with you?" she barked. "Who just walks into someone's house without knocking first?"

"Someone who has a key and is here to fix the closet? Someone who thought you were arriving on Friday?" The guy gave her a smile and a raised brow that was probably meant to charm her. But she was too angry to be taken in by a man with gleaming white teeth and who was built like a small mountain.

She stuck her palm out. "Hand it over."

He looked at her blankly.

She said impatiently, "The key. Give me the key."

"No." His deep voice was soft and firm. "The key belongs to Noah, who's paying me to do a job. I'll return it to him when I'm done installing the closet poles." He eyed her for a moment longer. "Now, I'm going to come up and do exactly that, so I'd appreciate it if you'd put the gun down and let me do my job."

Sarah took a deep breath and then another while he waited patiently on the stairs. Julie hadn't mentioned that anyone would be working on the apartment. However, maybe she didn't know. Maybe he wasn't who he claimed to be. What if he was one of Paul's goons? "Stay right there." She waved the gun at him. "Don't move. I'm gonna call Julie."

He plopped down on the top step and sighed. "You do whatever you need to do, ma'am," he replied with a grin. "Tell Jules I said hey."

Sarah tucked the gun in her back pocket and turned to get her purse before realizing that her cell phone was charging downstairs. There was a landline on the nightstand by the bed, though, so she dialed Julie's cell while keeping an eye on the very large man sitting on the stairs.

He simply grinned at her and she couldn't help the tiny pull of attraction that quivered through her at the dimples that bracketed his full lips. She quelled that thought as Julie answered briskly.

"Hey, sweets. You getting settled in?"

"I was," Sarah said, "until some guy let himself into the apartment. He says his name is Tony something and—"

"Reynard." The man supplied, his voice deep and gravelly before it rose slightly as he called, "Hey, Jules, tell her I'm okay."

"He's fine, Sarah." Julie laughed. "He's been doing some reno work on the apartment for Noah."

"Okkkkaaaay," she drawled in disbelief. How had Julie not mentioned some dude was working on the apartment?

Julie picked up on Sarah's doubtful tone immediately. "Honey, I'm so sorry. I should've remembered to tell you he might be there. Seriously, Tony's the best. You want to make friends with him. He's the deputy sheriff in town, so he's always only a 9-1-1 call away."

"Is that so?" Sarah eyed Tony Reynard, who was now digging through the big Target sack, emptying it on the floor. Sure enough, he pulled out two twelve-packs of velvet hangers and a couple of rolls of flowered drawer liner.

"That is so." Julie's grin was loud and clear over the phone line. "Breathe, Sarah. Just breathe."

Easy for her to say.

Sarah sighed. "Thanks, Jules." She hung up and gave Tony a short nod. "Do what you need to do."

Sarah kept an eye on Tony as he placed the four poles in their appropriate holders in the closet and opened the hanger packages and filled two of the poles. He scowled as he yanked a length of the drawer liner out, releasing the soft scent of lavender into the room.

"Dammit, I didn't bring my tool belt in, so no scissors." He turned the box around. "I guess I thought this thing would have a cutter on it, like waxed paper or aluminum foil."

"There's probably a pair around here somewhere." Sarah made the offer reluctantly, then backtracked. "But, I can do the drawers. You don't have to." She was too aware of him, his bulk suddenly made the master suite seem small.

He didn't have an ounce of fat on him; he was tall and broad and very male. He didn't frighten her anymore. Not after talking to Julie. And her sensible mind assured her he had no intention of hurting her. So why was her heart pounding? No, she wasn't afraid, not exactly, but he was a stranger and a man, clearly able to overpower her in a heartbeat. She wanted him gone.

It didn't look like that was going to happen as he stood there playing with the drawer liner. "Nope, I need to do it," he said as his shoulders filled the door to the bathroom. "Noah is paying me."

A shiver skittered up her spine at his determined tone. "I'll tell him I sent you away." Her breathing became shallow as she edged to the French doors, her hand behind her back on the grip of the gun. "Please." The word came out in a strangled gasp that exasperated Sarah. *Dammit, don't show him the fear.* Her heart pounded and tears stung her eyelids. She blinked them away as she stood her ground.

Tony's focus suddenly shifted from the drawer liner to Sarah. His brows drew together as he regarded her, clearly bewildered. Without leaving her view, he set the box on a shelf behind him and grabbed the hanger packaging and the empty bag from the bathroom floor. "Okay, I'm going to get out of your way now," he said and held up a single key with colored tag hanging from it. "Here's the key." He laid it on the nightstand by the bed. "Please give it back to Noah for me."

Sarah's heart rose to her throat as he moved toward her and she backed onto the loft landing. The little pistol pressed against her behind in her snug jeans—a small comfort against the vulnerability currently overwhelming her. She nodded, keeping as much distance between them as she could.

Tony slipped through the doors, sticking to the opposite side of the landing. At the top of the stairs, he stopped and gave her a cockeyed smile that lit up his brown eyes, making them glow almost amber in the late afternoon sun streaming in the front windows. "I wouldn't carry that gun in your back pocket if I were you, Sarah. You're gonna shoot yourself in the butt."

She took a shaky breath. "I know how to use the gun."

His steady gaze never left her face. "No, you don't, but you can learn." This time his tread on the steps was surprisingly quiet for a man of his size. She walked to the bedroom window and a few seconds later, saw him bound across the gravel parking area and get into a large late-model pickup. When she went downstairs to check the back door, she breathed a huge sigh of relief. He'd locked it up again.

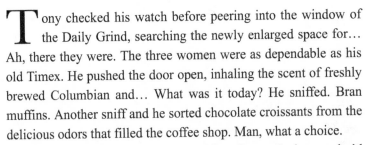

Tony checked his watch before peering into the window of the Daily Grind, searching the newly enlarged space for... Ah, there they were. The three women were as dependable as his old Timex. He pushed the door open, inhaling the scent of freshly brewed Columbian and... What was it today? He sniffed. Bran muffins. Another sniff and he sorted chocolate croissants from the delicious odors that filled the coffee shop. Man, what a choice.

"Morning, Deputy." Round, balding Perry Graham, who'd hopped on the designer coffee wave almost fifteen years ago to open the Daily Grind, greeted him with a smile. "Got your medium half-caf right here."

"I can wait my turn." Tony shouldered his way through the clutch of patrons waiting at the pick-up counter. "Warm me up a bran muffin, too, please?"

"These guys have all ordered. Kelly and Seth are working on their fancy-schmancy beverages." Perry grinned at the others as he handed Tony a cardboard cup. "You were next anyway. And put your money away. Law enforcement never pays at the Grind. You know that."

"I'll accept the coffee and thank you, but I'm paying for the muffin," Tony protested, even though he and Perry had this argument almost every single morning.

"Fine, I'll put it on your tab." Perry waved him away and turned away to put the muffin in the microwave. "Go sit. I'll bring it to you."

"And yet somehow that tab goes missing every time I try to pay it," Tony replied with a smile.

"What can I say, man? Computers." Perry shook his head and winked over his shoulder.

Sipping his coffee, Tony headed for the back corner. Like everyone else in town he'd been delighted when Perry had expanded into the space left empty by Bertie Chalmers, who moved her yarn shop to a sprawling house over on Cherry Street. Perry didn't use the extra space to crowd in more tables, although he'd added several; rather, he'd set up five new areas with deep armchairs, small sofas, and coffee tables. Each little space was a cozy spot for conversation, and they all contained accessible outlets for laptops.

Nearly every chair and a lot of the tables in the place were occupied despite the fact that it was past nine in the morning. That didn't surprise him one bit. In the city, a place like the Grind would've been emptied out by now with folks heading to work or school. Except for the bank and the drugstore and the market, most of the businesses in Willow Bay didn't open until ten and school, which was in session for another three weeks, started at eight a.m. Life in the little resort village was pretty quiet until summer got underway, and even with the tourist trade, it was a laid-back place that suited Tony just fine.

Pete Carvey and his charter boat crew sat together at one of the bigger tables, a large lake map spread out on its surface. "Morning, Deputy." Pete's white teeth gleamed through his dark bushy beard. He'd gotten new implants last month and grabbed any opportunity to show them off.

"Hey, Pete." Tony stopped for a moment and nodded to each of the crew in turn. "Kyle, Mark, Samantha, Kenny." He peered over Mark's shoulder at the map. "Getting ready for the season, eh? How're the salmon running?"

"They're not running, Tony, they're still just swimming," Samantha replied and grinned up at him. They indulged in the tired old joke damn near every morning during tourist season, but Tony still laughed along with the crew. The camaraderie of village life was something he'd never tire of after so many years of living in Chicago. He patted Samantha's shoulder before heading off to the three women sitting in the mini-living room in the corner.

"Tony!" Julie Miles grinned. "Hey, baby, pull up a chair."

"Thanks." He plopped down in the only empty armchair. "Hey, Carrie. Sophie. Where's Libby? I need to talk to you, Jules."

"Good morning to you too, Tony." Carrie looked up from the papers she had on her lap and stared at him over her reading glasses. "Libby's bottling pinot noir this morning. Is this official police business? Do you need Sophie and me to leave?"

"Um..." Tony turned to Julie. He was fairly certain that anything he wanted to say to Julie about her friend Sarah wouldn't be a secret from two of Julie's three best friends; however, he wasn't prepared to bet the farm on it. "It's about your friend."

"Oh, sure." Julie nodded. "You can talk in front of these two, they know the whole story about Sarah."

"Want to let me in on it?" Tony accepted the muffin that Perry's barista Kelly handed him. "Thanks, Kel." He took a bite as he waited for her to walk away. "What is the deal with that woman? She pulled a freakin' gun on me yesterday."

Carrie gasped. "Sarah Everett pulled a gun on you?"

"Shh." Julie tapped Carrie's wrist with her coffee stirrer. "And it's Sarah *Bennett*."

"Oops. Sorry," Carrie whispered. "I'm never going to get used to that."

"You'd better. It's her name now." Julie turned back to Tony. "I didn't even know she *had* a gun."

Tony settled back in his chair. "She does," he said quietly, "and my guess is she hasn't had it very long because it's a coin toss which of us was more frightened of the damn thing."

"Oh crap." Julie reached over, pulled off a piece of Tony's muffin, and popped it in her mouth. "I'll bet a nickel she... um...*acquired* it the night before we left. She slipped out while Will was over at the shelter packing up her stuff and I was in the shower. I caught her coming back in when I came out of the bathroom. She claimed she'd stepped outside to clear her head."

"Maybe she met up with someone who gave it to her," Sophie offered. "Jules, leave the poor man's muffin alone."

"Yeah, get your own for once," Carrie added as Julie snitched another bite of Tony's pastry. "Probably one of the women from the shelter brought it to her. Had she been on the phone at all?"

"She was texting." Julie's perfect brows came together in a V under her wispy blonde bangs.

He couldn't help smiling at the trio of women he'd referred to as the Posse ever since Sophie had moved up to Willow Bay permanently a couple of years ago. They'd adopted his nickname and, in a moment of true Julie-style irreverence, became the *Menopause Posse*. They had a fourth with Libby Nolan, who owned the winery up by the lighthouse, and they were the village's movers and shakers—always setting up town events and working to improve the park or the beach or some historic site. The four women single-handedly raised the funds to repair an old barge, and brought back the summer tradition of fireworks over the bay every Saturday night.

Only last month, they'd won a battle with the school board over free breakfasts for the underprivileged children who lived in the trailer park south of town by simply holding a huge town-wide rummage sale in Dixon's Marina's parking area. The money they earned would pay for breakfast for twenty-seven kids every morning for the next school year. Their newest mission was to open a battered women's shelter in the county.

Tony had assumed that Sarah, who he heard had worked at the shelter in Chicago where Julie volunteered in the winter, had come to help her with that project. Now, he suspected Sarah's sudden arrival in Willow Bay went deeper, and he was a little irritated that his friend Will Brody, who also happened to be Julie's significant other, hadn't filled him in.

"It's a pretty safe bet she doesn't have a permit to carry that thing in the state of Michigan, no matter how she acquired it, and she's gonna hurt herself or someone else." Tony munched his muffin thoughtfully for a few minutes while Carrie, Julie, and Sophie speculated in soft tones about Sarah and the gun.

"Are you going to tell me her story, Jules?" he interrupted.

Julie and Carrie exchanged a long look before Julie sighed deeply. "You probably should know, given you're the law around here, but it's not my story to tell. It's hers."

"She's carrying a weapon she probably got illegally, ladies. At the very least, I need to confiscate it." He kept his voice low, even though the coffee shop had started to empty. It might have been unfair to pull rank on three good friends, but Sarah's combination of vulnerability and bravado worried him. And, okay, he'd admit it. That mass of auburn hair and those flashing eyes intrigued him, too. He glanced around the group that had suddenly gone silent and none of the women could meet his eyes. "Can you give me the basics?"

When they didn't answer, he sighed deeply and gave humor a shot. "Don't make me ask Will, Jules. What kind of a cop am I if I can't get a few simple facts out of three witnesses?"

Sophie, sitting on the small sofa next to Julie, nudged her with her shoulder. "Go ahead and tell him, Jules. He can't protect her if he doesn't know anything."

"Protect her?" Tony had an inkling what was coming, so he wasn't too shocked when Julie reluctantly offered up Sarah's story.

"She was a battered wife. She opened the resale shop in the shelter and lived above it. Her ex-husband's been in prison, and now he's out and he came looking for her in Chicago a couple of days ago."

"He was in *prison* or jail for abusing her?" Tony asked. "There's a difference."

"I know that, Officer Krupke." Jules threw him a disdainful glance. "He was in *prison,* but not for anything he did to Sarah—although he should've gotten a life sentence for that, in my opinion."

Carrie and Sophie exchanged a quick look and nodded. Obviously, they knew Sarah's history too; however, neither of them added anything to the conversation. Clearly, getting information was going to be like pulling teeth.

"You might as well tell me what he was in there for. Save me a couple of hours on the internet."

"About eight years ago, he backed his car over their teenaged daughter and killed her," Julie whispered.

Jesus! Tony's heart dropped to his socks and surged back up into his throat, making swallowing the bite of muffin nearly impossible. He washed it down with a sip of coffee as Julie continued in the same unusually quiet tone.

"His name is Paul Prescott. He was some high-powered real estate mogul in Georgia. His family practically runs the little town they lived in outside of Atlanta. Apparently, he'd gotten abusive after he and Sarah had been married a couple of years; she got pregnant almost immediately and, like so many battered women in that situation, she stayed with her abuser. She's never told me everything, but I know the day the daughter died, he'd gone off the dial over something insignificant, smacked Sarah around in the kitchen, and stormed out of the house." Julie cringed as she spoke.

Tony's blood boiled at the thought of some bully beating the crap out of tiny Sarah, even though he couldn't picture the little firebrand he'd met this morning cowering on a kitchen floor. "What happened after that?"

Julie swallowed hard. "As I understand it, he backed his giant SUV out of the garage and right over the girl, who was sunbathing on a chaise lounge in the driveway. He was in such a rage, he dragged her almost to the end of the driveway before he realized what he'd done."

Nausea nearly overcame Tony as he sat gazing at his coffee cup, and he struggled to sit still and keep the muffin down. Finally, he looked up at the three women. "Holy shit," he breathed. "The WTF list is endless."

Julie nodded. "By the time the authorities got there, the girl was dead and that evil snake was screaming about Sarah, claiming to the cops that the whole thing was her fault. Of course, never mind that she was out cold in the kitchen. Fortunately, a neighbor saw what happened to the daughter and he testified as a witness. They put the bastard away. Involuntary manslaughter, I think, or reckless manslaughter or something like that."

"That was eight years ago?" Tony asked.

"Yeah. He got sixteen years for the manslaughter, but he was never charged for what he did to Sarah, or it probably would've been longer. I think he served like half of the sentence. All I know is that Sarah divorced him, left after the trial, and came to Chicago to the shelter. She managed to stay hidden from him all this time, but somehow he found her and showed up at her place a few days ago."

So many questions swirled in Tony's head he couldn't even form a coherent sentence, so he simply sat and gazed out the window. The street outside was bathed in sunlight, and a gentle breeze ruffled the yellow and purple pansies that had recently been planted in the flowerbeds along the sidewalk. The village was dressing up for summer, preparing for the onslaught of tourists who would soon arrive. Life was going to get busier for the sheriff's department, which consisted of himself and Sheriff Earl Gibson. He sighed. Apparently, it had already started. "Did he hurt her? Threaten her? Is she in hiding up here?"

"Yes, yes, and yes." July replied succinctly. "So can you sorta keep an eye on her?"

"I don't like it that she's got an illegal handgun." Carrie voiced Tony's own fears.

He didn't like it much, either. He couldn't simply show up and confiscate the damn thing. Well, legally, he *could*, but the woman was clearly terrified for her life and seemingly with good reason. He was just going to have to get to know this Sarah Bennett. Given that he couldn't stop thinking about the tiny little spitfire, with her mass of auburn curls and those big blue eyes sparking with false bravado, that didn't sound like such a bad way to start his summer.

CHAPTER 3

"Sarah? Sarah!" Julie's words carried through the closed windows and Sarah heard her rattling the doorknob. "Open up."

Sarah peeped out the shutter covering the wide front picture window. Julie wasn't the only one on her doorstep. She had Carrie and two other women with her, their arms loaded with grocery sacks.

Dammit. She was going to have to let them in.

"Come on, Sarah. Don't make me go get a key from Noah." Julie's voice rose another decibel.

Sarah glanced down at her coffee-stained T-shirt and crumpled shorts and raked her fingers through her messy hair. She looked like hammered shit. The women would know in a heartbeat that she hadn't showered in a couple of days. Okay, five days... maybe six. She couldn't remember. She'd showered the morning after she arrived—it had taken forever because she'd had to keep turning off the shower, thinking she'd heard something outside the locked bathroom door. Washing up at the sink was just easier—she could stay partially dressed that way and grab her clothes off the vanity if she needed them quickly. But the only way to wash her hair was to shower or use the big kitchen sink and sticking her head under running water left her too exposed.

Dear God, she sounded as irrational as those poor women when they first came into the shelter all battered and bruised. She was past all that. Wasn't she?

Damn that bastard. Damn him.

"Sarah?" Now it was Carrie's voice. "Let us in. We've got ice cream melting out here."

Sarah felt in her shorts pocket for the little pistol and slipped it into the drawer in the end table by the sofa before padding slowly to the front door. She pulled aside the curtain to peek out, making sure it was only the four women, then unlatched the chain, the deadbolt, and the doorknob lock.

Julie tugged at the screen door. "Come on, Sarah. It's us."

Sarah managed to unhook the wooden screen door and the women trooped in, carrying at least eight grocery bags that they dumped on the kitchen counter and table. Sarah re-hooked the screen door and firmly shut the front door, prepared to lock up when Julie stopped her.

"Leave that one open. It's musty as hell in here," she ordered as she took fresh fruit and vegetables from a bag on the table.

Sarah straightened her shoulders. "I prefer it closed."

"Hey, sweetie." Carrie hurried over to give Sarah a hug, holding on until Sarah returned the embrace. "Julie's right. You need to air this place out. It's getting into the seventies during the day now, and the breeze off the bay is delicious." She put both hands on Sarah's shoulders and held her at arms' length, chattering away as if Sarah had just arrived in town. "I'm so glad you're here. I've missed you! It's been months! Liam and I headed straight back here after Europe, so we didn't even get to the fundraiser this spring."

"It's good to see you, too, Carrie." Tears stung Sarah's eyes and she blinked them back, determined not to break down. Not in front of her two dearest friends and a couple of strangers who were putting away groceries as comfortably as if they'd been here a hundred times, which they probably had. If memory served, both Carrie and Julie had occupied this apartment at one time or another.

Carrie moved off to open the windows in the back while Sarah reluctantly opened the front door, verifying that the screen door hook was snugly latched. A pine-scented breeze blew through the back windows and Carrie gave her a sunny smile. "Isn't that better?"

Sarah nodded. The air stirring the musty atmosphere did feel good, although she kept an eye on the open front door.

"This is Sophie Dugan"—Julie pointed first to the tall, dark-haired woman and then to the slightly older lady who had a startling streak of pure white in her otherwise dark brown hair—"and this is Libby Nolan."

Sophie and Libby immediately stopped working and hurried over to greet Sarah with warm hugs and murmured hellos.

"We're so glad to have you here," Libby said, her blue eyes sparkling. "You'll love Willow Bay, I promise." Her voice was a little husky and that snowy streak in the front of her hair was so perfect, it had to be natural.

"Welcome, Sarah." Sophie gave Sarah's shoulders an extra squeeze before she headed back to continue unloading groceries. "Anything at all we can do for you, anything you need, just holler. We'll put our numbers in your phone, okay?" Sophie was as tall as Julie and curvy in a jeans skirt and a knit top.

Sarah tried to remember what Julie had told her about the two women. Was it Sophie who was married to a nerdy multimillionaire and Libby who owned a winery, or the other way around? What did it matter? She'd figure it all out eventually. In the meantime, she bit her lower lip and swallowed hard as tears threatened again at the kindness of all four women—their chatter and camaraderie reminded her of the shelter she'd left behind in Chicago. Was that a week ago?

How long had she been here?

"Okay, let me look at you." Julie closed the gap between them with three long strides. "Jesus, Sarah Jane, you look like hell. When's the last time you ate a decent meal? Or had a shower?"

"I showered a couple of days ago, I think," Sarah muttered, heat rising in her cheeks. Dammit, what did it matter to Julie how often she showered? Resentment flashed through her. She sure as hell didn't need Julie and Carrie poking in, dragging strangers into her house. How often she showered was none of their affair. Neither was how much she'd been eating for that matter. "And I've been eating. I finished that casserole and ate the pie and salad you left me." She gave them a nod, shoving down the anger her reasonable mind told her was silly. "Thanks, all of you, by the way."

Julie put a finger under Sarah's chin, gently insisting she meet her gaze. "Baby, you've been holed up for over a week. You've answered our texts, but put us off and put us off, claiming you were exhausted or had a headache or some other nonsense. I'm fairly sure you haven't opened the door once, because Noah and Margie said the place has been shut up tight since you arrived." She didn't even have the grace to look sheepish for having checked up on her with the Dixons. "The shutters were all closed when we got here, all the blinds are drawn—"

"And what's the deal with the chair wedged under the back door?" Carrie called from the mudroom. She appeared in the doorway, a new bottle of laundry detergent still dangling from her fingers.

"So what's going on? Did something else happen?" Julie led Sarah to a bar stool and practically shoved her onto it. "It's obvious you're frightened out of your wits, and now, you're scaring us, too. Jesus, Sarah! Tony said you pulled a gun on him last week when he came to finish up the closet." She peered into Sarah's face and enunciated firmly, "Paul's not here. He doesn't know where you are. You're safe."

Sarah folded her hands on the bar, opened her mouth to speak, and shut it again. She was a mess, Julie was absolutely right, but the terror was real and she had no idea how to express it without sounding like she'd completely slipped a cog. Perhaps she had. Maybe Paul had finally sent her 'round the bend. Wouldn't that be the ultimate in irony? She finally fought back, but lost her mind in the aftermath. She glanced around at the four women, who were all staring at her with various levels of sympathy and curiosity. "I-I..." The words clogged up in her throat.

How could she confess she'd spent the past few days curled up in the armchair in the bedroom because it was in the corner that faced the door so she would see anyone coming up the stairs? How did she admit that hourly she'd made the rounds of the windows and doors, assuring herself each one was securely locked? That she'd finally turned off the ringer on her cell phone because every time it rang, she nearly jumped out of her skin? That the sound of gravel crunching under car tires in the parking lot at the top of the hill sent her flying to the window to peer out between the slats of the shutters to make certain it wasn't a black Town Car with dark-tinted windows?

Libby held up a bottle she'd pulled from a six-bottle cloth carrier. "I think we need wine. I mean it's almost two. The sun is definitely over the yardarm somewhere." She yanked open a drawer and took out a corkscrew. "Soph, grab some glasses." She stopped for a moment to give Sarah a concerned smile. "Unless... I mean, unless you need Sophie and me to leave."

Sarah gazed around for a moment before closing her eyes and pressing her fist to her mouth—the only way she could hold back a wail of anguish. These women had no idea. Just looking at them, she knew. They were clueless. They'd never known the cold brick of fear that she'd carried in her belly for so many years. Not a single one of them had ever hidden in a closet from a ranting maniac or been kicked in the ribs as she cleaned up an entire pot of hot spaghetti sauce that had been swept from the stove because it didn't have enough basil in it; or re-ironed a shirt nine times while a monster stood behind her tightening an extension cord he'd wrapped around her neck.

No, they lived in this quiet, safe little place, married to gentle, kind men who wouldn't dream of yanking them upstairs by the hair and tying them to a bedpost. When she opened her eyes, Libby and Sophie were gathering up their purses and heading for the door. Oh shit, she'd offended them and probably pissed off Julie and Carrie.

"No, stay. It... it's okay." She managed to get the words out around the huge lump in her throat. She really didn't mind them being here. Surely, these women were the *Posse* that Julie always referred to when she spoke so lovingly of her friends in Willow Bay, and they probably already knew Sarah's circumstances. Besides, how many broken moments had *she* been privy to in the shelter? Experience had taught her that women were stronger together; it was simply a fact. And how she'd longed for the camaraderie of other women during her marriage—something Paul had never allowed. He'd even fired Della, her first housekeeper, when he'd walked in on them giggling in the kitchen over a sagging soufflé. No, she didn't have friends in Ames—he'd managed to make everyone there believe she was a little off, which of course made them cautious. Julie and Carrie trusted Libby and Sophie. She should trust them too. She should... but how could she trust anyone?

She tried again to speak, but nothing came out. They didn't know. They could never truly know. But their expressions told her that they wanted to understand. A tear trickled down her cheek and then the sounds came gushing out—raw, tormented sobs that she could no longer control. Through a veil of tears she saw Libby's and Sophie's eyes grow rounder as they tossed their belongings on the sofa and came rushing back.

"Sarah?" Two arms came from behind to gently embrace her and she caught the familiar scent of Carrie's lavender and musk perfume.

"Let it out," Carrie whispered, her breath soft in Sarah's ear. "You just let it go."

Sarah turned, dropped her head on Carrie's shoulder, and sobbed. Her entire body shook as hot tears poured down her face. Amid the storm, it occurred to her that she needed this—this surrender. If her friends thought they were scared by what they saw in her, they should've been inside her head. Even now as she wept copious tears, her logical mind continued to process her raw emotions. That ability to compartmentalize and watch herself from afar was the result of years of physical and emotional abuse. It was how she coped. How she survived.

Carrie was right. She knew she'd lost her grip on reality; she was aware that locking herself up in the apartment was over the top. However, Paul's reappearance had brought everything rushing back and her old instincts had kicked in. This release was probably what she needed, so she let it go, allowed the fear of the last couple of weeks to slowly dissipate with the sobs—that is, what she was *able* to let go. The fear was an essential part of her. Even though it had crippled her for the last few days, that tangible, almost material sense of terror was what had kept her sane—and safe—since she'd left Atlanta eight years ago.

Sarah became aware of Julie standing beside her, smoothing her tangled curls, murmuring soft comforts while Sophie brought a tissue box and a cool damp washcloth and offered them up. Sarah heard the pop of a cork as Libby opened a wine bottle. Glasses clinked on the bar and the glug of liquid being poured brought her completely back into the room. She raised her head, shuddery sobs still hiccupping through her. The washcloth felt like heaven against her grainy eyes and she held it there for moment before she tried to speak. "I–I'm so sor—"

"You never have to apologize to us." Julie cut in, quiet, but deadly serious. "Never, okay?" She peered into Sarah's face, tears filling her own eyes. "Not for this. Never ever."

When Sarah looked around, every one of them had tears brimming over their eyelids. Libby smiled at her and blinked quickly as she poured more wine. Sophie scooted the tissue box an inch or two closer, then pulled one out and used it to wipe her eyes. Carrie kept one hand on Sarah's shoulder and swiped at her own cheeks with the other.

They didn't know. None of them would ever fully comprehend, and God willing, they never would. But somehow…they empathized and they were with her. These four women had her back, and right now, that was what she needed most.

CHAPTER 4

The heavenly scent of cinnamon wafted up the stairs and Sarah sniffed appreciatively as she came out of the bathroom swathed in a fresh terry robe she'd found on the back of the door. Once again, evidence of the generosity and thoughtfulness of Julie and her friends—of Sarah's new friends.

Julie lounged on the bed, staring at her phone. "Better?"

"Much." Sarah offered the best smile she could muster as she padded across the room to pull clean underwear, a pair of yoga capris, and a long-sleeved T-shirt from the pile of clothing scattered on the floor on the opposite side of the bed.

"After lunch, we'll get that stuff sorted and put away in the closet, okay?" Julie's expression held no judgment as Sarah glanced at her when she passed by, the clothes clutched to her chest. "We can start some laundry, but we'll have to figure out how the new washer and dryer work."

"I'm a little surprised you didn't do it while I was in the shower."

Julie grinned, undeterred by Sarah's dry tone. "I thought about it, but, first of all"—she held up one finger—"I didn't know what

needed to be washed and, second,"—she held up another finger
—"I didn't want to make a bunch of noise in here and worry you
while you were in the shower."

Sarah stopped to gaze at her friend. How did she know? How
could she even fathom how vulnerable she felt in the shower?

Julie merely raised one brow and answered the question she
must have read in Sarah's eyes. "I saw it at the shelter, honey. I
watched you with those victims who came in so terrified that they
couldn't even take off their coats, let alone strip down for a shower." She rose and placed one arm around Sarah's shoulders,
leading her back to the bathroom. "Get dressed. I'm here and
anyone who tries to come near you will have to come through
me." She gave her a little push. "Go on. Smells like Carrie
warmed up her apple cinnamon muffins. You're gonna love 'em.
Hey, use some moisturizer," she instructed and left the bathroom
door slightly cracked. "Oh, and don't bother to dry your hair. You
can let it air-dry and Sophie'll French braid it for you. She's a
genius at it."

Sarah stared at the woman in the mirror. A sprinkle of freckles
stood out against the pallor of her complexion and she was certain
she'd developed a few new lines around her eyes in the past
week. She looked every moment of her forty-three years, and then
some. What had happened to the homecoming queen? To the
vibrant, red-haired vixen voted Most Likely to Become the Next
Miss Georgia?

Her lips tightened grimly. Paul Prescott had happened. Right
there at the country club pool. The day after she'd given the vale-
dictorian's address at the Ames High School graduation ceremony. The day after she'd been fêted by friends and family for
receiving a full ride to Ole Miss on a French scholarship. She was
going to get her degree and then go to Paris and be a translator at
the French stock exchange—the *Bourse*.

Well, none of it happened—not Ole Miss or the degree or

Paris. Instead, Paul Prescott had absorbed her into his glamorous world, where at first she'd been cherished and adored. Until...

Sarah shook her head and untied the belt to her robe. Nope. She couldn't go *there* right now. Not and stay sane enough to go downstairs and face Carrie and Libby and Sophie. Instead, she swiped on deodorant, dabbed her face with some moisturizer from the bag of cosmetics she'd managed to drag from the bedroom to the bathroom at some point during the last week, and brushed her teeth. She threw on her clean clothes and unwrapped the towel from her hair, letting the wet mass fall down around her shoulders.

She should cut the tresses off—it might be easier to deal with a short sassy cut like Carrie's. Grabbing the pick, she attempted to tame her curls, but Julie peeked around the door, then came in and plucked the pick right out of her hand.

"Here, let me." Very gently, she slid the wide-toothed comb from the top of Sarah's head to the ends of her hair, and Sarah closed her eyes and allowed the luxury of someone else's fingers on her scalp.

"Maybe I should cut it off," she murmured, tipping her head back as Julie detangled with deft strokes.

"You could," Julie agreed from behind her. "But I'd get settled in before you make any major changes. Right now, you can do a braid or clip it up or pull it back into a ponytail. If you go shorter, you'd have to do it every day. Besides, your hair's gorgeous—so thick, and the color's amazing."

Sarah opened her eyes. "Yeah, but I've been yanking out a couple of white hairs every few weeks. If that continues, I'm gonna be bald by the time I turn fifty."

"You're so tiny and cute, you could probably pull that off with no problem." Julie grinned at their reflections. "Come on, kiddo. Let's go eat."

~

Julie placed her fork on her plate, nudged it aside, and rested her elbows on the placemat. "We need to talk, Sarah."

"I know." Sarah played with a paper napkin, folding it into a fan shape and smoothing the wrinkles out again over and over.

"Lib and Sophie and I talked things over." Carrie set her coffee cup down gently. "We decided we're going to take turns staying here with you at night for a while."

"*What?*" Sarah gasped. "Why?"

"Not forever," Libby amended quickly. "Just until you get more comfortable."

"That… That's not necessary." Sarah was torn between frustration that they believed she couldn't even stay by herself and relief that she'd have someone near to help her listen.

"Given the past week or so, it seems like a good idea," Carrie replied. "But only until you get settled in and can sleep at night. That's my son Jack's old room." She tipped her head toward the door under the loft steps. "The daybed in there is very comfortable and with someone here, you'll always know help is downstairs."

Julie scooted her chair closer and put an arm around Sarah's shoulders. "And I'm giving you the name of a good therapist in Traverse City." She tightened her grip when Sarah automatically began shaking her head. "Yes, Sarah. You need some help. We can make sure you're eating and taking care of yourself, but you *have* to talk to someone. Dr. Benton is an amazing psychologist— she got me through the year after Charlie's death."

Tension built in Sarah's body and she struggled with the urge to flee, to run as far and as fast as she could.

But Julie held her firmly when she made the move to rise.

"This isn't negotiable, Sarah. You can't stay holed up in this apartment for the rest of your life."

"So we're coming to take you out each day," Sophie added as she stacked plates.

"I don't think…" Panic rose in Sarah's throat. Outside she was exposed. She might be recognized.

Libby laid one hand over Sarah's on the table. "There are lots of artists up here and tons of little shops with lovely crafts and antiques. And right now, the beach is covered in smooth stones and shells and other interesting things left by winter. You can collect some stuff, start making this place your own."

"That's right." Carrie rose, crossed to the living room, and brought back a bowl that was sitting on the narrow table behind one of the sofas, filled with all sizes of rocks that had been polished to a high sheen. "These are called Petosky stones—they're actually fossils of critters that lived under the lake thousands of years ago. They're all over up here, but you can't find them anywhere else on Earth. I found these when Jack was growing up. He and I wandered the beach all the time. The lake is very…calming."

Calming? There was a concept Sarah couldn't imagine. Even in the relative safety of the Chicago shelter, she'd never actually experienced a true sensation of calm. Oh, she'd managed to relax somewhat now and again, but that was always with the help of a glass of wine or a shot of tequila. She never had more than one drink, though. Alcohol clouded her mind and staying in control was crucial. Plus, tequila made her chatty, which meant she might start sharing secrets best left under wraps.

There *was* that one night after she and Julie had closed down the resale shop. They'd shared a few shots of tequila from the bottle Sarah kept tucked in the bottom drawer of her desk in the back room. The liquor loosened her tongue and she let down her reserve enough to share her story with Julie—something she'd never done outside of mandatory group therapy. That night was the beginning of their friendship and somehow Julie Miles had managed to worm her way into Sarah's heart and confidence.

Shivering, she crossed her arms and gazed out the front window at Lake Michigan. Someone had opened up the shutters, which filled the whole apartment with light and suddenly made it feel huge. The bay was quiet, except for one gleaming white yacht that was making its way in from the lake. A few others were already parked along the long wooden dock that extended into the bay, but there wasn't a lot of activity in the marina this afternoon.

She wondered how easy it would be for someone to blend in on a busy summer afternoon. Someone could be up the stairs to her deck and never be noticed by the kids she'd seen scrubbing down the docks, pumping gas, and planting annuals in the boxes along the dock. Fighting an urge to race back upstairs to her chair, Sarah pulled her attention back to the room.

"Absolutely," Sophie was saying from the kitchen where she was rinsing dishes. "Henry and I walk the beach almost every evening all summer long. By August, the water's almost warm enough to swim."

"That's debatable." Julie grinned. "You kids might be willing to get in it, but holy shit, that water is too dang cold for my old bones."

Libby snorted. "Old bones? My bones should look so good when I'm almost"—she paused, clearly for dramatic effect —"*sixty.*"

"I thought we agreed we weren't mentioning the *S* word ever again." Julie drawled.

"But the look of complete horror on your face every time we do is so priceless." Carrie laughed.

Sophie giggled and poured the last of the wine into her glass.

"And you keep giving us openings that are perfect to remind you that you *are* the old lady of the group."

"It's still years away." Julie's tone indicated that the matter was closed as far as she was concerned, but the others continued with the good-natured ribbing.

Sarah couldn't help smiling as the four squabbled with the ease of old friends, their affection for one another obvious. They'd done everything they could to include her in their conversation at lunch, to put her at ease, and it warmed her heart. Yet, except for Jules, she wondered if she could ever be at home among them. Julie was the first person Sarah had trusted since she'd left Ames, Georgia. Actually, the first person she'd trusted probably...*ever* in her adult life.

It had taken her several years to get comfortable enough to even speak to the other abused women when she'd moved into the shelter. She'd pretty much kept to herself and it hadn't been until after she helped start the resale shop that she'd opened up to her small therapy group about her past. She was perfectly aware that closing up was the natural instinct for an abuse victim. If you never opened yourself up to others, then you never risked getting hurt—in any way. Sarah had mastered that lesson early in her marriage to Paul Prescott. Dear God, how she had mastered it?

"Sarah?" Thankfully, Julie's voice brought her back before the memories began to wash over her again. "Did you hear what I said?"

"Sorry." Sarah blinked. She had to stop drifting like that—vigilance required focus. Besides, Julie was watching her like a hawk, so she needed to show her some semblance of normal. She plastered on a smile. "I wasn't listening. I got distracted picturing you with a walker and a hairnet."

Libby, Sophie, and Carrie burst into laughter while Julie shook her head and rolled her eyes.

"I like her," Libby said. "I like her a lot."

"Teasing Julie is our favorite sport." Sophie turned off the water and joined them at the table. "You're going to fit into the MP just fine, Sarah."

"MP?" Sarah raised one brow.

"Menopause Posse," Carrie supplied. "We stick together, have each other's backs, and do charitable work around the village, but our main mission is to make Julie feel like crap about being the oldest among us. And you've just proved you're worthy of full membership with all the rights and privileges therein." She rose, came around the table, and grabbed a daisy from the bouquet they'd brought in with them.

Sarah hadn't even noticed it until this moment, even though it had been sitting right there on the kitchen bar. Good God, they'd brought her flowers. Inanely, she wondered if the lovely blue glass vase had come with the bouquet or if it was already in the apartment. She didn't remember seeing it before.

Carrie bowed low, offering Sarah the flower. "You, Sarah Jane Bennett, are a true smart ass and, although you look about sixteen, I'm fairly sure you've reached or surpassed the magical age of forty, so you qualify as a Menopause Fairy. Will you accept our invitation to be an official member of the MP?"

It was now or never. Julie's friends were offering their strength, their friendship, and showing her they intended to protect and support her. She could accept their friendship, find her way here in Willow Bay, and begin to live like a normal person— or she could stay huddled in the chair upstairs. Alone. She could even cut and run again—maybe to Canada or France.

It was *her* choice. Just as it had been her choice eight years ago to finally divorce Paul and start over in Chicago. But would she find a readymade support group someplace else?

She gazed around the table at the eager faces—each woman's

expression warm and full of welcome. With a deep breath, she rose from her chair, curtsied, and accepted the daisy amid cheers from her new friends.

Blinking back tears, she cleared her throat. "Okay, so teach me the secret handshake."

CHAPTER 5

Tony paused in his vigorous rubbing of the teak deck to reach back and rub the sore muscles of his lower back. Sitting back on his heels, he admired the shining surfaces of Liam Reilly's yacht, the *Allegro*. Tony had been captain, first mate, and chief cook and bottle washer on the boat every summer for nearly fifteen years—the first five with a Chicago Bears linebacker who'd eventually grown bored with partying on the lake, and for the last ten years, with Liam. Tony had to confess that although the time with the linebacker had been glamorous, boating life with a symphony conductor was better, more peaceful, especially since they'd made the move to Willow Bay.

His phone vibrated against his leg and he swiped his palm on his jeans before he reached into his pocket. Caller ID showed him the faces of his daughter, son-in-law, and granddaughter as well as the time, six thirty, which meant it was an hour earlier in Chicago. No doubt Olivia had picked up Emma at daycare and was driving home.

Drive time was when his darling daughter caught up on phone calls and he figured Emma must have clamored to talk to Poppy.

He swiped the screen. "How are my girls?" he asked, trying

not to groan as he rose from the stern where he'd been kneeling. Was it possible he was getting too old to spend an entire afternoon on his knees waxing decks?

"Hi, Dad." Olivia's voice had the tinny quality of someone on speakerphone, which confirmed his guess that they were driving. "How's it going?"

"Poppy, I petted a bunny," Emma's little voice broke in.

"A bunny?" Tony dropped down on the wooden seat that lined the deck, grinning as he always did when the four-year-old called him Poppy. She'd stolen his heart the day she was born and he was her slave, which both delighted and annoyed her mother. He'd pull the moon from the sky if Emma asked him for it, but Olivia couldn't get too upset with him because he'd do the same for her and she knew it. "Was there a bunny at school?"

"A white one," Emma affirmed and Tony pictured her in the backseat, strapped into the car seat with that damn five-point racing harness that drove him crazy every time he tried to buckle the kid into it.

"That's pretty cool. Was it bring-your-pet-to-school day?"

Emma's sweet laugh carried over the miles and warmed her grandfather's heart. "No, Poppy. I can't take Gwennie to school. She'd poop on the playground!" She had a point. Gwennie was the family golden retriever and Tony had no problem imagining the dog doing her business in the schoolyard.

"A petting zoo brought some animals in today." Olivia sounded tired.

"Hard day at the hospital?" He reached down for his bottle of water and took a long pull as Olivia proceeded to vent about her job as an ER nurse.

He was so proud of his only daughter, but he worried about her working in an urban Chicago emergency room. When she switched from twelve-hour weekend shifts to three eight-hour days, his mind had eased somewhat—at least she wasn't driving in the city at all hours of the night anymore. Her husband, Brian, had requested she change her hours to coincide more with his job as a professor of physics at Northwestern, and Tony had supported him fully. Not only was it safer, but it allowed them more time together as a family.

"Do you have plans for the weekend?" he asked when she stopped to take a breath.

"We're going to Mom's—she and Francie are having a Memorial Day cookout," Olivia offered, sounding cautious. No matter how often he reiterated how pleased he was that his ex-wife had finally found happiness, their only daughter still worried about mentioning her to him.

Tony had always been aware that something was missing from his marriage to Olivia's mother, but Shannon had gotten pregnant their junior year in college. In the eighties, you married the girl you knocked up. She dropped out and cared for the baby while he finished up his engineering degree. Shannon had tried hard, but Tony, who was getting a career off the ground and putting food on the table and a roof over his family's heads simply wasn't paying attention. Somehow, they held it together, and it wasn't until Olivia was a junior in college that Shannon finally came out of the closet. The news that she'd fallen in love with her best friend, although startling, hadn't been a shock. It explained a lot.

"That sounds like fun," he said and he meant it. "Give her and Francie my best, okay?"

"What are *you* going to do for the holiday, Dad?" Olivia hesitated, then continued, "Why don't you drive over? I know you'd be welcome at the picnic and we'd love to see you."

"Thanks, sweetie, but I've already got plans." He had no doubt Shannon and Francie would welcome him with open arms, but thankfully, his weekend was already set. He loved seeing his daughter and granddaughter, but he didn't want to spend the holiday weekend with his ex-wife and her... wife. Even though he wished them well, it was just too uncomfortable. "We're taking the *Allegro* out for an overnight. I'm shining her up right now."

"Who all is going?" She was fishing. Olivia worried about him being single in a small town where most of the women were married or widows old enough to be his mother.

"Liam and Carrie, Will and Julie, the Dugans—you know, the usual crowd."

"By any chance at all, are *you* taking a date?" Olivia asked.

"I'm driving the boat, kid. No time for a date," he said. "Besides who would I take? Mrs. Boerger from next door? She baked me a pie last week after I helped her fix her walker. Or how about Bertie, the yarn shop lady? She's single and she knitted me a great scarf this past winter."

Emma chortled in the background when Olivia burst out laughing, probably trying to picture her big, brawny dad with either of the two septuagenarians. "Okay, Dad, I hear you. I worry about you being alone, that's all."

"I'm not alone, sweetie. I have plenty of friends."

"But you need a woman in your life. Even Mom worries about you," Olivia said. "She's terrified she put you off marriage forever."

"Neither of you needs to worry about me. I'm fine. Someone will come along one day, but I'm not actively looking right now." Tony's gaze drifted up to the apartment above the boathouse and his mind went to the tiny redhead he knew was up there. The shutters were open for a change. He bit his lower lip as an idea took hold. "Actually, I think Julie might bring along her friend Sarah. She moved here a few weeks ago." He was thinking out loud, but decided he'd dial Julie as soon as he hung up with the girls.

"That sounds interesting."

"Poppy, are you driving Uncle Liam's boat today?" Emma broke in, heading off any nosy questions or innuendos from

Olivia. "Will you come and get me at Granny and G-maw Francie's house? I can wait on the beach for you."

"We're not headed to Chicago this trip, angel face."

Olivia giggled. "Mommy, Poppy called me angel face."

"I heard him, Em," Olivia said. "That's 'cause he thinks you are an angel, but we know better, don't we?"

"I don't have wings."

"Are you sure?" Tony asked. "I'm going to check you out next time I see you. I thought I saw some feathers on your shirt last time." Grateful for the change of subject, Tony allowed the nonsense with Em to continue until Olivia said they were pulling in the driveway. They lingered over good-byes for a moment and after one last *I love you,* broke the connection.

Tony sighed and stared at the picture on his phone for another second or two before he scrolled through his contacts for Julie Miles's number. It might be a long shot, but he hadn't been able to get Sarah Bennett out of his head. Maybe it was time to do something about it.

~

"Sophie, I don't know if this is such a great idea." Sarah regretted agreeing to the boat trip on Lake Michigan and now she was inventing excuses even as she tucked a change of clothes and her makeup kit into the small bag Sophie had brought her. "What if I get seasick?"

"If you didn't get seasick on the ferry coming over here, you won't get nauseated on Liam's boat." Sophie handed her a folded T-shirt. "Seriously, it's like a floating house."

"But I'm not ready. I've barely been out in public yet." Sarah's stomach was churning at the thought of having to be social for two whole days. She *was* doing better. She'd been to town for coffee with the MP twice this week, and she'd gone with

Carrie to the market and to Libby's winery up by the lighthouse. Last night, she'd even slept through the whole night for the first time since she'd arrived in Willow Bay, thanks to Sophie, who'd graciously taken her turn sleeping in the daybed downstairs.

But this was different. The husbands would be there. She knew and trusted Will Brody, Julie's long-time "gentleman friend" as Julie described him. She'd met Liam Reilly on several occasions in Chicago, but she didn't know Henry Dugan at all, and Sarah didn't do well with men. Two days in an environment she couldn't escape from scared the crap out of her.

She'd never been on a yacht in her life—her privileged child-hood in Ames, Georgia, had been all about golf, the country club, and fancy events in Atlanta. When she got married...well, Paul had hated the water, so the question of boating or even the beach never came up.

The knot in her stomach tightened.

"Do you have a sweatshirt?" Sophie asked. "You're going to need one tonight. Liam has heaters for the deck, but it can still get chilly out there on the water this time of year."

"I don't have a sweatshirt. All I have is my raincoat. Will didn't get anything out of my coat closet." Sarah latched onto that thought. "I don't have enough warm clothing to wear out on the water."

"No problem." Sophie pulled her phone out of her jeans pocket and swiped the screen. "I'll call Henry and have him bring one of mine for you." She was speaking to her husband before Sarah had a chance to object. "There. All set." Sophie tucked the phone back in her pocket. "We caught him on his way out the door."

Sarah tried another tack. "Do I need to bring any food or anything? I didn't even think to prepare anything to contribute."

"Nope." Sophie smiled. "The *Allegro* has a fully stocked kitchen and a chef. Come on."

Sarah verified the contents of the bag one more time before zipping it shut. She followed Sophie down the steps and made a final pass through the house, checking doors and windows.

"We checked everything twice before we went to bed last night." Sophie led her gently but firmly away from the back door, which now had a deadbolt on it, thanks to Will and his toolbox. "Nothing's changed. The apartment is secure."

"Are you sure you didn't open your window during the night?" When Sarah headed for the guest room, Sophie stopped her.

"I didn't open it. We're all good." She gave Sarah a hug. "Stop stalling, Sarah. The others are waiting down on the dock. Let's get moving."

Patting the pocket of her white jeans to make certain she had her phone, Sarah gave a longing thought to the pistol tucked in the drawer by her bed. She'd seriously considered putting it in her bag, but she'd promised Dr. Benton in their first session that she wouldn't carry it without getting a permit first and she hadn't gotten to that paperwork yet. Besides, it wasn't like they were going to get hijacked by pirates on Lake Michigan. Surely there were no pirates on the Great Lakes.

She locked the front door slowly, then leaned against the wooden screen door for a moment. "Have any boats ever been… you know, like…stopped or taken over out there?" Her heart rose to her throat as her imagination went wild with pictures of fierce bearded men in a beat-up scow brandishing guns and shouting obscenities, á la that Tom Hanks movie where his ship had been taken over by Somali terrorists.

Sophie blinked and shook her head as if to clear it. "Do you mean by the Coast Guard?"

"No, by like thieves or drug runners or"—Sarah suddenly felt very foolish as Sophie's grin extended practically ear to ear —"never mind."

"*Pirates*?" Sophie chortled. "You're not seriously worrying about pirates."

"I said never mind," Sarah said defensively. She was being ridiculous. Closing her eyes for a moment, she took a couple of deep cleansing breaths just as Dr. Benton had taught her in their session earlier that week. In for five and out for five, in for five and out for five. When she opened her eyes, Sophie wore a cock-eyed grin.

"Argh, matey." Sophie closed one eye and offered up her version of a pirate's grimace. "We need to be boardin' that ship now before they set sail without us."

"Cute, Soph, very cute." Sarah's sense of humor, which had been slowly reappearing over the past week, kicked in and she chuckled as they made their way down the stairs and down to the docks. They were steps from Liam and Carrie's gleaming white yacht when something Sophie had said earlier struck her. "Wait. Did you say there's a *chef*?"

"Well, sort of." Sophie glanced over her shoulder as Sarah lagged behind. "It's Tony, he pilots the boat and does all the cooking."

"Tony?" Sarah squeaked and stopped dead in her tracks. "The deputy sheriff?" This time her heart rose to her throat for a completely different reason. She'd seen the handsome burly sheriff around town, but only at a distance and she hadn't spoken to him. However, she had thought about him, more than once—thoughts that disturbed her, because she wasn't at all interested in getting involved with any man.

"*He's* coming on this trip?" She let her bag drop to the dock. "Shit, Sophie. You guys never said—"

Turning, Sophie fixed her eyes on Sarah. "Somebody has the drive the boat."

"Why can't Liam drive? It's his boat." Sarah's stomach roiled. She simply wasn't ready to face Tony Reynard again, not after she'd threatened to shoot him through the heart last time they'd met. And it wasn't only that he was one more man she'd have to deal with for forty-eight hours, either. Even in her agitated state on that first day, she'd felt the pull of attraction to the handsome deputy and she simply wasn't prepared to deal with that.

"Look, Tony's the captain of the *Allegro*," Sophie explained patiently. "It's a big yacht. Big enough, I think, that the last guy who owned it had a whole crew, not just a pilot. Tony came with the boat; it's how he and Liam met."

"I thought he was the town handyman. That's what he told me. And a deputy sheriff."

"He wears a lot of hats. He's also a housepainter and an amazing cook, which you'll soon discover if we get our butts on the boat." Sophie crossed the few feet between them. "Tony's one of the good guys, I promise. There's nothing to be afraid of."

Sarah shivered, suddenly cold in the breeze coming off the bay. "Is *his* wife coming too? I'm not up for all this, Sophie, especially not if I'm going to be the odd woman out in a group of couples. Don't make me do this."

"He's not married, so you won't be the odd person—there'll be eight of us, and Dr. Benton said you need to get out and be with people again." Sophie laid her hand on Sarah's trembling shoulder. "We'll be on the water where no one can follow us. You can sit with a group of friends and have a meal without constantly looking over your shoulder. You can truly relax." She put an arm around Sarah and pulled her into a warm hug. "Come on. This will be good for you."

Sarah stood stiffly in the embrace, struggling against the fierce urge to bolt, to turn and flee back to the safety of the apartment. In her head, it all made perfect sense—the boat was the ideal environment for her first social gathering and the MPs were her friends. This wasn't a crowded city venue; it was a boat headed out on Lake Michigan for a sunny warm May weekend.

Sophie had a valid point. She wouldn't have to wonder if she was being followed or be sure to sit in the chair facing the entrance or keep a vigilant watch over every exit door. Dr. Benton had encouraged her to take the trip, to do anything that got her out of the apartment. Sarah's rational mind understood why that was important if she was ever going to live a normal life.

But was it even possible for her to have a normal life?

"Besides, what's safer than traveling with friends who love you, and having your own personal cop right there?" Sophie held her at arm's length to peer into her face. "It's another step forward, Sarah. One more tiny step toward freedom."

"Okay, okay." Although Sarah picked up her bag and marched toward the vessel, she stopped again as they arrived. "Hey, Soph." She offered her new friend a beseeching look. "Could you… Could you not mention the whole pirate thing, okay?"

Sophie's smile was tender. "Our secret, cross my heart." And to make the point, she drew an imaginary X on her chest.

"Thanks." Sarah squared her shoulders. "Well then, let's get on the damn boat…matey."

CHAPTER 6

S arah peered down the stairs to the main deck, trying to remember which side of the boat the kitchen, er, the galley, was on—left or right. Or was that starboard or port? She hadn't mastered which was which yet, although she'd learned more about boats and the lingo that came with them in the last twelve hours than she'd ever cared to know. Somehow, the captain of the *Allegro* had managed to find the time to give her a tour of the yacht that included every square inch of the huge vessel.

She'd been duly impressed by the massive boat with its dark-paneled main salon, a dining room, a gourmet kitchen, six sleeping cabins, each with a beautifully outfitted en-suite bathroom, and upper and main decks. Below deck was storage, an engine room, and space for what Tony referred to as *mechanicals*, which from the look of it, meant laundry, plumbing, and electrical. The lowest area also included the crew's quarters, which this weekend consisted only of Captain Reynard.

It *was* like a floating house; Sophie had been right on about that. Except for the lifeboats tucked into the ceiling of the main deck, Sarah could've been staying in lovely B&B. Well, that and the fact that she was surrounded by the gray-blue waters of Lake Michigan.

She found the door to the kitchen and pushed it open. She needed some crackers or something so she could take the damn antidepressant she'd forgotten to take with her breakfast a couple of hours earlier. She'd discovered she needed to take the medicine with food or it nauseated her, which was why she normally swallowed the pill with her morning coffee and bagel. She had only been on the drug about a week, so the effects of the medication weren't noticeable yet. But Dr. Benton had insisted on the prescription—just for a little while, she'd said. Sarah had agreed reluctantly—she hated drugs of any kind.

"Hello!" Tony Reynard, swathed in a spotless, if wet, white butcher's apron, stood at the sink loading dishes into the biggest dishwasher Sarah had ever seen.

She stopped in the open doorway. "Oh, hi."

Well, that was scintillating.

"Can I help you?" His smile crinkled the lines around his amber-brown eyes. "You need something?"

Sarah felt that smile all the way to her toes. "I was looking for something to nibble on—a cracker or something."

"Oh sure." He shut the dishwasher and dried his hand on the towel he'd slung over his shoulder. "How about these?" He pulled a box of Wheat Thins from a cabinet. "I can slice you some cheese to go with them."

"No thanks, just the crackers are fine." Sarah accepted the box, shocked at the zing that went through her when their fingers touched. This man's effect on her was bewildering and alarming and heady. She let the process of opening the box and pulling out a few crackers cover her confusion.

"Who's driving the boat?" she asked, reaching for a napkin from a basket on the stainless steel island.

"Liam. He and Will take turns out here on the open water. It's not a problem. I probably wouldn't trust either of them to bring the old girl into the bay or the marina, though." He folded the towel over the handle on the dishwasher. "Have a seat, why don't you?" He indicated a couple of stools with a nod. "I was just thinking about having another cup of coffee while I figure out what I'm going to make for supper tonight, if you'd care to join me."

Astonishingly, curiosity won out over anxiety if it meant a chance to get to know Tony Reynard, so Sarah pushed down the ever-present urge to cut and run and walked slowly to the stool. Unlike many abused women, she'd never had any desire to find another relationship. The very idea of a man touching her was repellant, which meant there was never any hoping against hope that this time she'd choose more wisely. She'd simply avoided the cruel cycle altogether by not dating again after her divorce. Her interest in Tony both intrigued and worried her, but what was the harm in having a cup of coffee?

Tony poured two mugs of coffee and put a handful of creamer pods in front of her. "Two creams, no sugar, right?" He settled on the stool next to hers.

"Right. Thank you." Sarah sipped her coffee, very aware of how big this man was—at least twice her size.

"What's everyone else up to?" Tony asked, looking relaxed and handsome in his jeans and a wild Hawaiian print shirt, which Carrie had told her was his uniform on the boat. Today's was all shades of tangerine, hot pink, and navy blue, and she had to confess the look worked for him. He sported a backward baseball cap that he yanked off to run his fingers through his salt-and-pepper hair.

"The women are upstairs playing that dice game again. Will and Henry are fishing off the…stern?" She hesitated over the term.

"The back of the boat?" He grinned when she nodded. "Yup, that's the stern. And the front is the…?"

She smiled. "The bow."

"Excellent. And what do we call this?" He indicated the kitchen and she couldn't help but notice how big his hands were.

"The galley," she declared. "And the living room is the main salon and my bathroom is a head."

"You've learned well, grasshopper." Tony chuckled. "Here's one for you to research. What do we call the space below deck where we store extra supplies?"

"Ah-ha," Sarah said, triumphantly. "I don't need to research—it's called the *hold*."

"That's right. How'd you know?"

"I have to confess I heard Liam refer to it when I got on the boat yesterday."

"Um, you mean when you *came aboard ship*?" His lips quirked as he corrected her.

"Oh sorry, Captain, but I'm just a little ol' country girl from Georgia." She played along, allowing her Southern drawl to show. "One day I'll master all these fancy yachtin' terms." Good God, was she *flirting*? She didn't flirt. Well, maybe she was a little bit —it had been years since she'd used those rusty skills.

As they laughed together, Sarah was surprised to realize her tension had eased somewhat as she sipped her coffee. Tony no longer frightened her. For that matter, none of the men she'd spent the last day with had given her any reason to worry. Will and Liam, whom she already knew, had been kind as always and Henry Dugan was a quiet, intelligent man who'd engaged her in a discussion about shipwrecks here in Lake Michigan. He was new to the area too and still discovering the fascinating history of the Great Lakes.

And then there was Tony, who'd welcomed her aboard and somehow managed to be present even though he'd also been cooking and piloting the boat. She couldn't help being curious about this man whose list of talents seemed endless.

"Do you ever have a crew?" she asked.

"It depends." He shrugged and a lock of hair fell over his forehead. "If we're going out for longer than a couple of days, I might round up a couple of college kids to help me keep things running smoothly. Liam can pilot us, too, and Carrie loves to cook, so we all pitch in on trips like this one."

"Sophie told me you came with the *Allegro*. Have you always been a boat pilot?"

"Nope. I was an engineer for a lot of years. In Chicago. I was a partner with Franklin Electric."

"I know them," Sarah exclaimed. "I used to see their red-and-white trucks all over the city. How'd you make the leap from engineer to boat captain? I mean, the engineer to handyman makes sense, but…boat captain? Oh, and deputy sheriff? And then there's the whole chef thing."

"A couple of years after my divorce, I just sorta realized my life was pretty boring. My wife was gone, my daughter was away at college, and I lived in a very…sterile apartment not far from the office."

"You have a daughter?" She clutched as she always did when someone mentioned their children. Even though Macy had died almost ten years ago, Sarah's heart ached over her daughter every single day.

"Yup." His expression filled with pride. "And a granddaughter, Emma, who just turned four."

"Are they in Chicago?"

"Yeah, they live in Evanston. Olivia is an ER nurse and Brian, her husband, is a physics professor at Northwestern."

She pictured a tall young woman with her father's dark hair and amber-brown eyes and wondered about her own daughter. Macy would have been twenty-five. Sarah could've been a grandmother by now. The possibility made the ache in her heart throb even deeper, and her voice quavered ever so slightly when she prodded, "So you were tired of the rat race and you left your engineering job?"

"I did." He gave her such a concerned look that she hurried on to another question before he began asking his own.

"But you still had to make a living, right?" God, had she really just asked a guy she barely knew about his financial situation? Heat rose from her neck to her cheeks. But Tony didn't seem to notice...or mind the question.

He rose and brought the coffee carafe over, refilling first her cup and then his as he resumed his story. "I'd met Will several years before through another partner at the company and put our investments in his hands—"

"Ah, the Sorcerer of LaSalle Street strikes again." Sarah chuckled, grateful for a chance to release painful memories. "So not to pry, but could *you* conceivably be the owner of this tub?" *Crap!* She did it again! Her social skills had deteriorated worse than she thought. "Sorry, that *was* prying. Ignore me."

"Madam, kindly never refer to the *Allegro* as a *tub*." Tony replied in feigned horror. "She is a state-of-the-art motor yacht." His deep laugh sent a flutter through her.

"I beg your pardon, captain." She kept her grave expression with difficulty.

"As well you should." His eyes twinkled and Sarah was struck by the way the lights overhead made them appear almost honey-colored. "And I don't mind answering your question at all. Yes, Will did well by us, so both Shannon, my ex, and I are comfortable. Thankfully, Olivia left school debt-free. When I retired early, I needed something to do, so I decided to buy a small boat like my dad had when I was a teenager. We spent every summer cruising the Great Lakes until"—his expression sobered—"until we lost him to cancer not long after Shannon and I got married."

He took a long drag on his coffee, then said, "I love boating. Always have. That's how I met the previous owner of this magnificent vessel."

"Obviously he wasn't at the yacht store looking for a *small* boat." Sarah smirked.

Tony snickered. "Nope, he was at the marina looking for someone to pilot his brand-new, very large, very expensive party barge."

"So instead of spending money on your own boat..."

"Exactly." He nodded. "I applied for my license and suddenly I was Cap'n Tony—pilot, cook, and chief babysitter to a kid who became a millionaire overnight because he knew how to run with a football."

～

Embarrassed that he couldn't keep the note of disdain from his tone as he told the story of how he ended up on the *Allegro,* Tony hurried the rest, "After five years of partying and snorting money up his nose, he finally sold the boat to Liam." The football player's story wasn't all that uncommon—talented kid gets recruited right out of college, signs a huge contract with an NFL franchise, and can't handle the wealth and fame, but he'd had a front-row seat to the whole debacle and hadn't been able to do a thing about it.

"Why'd you stay?" Sarah asked the question he'd asked himself for four of the five years, but the answer was complicated.

Tony would've liked to have said his intentions were entirely altruistic, that he hung in there and tried to help because he saw how much the kid wanted to play football and how hard he worked to stay clean during the season. Although the desire to keep the athlete on the straight-and-narrow had played into it, the simple truth was that he loved the *Allegro* and he loved being on the lake. It still rankled that he'd had to protect the boat from the drunken groupies who trashed it every summer.

"I dunno." He shrugged, reluctant to confess how relieved he'd been when the kid ended up in rehab and the yacht was sold. "But I'm happy to report that he finally got his act together."

"And happy that you got to stay and continue taking care of the *Allegro*," she said, and he had the feeling she'd seen right through him. Clearly, she was smart as well as beautiful, and those blue eyes held such sadness and such wisdom he knew she'd seen too much of the ugliness in the world.

A longing to show her the beautiful parts welled up in him. He grappled with the urge to simply take her in his arms as he nodded. "Thanks to Will, who steered Liam to the old girl when I told him she was up for sale. The rest is easy—I stayed with the *Allegro*, became good friends with Liam, and ended up moving to Willow Bay when he and Carrie got married. I've always been handy with tools, so when I'm not being Cap'n Tony, I do odd jobs around town."

"And the sheriff thing?" The longer they talked—well, *he* talked while she listened—the less nervous Sarah seemed, although she was still fidgeting with a tiny pillbox she'd pulled out of her pocket. It was obvious she had no intention of bringing the conversation around to herself, so he kept answering her questions without asking any of his own, even though they swirled in his brain.

"Yeah, that just happened a couple of years ago. The other deputy left for greener pastures and I'd done some work on Sheriff Gibson's kitchen. It's not a very interesting story."

"And you're a chef? You really are quite the renaissance man, Cap'n Tony." She gave him a hint of a smile.

"Oh yeah, that's me. And I'm no chef. I just like to cook." Tony watched a bit longer as she opened and closed the little green box before he finally asked, "Do you need a bottle of water, Sarah?"

Her fingers closed around the little container and she looked away. Tony could almost see her shut down and he cursed inwardly. He shouldn't have asked about it; he'd taken a step too close. He backtracked, casting around in his head for something casual and impersonal to say. "So I can either do a taco bar or make salmon on cedar planks tonight for supper. What sounds good?"

"I've got water, thanks." She rose, shoved the pillbox in her jeans pocket, and wrapped the small stack of crackers in a napkin. "They both sound great, Tony." She headed for the door. "Thanks for the coffee."

Dammit, he couldn't just let her bolt. They'd made some real progress and he sensed a couple of minutes ago that he might have had a shot at a date when they got back to dry land. "Sarah?"

Wordlessly, she stopped, one brow quirked in an expectant gaze, but her expression was cool. Shuttered.

"I...um...I'm thinking taco bar." He sounded like an idiot, but he pushed on, determined to reach her at some level. "It's kind of work intensive though. Would you be interested in helping me chop vegetables and heat up tortillas?"

Was that a flicker of interest in her eyes? Hard to tell, but finally she nodded briefly. "Okay." She turned back toward the door, but spun around, almost catching his silent cheer. "Do you have sweet onions, jalapeños, and roma tomatoes? I make a mean pico de gallo."

"I do." Heat flushed his cheeks at the near-miss. Wouldn't the sight of his mini fist-pump scare the crap right out of her? "I love pico de gallo. That sounds great!"

"Okay." The barest hint of a smile crossed her lips. "See you later."

CHAPTER 7

"Jules, I don't know." Sarah shivered in spite of the afternoon sun warming her bare arms as she lay in the chaise lounge on the upper deck of the *Allegro*.

The day had been lovely—so enjoyable in fact that she'd managed to shove her fear to the very back of her mind. They were far enough out on the lake that they hadn't passed another boat in hours. There was only the sun, the breeze, the hum of the engine, and the quiet whoosh of the water against the sides of the yacht as they cruised along. She'd even gotten comfortable enough around Liam, Will, and Henry that she didn't clench every time she heard a deep male laugh.

And then there was Tony. Although the captain had spent a good deal of time on the bridge, when he did appear all smiling and warm, she felt his presence right down to her core.

"You'd be perfect." Julie raised the back of her chaise another notch. "Don't you think so, Caro?"

"I do." Carrie sat up also, shoving her sunglasses on top of her head and twisting in her chair to face Sarah. "You're the one who inspired Jules in the first place, Sarah. She wouldn't even have tried for the grant if hadn't been for your work at the shelter."

"I haven't said anything to you until now because I was waiting to hear if I got the money from the Conroy Foundation," Julie said. "I asked for five hundred thousand, thinking we might possibly get a quarter million. You know better than anyone how these things work." She reached for her book on the low table beside her, pulled out an envelope that was stuck between the pages, and tossed it on Sarah's lap. "Look, Sarah! They're giving us the whole half a mil! And now *you're* here—it's a sign that I should be doing this thing."

Sarah opened the envelope and scanned the contents as the knot in her stomach got tighter. *Dammit anyway*. For the first time since she left Chicago, she was almost relaxed. Sophie had been absolutely right—she'd needed this weekend to clear her head, to make the conscious choice to move on. But now, when her friends offered her what she knew in her heart was the perfect opportunity to do just that, her belly dropped at the mere thought. Not only because of her last encounter with Paul, although that was still raw, but it was also the thought of the shelter and all she'd left behind there. She'd literally run away from everything she'd worked so hard to accomplish for the last few years and was back to square one again. Physically, emotionally, and mentally.

Now this? Julie wanted her to help open a shelter here in Willow Bay?

Sarah folded the letter and slipped it back into its envelope. "I'm not ready to help other women right now, you guys—I can barely leave my own apartment."

"But this is perfect, don't you see?" Julie accepted the envelope. "It's going to take months to get everything up and running. You'd have something to do every day, something to focus on…a mission that would take you away from the apartment."

"And out of yourself," Sophie added, ascending the steps with a tray full of drinks in salt-rimmed glasses. "It's five o'clock, ladies, and Henry's below at the bar doing wonderful things with tequila and a blender. Sarah, this one's yours—it's a virgin, but trust me, still amazing. The man makes a genius margarita either way." She served Sarah first and then passed a beverage to each of the others before settling into a chair and putting her feet up on the end of Julie's chaise. "Please think about this, Sarah. Jules already has a house on the east side of the village all picked out. It's a bit dilapidated, but it's big and would be ideal for a shelter."

Sarah tasted the drink—the blend of salt and the sweet-tart of lime and sugar was indeed spectacular, even though it didn't contain a drop of tequila. She didn't mind Dr. Benton's admonition about not mixing the antidepressants with alcohol—she wasn't much of a drinker anyway. She learned many years ago that even though wine or tequila might dull pain, it also dulled her ability to think clearly. She gazed around at the women's eager faces. "Why do you think this town needs a battered women's shelter? I mean, I know abuse goes on everywhere, but surely there's help in a bigger town nearby. Traverse City?"

"I want *us* to be a part of the Violence Against Women Coalition—not only help victims of domestic abuse, but also girls caught up in sex trafficking. This is important...and so necessary. We can be a safe haven on the road to a new start." Julie bounded out of her chair without spilling a drop of her drink. "Obviously, we wouldn't be as big an operation as the shelter in Chicago; we'd be more of an emergency stop. But it's perfect, don't you see, because who'd look for a runaway in a town like this one?"

"Do you really want to bring this crap to Willow Bay?" Sarah doubted Julie knew what she was undertaking. "Does your town council know what you're planning? You're never going to get zoned for it."

"The village board has already tentatively approved it. I had to have a letter from the board when I applied for the Conroy grant. Everything's in place. I'm dying to show you what we've already gotten done." Julie's eyes sparkled. "Oh, Sarah, you're the one who made me see how important this work is and, besides, you need a job, dammit."

"Actually, I *don't* need a job." Sarah set her glass down and hauled herself out of the lounge chair. Irritation snaked through her and she pushed it down with effort. Of course, Julie would bring this up here, now. This cruise couldn't simply be a couple of days out on the water to relax. Everybody always had an agenda.

Julie must've remembered a late-night conversation they'd had when Sarah had gotten on her soapbox about how few places there were in the country where women could feel safe enough to regroup after fleeing domestic abuse. How ideally, an underground railroad–type network of shelters would extend into every city and town in America. At the time, she hadn't been talking about opening and operating these places herself.

But now the idea got her attention in spite of everything else roiling around in her head. Running an emergency shelter for victims of domestic violence touched her heart exactly the way Julie knew it would. And truth be told, they'd chosen the perfect moment to spring it on her—when she was halfway calm—because *dammit*, ideas, to-do lists, and mental pictures of bright, cheery rooms and a large family-style kitchen where women could gather were already shoving the doubts aside. Her back to the others, she stared out across the sparkling lake and took several deep, cleansing breaths.

"It's a chance to serve others here the same way you served all those years in Chicago." Carrie appeared behind her and put a gentle hand on Sarah's shoulder. "We'd all pitch in. You wouldn't be doing this alone. Julie has a business plan full of costs and financial projections and all that stuff. She's been working on this idea for over a year, and it's because of you."

"Me?" Sarah stared at Carrie, whose open, loving expression didn't hold even a hint of the shrewd coerciveness she'd expected to see.

"Of course you." Carrie's smile grew. "We're so unbelievably proud of you and your work in Chicago. You're the one who can make this place a huge success. You've got the know-how and the connections and the experience and the *heart*, Sarah. We both saw you in action in Chicago."

"I ran a damn resale shop." Sarah's tone came out rougher than she intended. "Not the whole shelter."

"But you were on the board and you lived with the day-to-day operations." Julie joined them at the rail, covering Sarah's other side. "*And* those women trusted you."

"Those women were desperate." Sarah shuddered at the memory of her own desperation when Paul turned up at her door. No way was she prepared to cope with that again. "I was just someone who'd been in their shoes. I'm no counselor."

Sophie nudged into the group and handed Sarah the drink she'd left on the table. "We can find counselors, but according to Julie, you're a helluva manager, and that's what we need."

"You're in on this, too?" Sarah accepted the beverage and gave Sophie a brief smile.

"Yep," Sophie raised her glass in a toast. "Libby, too. She's already got some summer fundraisers planned over at the winery, and I have a feeling this is going to become Henry Dugan's new favorite charity."

Julie placed a bolstering arm around Sarah. "We aren't talking about a hundred beds. The place will hold up to five or six families or maybe a dozen single women at most, and no one would be staying longer than a couple of weeks." Her tone lowered to a more persuasive timbre. "You know, a stop to get them fed and clothed and provide new IDs before we send them off to wherever they want to settle. A safe house. That's all. I'm gonna do this no matter what, but we need you." Her eyes narrowed. "Before everything went down with your bastard ex, I'd been intending to ask you to consider coming up here. He just moved things along."

Sarah trembled, her mind awash with scenarios, both good and bad. However, she had to confess she was ready for something more to do. She'd been thinking more along the lines of maybe learning to knit. That yarn shop in the village was pretty interesting and she remembered watching her grandmother knit. It seemed like a soothing activity. But starting a new shelter for women who'd experienced the very thing she was hiding from here intrigued her exactly as her friends knew it would.

If she got involved, there was a better-than-good chance Paul would find her. Hell, she hadn't a single doubt that he'd turn up in Willow Bay at some point anyway. That was inevitable. Paul Prescott didn't lose—ever. Hiding here wouldn't deter him forever.

But for now, in this moment, she was breathing, and for the first time in longer than she could remember, anticipation, not dread, stirred inside her. When she gazed across the peaceful water of Lake Michigan, that cold brick of fear almost, but not quite, began to thaw.

She caught her lower lip with her teeth. "Five hundred grand is a good start, but it's not even close to what we'll need to open."

CHAPTER 8

Raucous chatter and laughter met Tony as he came down the stairs from the bridge. "I'm looking for that *sous*-chef who claims to make a mean *pico de gallo*," he called as he approached the group who, it appeared, had just refilled their margarita glasses from an icy pitcher set between them.

Sarah sat with her back to the wall at the big teak table, which didn't surprise him in the least. She may have relaxed some as they'd been out on the water; however, he noticed her constant vigilance, always checking the area, going on hyper alert if another boat came within a few hundred yards of the *Allegro*.

"I can do that if you show me—" Carrie's offer was interrupted by an elbow to the ribs from Sophie. "What?"

"I think he's looking for Sarah," Sophie stage-whispered, then looked at him with pleased approval while Julie raised her brows.

"Well, *that* was subtle." Sarah slipped out of her chair, drink in hand. "As a matter of fact, he *is* looking for me. Ready for KP, Captain." She turned those Caribbean blue eyes on Tony and his knees went weak.

"Oh. *Oh*. Okay." Carrie's face beamed with comprehension, and he realized a little come-to-Jesus talk with the Posse was going to be necessary in the very near future. He certainly didn't need these three tag-teaming her about him. He wanted to get to know her better, but this was *his* ballgame and he sure didn't want this well-meaning bunch scaring the crap out of her before he even got up to bat.

"Who's got the con?" Sophie asked as Henry and Will sauntered around the corner, Will carrying a tray laden with bags of tortilla chips and jars of salsa. "Ah, okay, so Liam's on the bridge."

He nodded, basking in the warmth of good friends, a beautiful boat, and a Lake Michigan sunset. It was good to be captain; he couldn't deny how much he loved his life—especially today. He glanced around, his focus settling on the tiny redhead who'd come around the table to stand beside him, and he fought an urge to yank the clip out of that mass of thick hair so he could watch the waves spill over her shoulders.

In one smooth move, Henry passed behind them, handed Sarah a new drink, and collected her used glass. "A virgin marg for the lady rocking my wife's Stanford sweatshirt," he said with a grin. "Looks good on you. We'll bring you back one of your own next time we go west."

"Thanks, Henry, I'd love that!" Her smile lit up the deck and Tony's heart lurched.

A little worried that his infatuation was showing, he gave Will and Henry the evil eye. "Good God, men, don't you have any couth at all? You could've at least stuck a spoon in each jar and brought out some plates."

"Hey, Martha Stewart, we used a tray." Will held the snacks out. "What more do you want?"

"How about baskets for the chips? Napkins? Oh hell, give me that." He took the tray and with a head tilt toward Sarah headed for the galley. "We'll be back in few minutes."

Hoots of laughter followed them down the gangway and the

impish grin she tossed over her shoulder sent a twinge of longing through him. It'd been a long time since a woman had intrigued him like Sarah. He eyed her cute little backside as she shouldered the galley door open and he wondered how any man could ever want to harm her. Fury replaced desire for a moment when she turned those amazing eyes on him and asked how she could help.

What kind of monster wallops the crap out of a woman? Who does that? What kind of sick son of a bitch tears into a person half his size and intimidates and abuses her for years on end? And why, dear God, does she stay and take it? He had so many questions he wanted to ask her, but they weren't there yet.

Julie hadn't given him any details about what happened to Sarah. However, he'd learned about domestic violence in the criminal justice and psychology classes he'd taken at Western after Sheriff Earl Gibson deputized him. He'd even been called to a couple of domestic disturbances right here in Willow Bay since becoming a deputy. Bucolic as it seemed to tourists, the village had all the drama of any other town, only on a much smaller scale.

Last week, after coaxing a bit more information out of Julie one evening, he'd used the computer at work to check out the case file on her ex-husband, Paul Prescott. He'd found more details than he'd ever wanted to know. Crime scene photographs of her teenaged daughter taken after she'd been run over and dragged down the driveway made his gorge rise. The autopsy report showed that, mercifully, she'd died on impact.

His heart ached at the pictures of Sarah in the file—the bastard had broken her nose that last round, yanked out a handful of that beautiful red hair, and blackened one eye. Her face was so cut and swollen he'd barely recognized her. She had four broken ribs and was a mass of bruises on her back and thighs. According to the report, she spent more than a week in the hospital before she could even bury her child. Most infuriating was the mug shot of Prescott, who looked as if he was posing for an ad in *GQ*—not a hair out of place and wearing an arrogant smirk that made Tony want to punch the computer screen. He'd killed his daughter and beaten the living crap out of his wife. The man was a monster.

"Where are they?" Sarah's question brought his focus back to the galley.

"Where are what?" He blinked and realized he was just standing there holding the tray.

"The baskets." She peered at him. "Are you okay?"

"Yes, yes, I'm fine." He set the tray on the island and gave her a warm smile. "Sorry, senior moment."

She laughed, a rich delicious sound that filled the galley, and once again, he was overtaken with the urge to wrap her in his arms and keep her safe so that laugh would never disappear again.

What the hell was going on? He hadn't been this distracted by a female since he'd gotten hit in the head with a basketball while drooling at Mary Jane McDonald in her cheerleader outfit.

"Senior moment?" she scoffed. "You hardly qualify, my friend."

"I'm fifty-two. Hell, woman, I'm a grandfather, remember?" He pulled three large wicker baskets from a cupboard under the island and pointed to a drawer behind her. "Napkins for lining the baskets in that drawer."

"As I said, you hardly qualify." She shook out three red-and-white-checked cloth napkins and tucked them into the baskets while he ripped open the bags of chips. "I can't believe you're a grandfather."

"I am." He nodded toward the bulletin board beside the door. "To that little heartbreaker right there in the pink overalls."

She wandered over to examine a photo posted among the detritus of fire exit instructions, carryout menus, and recipes. She stood for a long moment, running her fingers over the matte surface of the picture. "How gorgeous," she whispered and swallowed visibly.

"Thanks." Although he was longing to ask about her daughter, this wasn't the time, so he redirected her attention to the food. "Okay, so yellow corn tortilla chips in this one for Henry and Julie and me"—he filled one basket—"and white in this one for Will, Liam, and Carrie because they're not crazy about the yellow." He poured thinner white corn chips into another basket. "Potato chips in this last one because Sophie doesn't like tortilla chips at all— she's always the odd man out on Mexican night."

"You really do take care of them like you were their daddy, don't you?" Sarah's face brightened—clearly, she was grateful for a chance to change the subject.

Tony shrugged. "It's my job. Besides, when you've been together as long as we have, you kinda learn what people prefer."

"You guys are all so close—it's nice." Wistfulness edged her tone.

"We've been friends a long time and it's a small town." He stuck the baskets of tortilla chips in the microwave and gave them forty-five seconds each. "But we're always open to new friends. Love 'em in fact." He handed her some small bowls. "Here, dump the salsas in these, and the French onion dip for Soph goes in the clear glass dish. Believe it or not, Carrie bought colored spoons for the salsas so she could tell which was hot, medium, and mild. She hates anything too spicy."

"Oh, this is too cute. Red for hot"—Sarah put the spoon in the hot sauce—"yellow for medium and green for mild." She placed the other spoons appropriately. "And is that sugar? What's that for?"

"The sweetness makes the mild sauce even milder." He'd crowded a sugar bowl onto the tray with the other dishes and added small paper plates and napkins. "Carrie's hard over about not wanting food to burn her mouth."

"Somehow that doesn't surprise me. Personally, I like a little heat."

He almost dropped the baskets of warm chips as he watched her dip her finger in the hottest sauce and suck it off. Unquestionably, it was the sexiest thing he'd seen in ages simply because the gesture was so innocent. Sarah wasn't flirting with him; she had only relaxed enough to be herself. He handed her the baskets. "So do I." Anticipating the great view, he picked up the tray and, with a nod, indicated for her to lead the way.

Sarah blinked back tears as she diced a sweet onion into tiny pieces and dumped them into a bowl. No matter how sweet the onion was, it always made her cry. She swiped the back of her gloved hand across her cheek as the tears spilled over.

"Here, try this." He set a lighted votive candle on the counter next to her cutting board. Gloved himself, he was seeding and chopping jalapeño peppers. "I saw Alton Brown do this. Claims the smoke from the candle draws away the odor of the onion."

They were back in the kitchen preparing the taco bar after delivering the snacks to the main deck and hanging out with the group for a while. Sarah had ignored the knowing glances from Carrie, Julie, and Sophie as she nabbed a plate of hot salsa and some chips. No question those three were matchmaking, even though they had to know this wasn't the appropriate time in her already-confused life for that.

"The gloves are genius." She sniffed, grabbed a paper towel, and blew her nose. Very elegant, but what else could she do? "Where did you learn about that?"

"Life lesson, actually." He grinned as he added his peppers to her bowl of onions. "Is that enough or do you want more?"

"That looks like plenty, thanks."

He moved to the sink to rinse the roma tomatoes he'd produced from a bowl on the counter when they got back to the kitchen, no, *galley*, after they'd delivered snacks to the main deck.

She was still working on the lingo, determined to get the terms right. For some odd reason, she felt Tony would be pleased, although why she cared about that was a mystery. She'd decided long ago that she would never again try to please another man. Maybe *please* was the wrong word. Perhaps the boat was simply a place to connect with him, and she was shocked down to her socks at how badly she wanted to connect with this man on any level. But she did.

"I got the box of gloves after I damn near blinded myself rubbing my eye when I'd seeded hot peppers once." He grimaced as he told the story. "I washed my hands; I guess the essence stays, because I didn't think I'd ever open my eyes again. I saw a chef in Puerto Vallarta using them after I'd figured it out, so not original thinking, just a good idea. How many tomatoes?"

"Why don't we chop all of them? Then we'll have them for the taco bar, too." She reached into the colander the same time he did. When their hands bumped, her stomach fluttered in a way so unfamiliar she stopped mid-grasp and almost dropped the tomato. She recovered quickly enough, although heat flushed her cheeks. "The gloves are great, but they do make things slippery." A pretty good save considering her knees were shaking under the giant apron he'd given her earlier.

Well, crap.

Was she really becoming smitten, as her Southern belle grandmother used to say? This was so not the time for her to get all dewy-eyed over the local deputy sheriff—she had way too much emotional baggage to add anything else right now. She was fairly sure Dr. Benton would agree. The pull was there, though, and she wasn't sure what made Tony Reynard different from any of the other men she'd met since leaving Atlanta. He was handsome, but so were plenty of other guys. Although he was twice her size, his warm brown eyes and ever-present easygoing smile kept him from seeming intimidating. She stole quick peeks at him as they chopped tomatoes in peaceful, companionable silence.

And there was the real rub—the reason she was so attracted. He was obviously a serene soul. With a few notable exceptions like Will Brody and Liam Reilly, Sarah had grown so accustomed to men simmering with rage that she'd come to expect all men to be like her ex-husband. Most didn't disappoint her as they came storming into the shelter looking for errant wives or girlfriends. Not all were openly violent; some seemed perfectly harmless, charming even. Those were the ones you truly wanted to watch. Turned out that the more charismatic a guy was, the more dangerous he could become.

For all his size—and Tony Reynard was a very big man indeed—he was also obviously a gentle man. And a *gentleman* in the old-fashioned sense of the word. Sarah could let her guard down a bit with him—not completely, perhaps never completely, but for now, they could be friends.

Friends would be nice.

CHAPTER 9

The house needed work, no question about that. Sarah shook her head as she stood with Julie in front of the dilapidated old structure on Eastern Avenue. "A diamond in the rough," the real estate listing sheet read. At the moment, Sarah was having a hard time even considering the place a "fixer-upper."

"Do you think it's even structurally sound?" she asked. "What if all we can do is rent a bulldozer and start over? We don't have that kind of money."

"The house is sound," Julie said with way more confidence that Sarah felt. "Mattie assured me there's good bones and Will's gone top to bottom. It just needs a little work."

"You keep saying that, like all we have to do is sweep out the cobwebs, paint the walls, and wash the windows." Across the front, a wrought-iron fence was still intact, including an ornate gate that must have beautiful at one time, but was now all rust and peeling black paint. However, along the sides as far as she could see from the street, gaps showed where chunks of the old fence had been taken, probably to be sold for the metal.

"I know it's going to be a lot more work than that." Julie's perfect brows pinched together in a frown, then she brightened just as quickly. "But the historical society is ready to be rid of it, so they're practically willing to give the place away."

Sarah doubted that seriously—nobody *gave* anything away. "Two hundred and fifty-seven thousand isn't giving away—that's half our grant. And how does a nonprofit sell off an asset? Does our purchase price come to them as a donation or what? Are we going to be tied up in IRS red tape for years?"

"Oh, who knows? I'm sure the attorneys for the society have that all worked out or they wouldn't allow them to sell the place. And a quarter mil isn't even close to what we'll be offering. Truthfully, I'm hoping we can convince the society to donate the place or sell it to us for ten bucks. Can't you try to look past all the warts and see the perfection?" Julie threw her arms out as if to embrace the property. "It's a big sturdy house built at a time when people had lots of kids, so there are six bedrooms and a huge kitchen and dining room. The downstairs has a library and a solarium and two parlors, and a maid's room off the kitchen that would be a perfect office for you. There's even a freaking butler's pantry, for Pete's sake. Plus a full finished basement where we could put a space for the kids to play and storage for supplies and donations." Her eyes sparkled as she headed off on a tangent. "Oh, donations. Most of these women are gonna arrive with only the clothes on their backs. We'll have to start collecting stuff as soon as we can."

Sarah couldn't help smiling at Julie's enthusiasm and even catching a little of it herself. The rather overgrown yard was vast —the listing had said nearly two acres—and although it wasn't easy to imagine it cleaned-up, she was picturing an expanse of green lawn in front under the ancient trees that desperately needed trimming and maybe a playground out back. The rambling house had a wide porch along three sides where they could put wicker settees and rocking chairs, maybe hang a Boston fern right there in that section that rounded out into a little gazebo at the far corner.

The fact that the house was on the edge of town and yet walking distance to all the shops and restaurants and the harbor made Sarah glad. Neighbors weren't so close that post-midnight arrivals would be an issue—that was a good thing, because experience had taught her that often victims showed up in the dark of night. Chewing her lower lip, she peered down the drive that curved from the road, wondering if parking was going to be a problem and if there were any outbuildings. Didn't the ad mention a carriage house or a barn or something?

She tugged on the padlock that held the tall gates together before running her hands over bricked columns on either side of the driveway.

"What are you doing?" Julie asked.

"Seeing if there's a loose brick where they'd hide a key to the gate." Sarah tested a couple at eye-level and mortar rained down.

"I'd guess a bunch of them are loose," Julie said wryly. "This place has been empty for years. I remember Lillian McCartney—the last one to live here. She was ancient, but she died right before the twins were born, so about twenty-five years ago." She leaned against the front fender of the car to reminisce. "I drove Charlie crazy because I was convinced that old lady's death was a sign that the babies weren't going to survive birth." She shook her head at Sarah's puzzled look. "Don't ask—I was weird when I was pregnant. Her funeral was so sad because only about a dozen people from the village showed up; no family came because she was like the last of her line."

Sarah couldn't imagine anything more depressing than a funeral where no one came to mourn the deceased. Macy's service was packed to the rafters. The funeral director had set up chairs in the hallway and into the next room. "She didn't have kids?"

"No, she never married and, if there were any relations left, they were so distant they didn't even know she existed."

"Did she die without a will or something?"

"Oh no, she had a will all right." Julie's eye roll made Sarah's heart lurch. "She left the entire estate in trust to the county historical society with the caveat that we keep the property maintained for her cats."

Sarah snorted a laugh. "You've got to be kidding me. That doesn't happen in real life." She gaped at Julie. "Does it?"

"Oh, it does. She said the society was free to do whatever they wanted with the place after the last cat died." Julie sighed. "Unfortunately, there wasn't a lot of actual cash left in the estate, so by the time I got on the WBHS board, the only thing they'd managed to maintain was keeping the damn cats spayed and neutered, and don't think *that* was easy. The last cat died about a year ago, and we don't have the budget or the desire to keep this white elephant. About ten or fifteen years ago, they got permission from the court to auction off the contents, which added to the cat care fund. Thank God for the feral cat folks or we'd still be chasing down kittens."

What a story! Fascinated, Sarah gazed at the house, half-expecting to see a platoon of cats curled up on the porch rails and wandering along the weedy gravel drive. "Where is the realtor? She was supposed to meet us twenty minutes ago." She was impatient to get inside, her curiosity growing by the second.

"Here she is!" Julie waved as a big SUV pulled up behind Julie's little BMW and a woman slid out, leaving the car running.

"Hey, Jules, sorry I'm late." A chipper woman in her late fifties, she managed to give them a sunny smile and look abashed all at the same time. "We had a little paperwork disaster at the office." She extended her hand. "I'm Mathilda Fry—folks call me Mattie unless they want to irritate me. Welcome to Willow Bay." Mattie's handshake was firm and friendly and her smile warm.

Her gray hair, shining silver in the noon sun, was cut in a cute pixie style that Sarah envied.

"Sarah Ev—Bennett." *Dammit*. Was she ever going to get used to the new name?

"Okay. Let's take a look." Mattie used one of the keys on a laden keyring to open the padlock on the gate, which swung open smoothly without the creak that Sarah was expecting to hear. "Hop in and I'll drive us up to the house."

"We can walk," Sarah protested. She wanted to get a feel for the size of the property.

"You can if you like, but I've got a bum knee." When Mattie headed for her open car door, Sarah detected a slight limp, although the bad knee didn't seem to affect the amount of pressure she could apply to a gas pedal. The realtor spun gravel as she careened up the driveway and came to a hard stop right in next to the wide front steps.

"She's a bundle of energy," Sarah observed as she and Julie trotted up the drive.

"She's a hoot," Julie said. "A little scattered sometimes; however, she knows her stuff and she does a mean karaoke at the Harbor Bar. You should catch her act some Friday night." She stepped carefully around a small pile of tree branches that someone had raked up on the side of the drive. "I see the beautification committee has been out."

"Beautification committee?" Sarah scanned the unkempt yard. The grass was green, and from this vantage point, apparently it *had* been cut in the last month or so in spite of the tall weeds growing along the fence. The gardens were overrun with weeds, and Virginia creeper vines hung from the tall trees that shaded the house. A pair of Michigan's famous black squirrels scampered away as Sarah and Julie approached. A few late spring flowers added a little color, as did the peonies blooming up by the porch.

Those could be saved. And was that wisteria growing up over the porch rail?

"Oh, about four times a summer, a group of retired villagers head out here with their riding mowers and make a run around the property. Sometimes they pick up sticks and, usually in the fall, they have a bonfire out back to burn them."

Sarah stopped for a moment to take in the scene before her, which wasn't so daunting close up. A wide porch almost seemed to welcome her and cockeyed shutters lent an air of whimsy rather than neglect. This could work—if the inside was halfway decent and the ceilings weren't falling in and the floors weren't covered in cat crap or reeking of urine.

Yeah, this could work.

"C'mon"—Julie gave Sarah's shoulder a little nudge—"let's go look inside."

~

Almost two hours later, an exhausted but exhilarated Sarah stood in the expansive foyer gazing up at the ornate ceiling fixture and shaking her head. "Un-freakin'-believable," she said for what seemed like the hundredth time.

"Right?" Julie agreed, brushing her hands together in a futile attempt to remove the grime she'd picked up as they wandered the property. "So what do you think?"

Sarah turned a complete circle and took in the double parlors, the dining room beyond, the wide staircase with its glorious carved walnut bannisters, and the sun shining through the filthy stained glass window on the landing. How had that thing survived?

Somehow, the historical society had managed to save the house from vandals and scavengers. All the built-ins—the corner cupboards in the dining room, the glass-front cabinets built into the walls around the fireplace in the east parlor and the floor-to-ceiling bookcases in the library off the west parlor—although dusty and in need of refinishing were still in good condition. Only a few panes of cracked glass would need to be replaced in the solarium that opened from the east parlor, and all the gorgeous painted tiles around the dining room and parlor fireplaces were intact. Hell, even the rolling ladder in the library was still in place.

"How did the society keep this place pristine for so many years?" Sarah asked Mattie, who'd settled with a *thump* on the second-to-the-bottom step of the ornate staircase, heedless of her black pants and the dust. "I mean there isn't even any graffiti anywhere in here or any broken windows."

Mattie leaned against the newel post, her face streaked with dirt and sweat. "We've kept an eye on things, fed the cats, made sure the windows and doors were locked up. As you saw, the house is alarmed, although it's an ancient system that will need to be replaced. Every year, a group comes out and makes a run through with mops and buckets and dust rags."

"And there is the fact that the old place is haunted," Julie said with a twinkle in her eye.

"Seriously?" Sarah shivered, half-expecting to see a shadowy shape float by, which was ridiculous because the house had welcomed her from the moment she'd stepped on the porch. It most certainly wasn't haunted or if it was, she'd bet they were friendly ghosts.

Julie tossed her a wry smile. "Of course not, I'm kidding. Everyone got to come through the place when we auctioned off all the contents a few years ago, so curiosity has pretty much been held to a minimum."

"It's off the beaten path enough that tourists don't even know it exists," Mattie added from her perch on the stairs. "And frankly, I haven't advertised it since we got the listing a few months ago because Julie here asked me to hold off. When she told me what she wanted to do, I was happy to oblige." Her eyes darkened and she cocked her head to one side. "My daughter was in an abusive relationship when she was a teenager—some punk from Traverse City that she met at a football game. If I could've cut the kid's balls off, I would've done so with glee the night she came home with a black eye."

"How is she now?" Sarah asked, suddenly seeing the gruff realtor in a new light.

"Happily married with two kids and another one on the way." Mattie grinned. "We saved her early, got her into therapy. I wasn't about to let violence become a pattern for my baby girl."

"You were smart," Sarah said. "She's lucky to have you."

Mattie pushed up off the step. "She's the light of my life, and those grandkids… You got grands?"

"No." Sarah wandered through the wide arched doorway to the east parlor and beyond to the solarium that looked out on the backyard.

"I guess you're a little young for that yet. Got any ki—" Mattie's questions cut off so quickly that Sarah was sure Julie had given the realtor a signal to shut up. A few muffled words behind her made her smile—good ol' Jules always had her back.

Surprisingly, the questions hadn't bothered her. She was too wrapped up in the house. Julie was right—it was perfect and Sarah's mind ran riot imagining the walls stripped of the old faded paper and gleaming with fresh paint. Once the trees were trimmed and the dead ones taken down, sunlight would stream into all the windows. The hardwood floors would shine again. She and the Posse could haunt secondhand stores and discount places for bright rugs and comfy furniture.

She pictured a huge table in the dining room—one that would seat fifteen or twenty—and white wicker furniture with flowered cushions for the solarium. All the wallpaper could be removed from the bedrooms and each one made bright and cheerful with paint and curtains. No doubt the whole place would need to be replumbed and that behemoth of a furnace in the basement had to be at least seventy years old, so there was another huge expense. Maybe new ductwork, unquestionably new electric throughout. "New bathroom fixtures in four and half bathrooms." Sarah didn't realize she'd spoken the words out loud until Julie's voice behind her made her nearly jump out of skin.

"Yeah, definitely all new tubs, stools, and sinks. Do you think the jack-and-jill bathrooms between those four bedrooms will work or do we need separate bathrooms for each bedroom? Right now only two of the bedrooms have en-suites."

Sarah blinked, wishing like crazy she'd brought a notebook and pen with her. That she'd fall immediately in love with the old house had never occurred to her. She had come along just to mollify Julie. Lunch in town and a trip to the yarn store were next on her agenda. This morning, the idea of opening a shelter in Willow Bay had seemed far-fetched at best, in spite of all the plans Julie had shown her when they'd gotten back from the cruise.

Sarah had been impressed with how well Julie had done her homework—how she'd already set up the nonprofit and registered it with the state of Michigan. How she'd gotten the grant to get started and even had an intricate budget that included everything from staplers to paper towels.

An attorney was in place, fundraising events had been discussed, and costs of renovating the old house had been projected. Will was in the thick of everything, bringing his financial expertise to the mix. Henry Dugan's company had pledged a million dollars to the project, so Sophie had been right about his interest. This wasn't some pipe dream. In spite of everything, Sarah hadn't been able to picture herself as a viable cog in the works—until now. Until this house had gripped her imagination.

Julie touched Sarah's shoulder. "So what do you think? Do you think the shared bathrooms will work?" She peered into Sarah's eyes. "Hey? Are you okay?"

Sarah's full-to-bursting heart suddenly overflowed into her tear ducts, and she swiped at her cheeks. "I'm fine," she choked out.

"What is it?" Julie draped an arm over Sarah's shoulders. "Oh, babes, I'm pushing too much, aren't I? I'm sorry. Let's go. We'll get some lunch in the village and—"

"I'm okay, really." Sarah realized she *was* okay as she laughed through her tears and dug in her pocket for the tissues that had become a part of her everyday wardrobe accessories. Tears threatened frequently, and Dr. Benton had told her to let them come. Sarah wasn't a weeper by nature—crying *was* cathartic, just sometimes inconvenient. However, these weren't her usual tears of fear or sadness or anger or desperation. These were the good kind. "I'm just…a little stunned by how much I want this."

"Yeah?" Julie's lovely face lit up. "Really?"

"Yeah." Sarah nodded and took a deep breath. "I'm in, Jules. I'm all in."

CHAPTER 10

The knock on the door came just as Sarah got her hair pulled up into a ponytail. Alarmed, she peered over the loft rail trying to get a glimpse of whoever was on her deck. Unfortunately, the half-open shutters hid the view, so she hurried to the nightstand, grabbed the little .22 pistol, and stuck it in the pocket of her jeans before heading downstairs. She'd told Julie she'd meet her at the Grind. Who else would knock on her door at eight thirty in the morning?

When she pushed aside the curtain on the door, her heart beat a little faster. Tony Reynard's big frame filled the window glass. "Hello," she said, pulling the inner door open without unlatching the screen door.

Tony was in uniform and, dammit, he looked good. His tan shirt was crisp and the crease in his pants so knife sharp that she wondered if ironing was another of his many skills or if he sent his uniforms out to be laundered. He wore the same quiet smile he'd charmed her with on the boat.

"Hey, Sarah."

She was struck again at the unusual honey-brown color of his eyes. He had the longest lashes she'd ever seen on a man.

"We need to talk." His tone and expression told her he wasn't here to shoot the breeze.

"We do?" Sarah was mystified. She and Tony had crossed paths in the three weeks since the boat ride—they'd waved at one another on the dock and exchanged smiles and casual greetings in line at the Grind. Just last night, he'd represented the sheriff's office at the first official meeting of the shelter's board. They'd even had one short, official, and rather uncomfortable conversation about why she hadn't gotten her gun registered with the state —something she'd put off doing, even though she'd assured him she would.

He'd been very pleasant, and fact was she'd been half-expecting him to ask her out after Memorial Day weekend. He'd clearly indicated interest and Julie told her he'd asked questions about her. Sarah had enjoyed their mild flirtation on the boat. Dr. Benton was frustratingly neutral about the possibility of dating again, neither encouraging or discouraging it. In spite of being attracted to the burly deputy, Sarah hadn't pursued it. The house on Eastern Avenue occupied every moment of her time, every corner of her brain, and her heart.

"It's about your gun." Tony's expression turned solemn.

She bristled. "What about it?" If he thought she was going to leave the apartment alone without it, he was crazy.

"You still haven't been in to apply for a permit to carry—I checked—and I saw the gun in your pocket last night at the meeting." He took a step back and squinted at her through the screen door. "It's in your pocket right now, and I know you're meeting Jules and Carrie at the Grind before you head to the shelter. You've been here almost two months; you need to get the thing registered if you're going to carry it."

"You here to arrest me or confiscate my little ol' pistol, Deputy?" Sarah smiled, deciding playful might be the way to go.

No way was she turning her only means of protection over to local law enforcement.

"I'm here to take you down to the office to register the gun with the state of Michigan and fill out an application for a permit to carry," he insisted. "The process takes about forty-five days, so while you're waiting, I'm going to take you to the shooting range and teach you to use the damn thing." He blew out a frustrated breath. "You can have the gun here at the apartment once it's registered, but you can't carry it around anymore—not until you're legal."

Sarah couldn't believe what she was hearing. "Are you seriously pulling rank on me?"

"Can I come in?" He reached for the door handle and tugged against the latch.

"No." Sarah put one hand over the hook on the door, as if Tony couldn't simply yank the thing open if he wanted. The very thought of going out without the gun terrified her. The gun was her security blanket and that shocked her as much as anything else that had happened since the night Paul had showed up at her apartment in Chicago. She hated guns. She'd never owned one, never touched one before she'd *acquired* the .22 right before she left for Willow Bay.

Her fear of guns was no big psychological mystery—her parents had been shot dead in their bed during a robbery of their elegant home in Ames, Georgia, an expensive bedroom community outside Atlanta. The thieves had used her dad's own hunting rifle to execute them as they lay sleeping one freezing January night not long before Macy was born. The crime had been cold-blooded and devastating, and after they'd returned from the funeral, Sarah had begged Paul to get rid of the guns he kept in a locked cabinet in his study.

Of course, he'd refused and later, after the abuse began, the rifles became part of the evil—once he'd even pointed one at her and cocked the trigger while he forced her to—

She closed her eyes against that particular memory and put her hand in her pocket to wrap her fingers around the grip of the pistol. Things had changed. *She* had changed. "I'm not giving you my gun, Tony. So I guess you're going to have to arrest me."

"Sarah, we talked about this. I told you a few weeks ago that you had to register that thing and to stop carrying it until you had a permit. You agreed to do it, but you haven't." Tony's tone was the same one he'd have used with his four-year-old granddaughter, Sarah was sure of it. "I'm not going to take it away from you; however, I do need to get the serial number off it, take a photo of the damn thing, and take you down for fingerprints."

Her heart stuttered. "Fingerprints?" she squeaked. "Are you kidding me? I don't want my fingerprints on file anywhere. I know Julie's probably told you some of my story. *Jesus!* My ex would find me in two seconds." Tony had to be joking—her *fingerprints*? Did the man truly not understand what kind of manipulative monster she was dealing with?

"He has no access to the gun registry in Michigan. In fact, he doesn't even know where you are, so I doubt it would even occur to him to check," Tony explained. "Besides you're not registering as Sarah Everett. You're safe here."

"I'm not safe anywhere, Deputy, but this"—she held out the gun—"at least makes me feel like I can fight back."

"Do *not* point that thing at me." He reached for the door handle, then dropped his hand just as quickly. "Come with me and let's get you legal, okay? I think I've figured out what you can do during the waiting period."

~

Tony waited while Sarah contemplated for a moment. Her white teeth caught her lower lip, and she gazed at the gun and then back at him. He'd hated "pulling rank" on her—hated that was how she saw it. This wasn't really the encounter he wanted to have with Sarah Bennett after the tentative friendship they'd started on the boat. He'd been waiting for the right time to ask her out, but somehow, the cool shell she'd managed to put up since they'd returned from the cruise had daunted him. He'd almost stopped her last night as she and Julie had left the board meeting, but he'd been waylaid by the mayor asking more questions about the sheriff's department being able to handle the extra burden of the shelter.

When he checked with the county clerk and realized Sarah hadn't been in there or to the sheriff's office to register the gun, he formulated a plan. He wasn't going to be able to make her stop carrying the wretched thing around unless he confiscated it, and she was in clear violation of Michigan law if she did, so there was only one way to make her feel safe without it when she was out of the apartment. However, first he had to get her out of the apartment.

"What have you figured out?" Suspicion dripped from her question.

"I have a plan." He cocked his head and gave her his best persuasive smile. The one that always worked on Emma. "Come on. Let's go down to the office and I'll tell you all about it."

With a sigh, she unlocked the screen door. "Come in."

"Thank you." He crossed the threshold and followed her to the table. "Set it down on the table, and I'll take a quick picture and get the serial number."

Reluctantly, she did as he instructed and backed away from the table. He remained all business as he examined the gun, which was a cheap model anyone could pick up on the streets of

Chicago. The weapon was beat-up and the serial number had been scratched off. He turned it over in his hands and came to a decision. If she wanted a gun, she needed a real one, not this piece of crap.

Sarah had wandered over to the big window overlooking the bay, her back to him.

He left the gun on the table. "Okay, tell you what," he said as he closed the space between them in three wide strides. "Let's go to Traverse City and buy you a decent gun. You can buy one from a federally licensed dealer, then we'll come back and process you for a carry permit." Since he was still speaking to her back, he moved closer. "While you're waiting for the paperwork, I'll take you to the shooting range and teach you how to use it."

"And until I get processed?" Her voice trembled. "How do I protect myself at the shelter? In the village? If I have to go into Traverse City?"

"You can keep the new gun in your nightstand until you have the permit to carry. While you're out and about, well, like I said, I have a plan."

"What's your plan?" She turned around and he could read doubt and fear in her expression.

When he reached for her, she jumped back, her eyes wide and he cursed inwardly. He'd only meant to turn her attention to the window again. He dropped his hand. "Look down there." Instead of touching her, he pointed to the docks below. "See that big blond kid scrubbing the top deck of the *Allegro*?"

With a quick glance back over her shoulder Sarah's focus switched to the yacht in berth 38. "Yes," she said cautiously. "What about him?"

"That's Chris Waggoner." Tony edged closer, trying to figure out how far he could go into her personal space without freaking her out. "He got into some trouble last month and now he has three hundred hours of community service to do to clear his record."

"Okaaaay." Doubt edged her tone. "What does that have to do with me?"

"Yesterday afternoon, I got the judge who handed down the sentence to agree that being your personal assistant and helping work on the shelter qualified as service hours. Chris is your new PA and bodyguard. If you'll have him."

She stared at him in disbelief. "You're giving me a juvenile delinquent as an assistant? What did he do?"

"He and a bunch of his frat brothers from MSU had some beers, stole a dune buggy, and headed up to Sleeping Bear."

"Sleeping Bear?"

"God, you really have been focused on the shelter, haven't you? Remember we showed you Sleeping Bear when we were out on the boat—the national lakeshore a few miles north of here," he explained. "Great big sand dune?" he added when her expression remained bewildered.

Realization dawned on her face. "Oh, yeah, okay. I do remember now. Jules wants to take me up there for a picnic. They don't allow dune buggies there?"

Tony shook his head. "Nope, no dune buggies are allowed in the park, stolen or otherwise. Plus they'd been drinking. They hit a tree and roughed up some of the lakeshore and dune pretty bad, and then had the unfortunate luck to get a judge who does conservation work in the area." He grinned. "She was plenty pissed that a bunch of over-privileged frat boys would have such disrespect for nature."

"How old is this kid?" She craned her neck to stare down at Chris, but she didn't move away, which Tony counted as a small victory.

"He's nineteen, gonna be a sophomore at MSU next fall, majoring in business and finance. He's a good kid. Honor student.

Never been in trouble before. Just happened to go along for the ride with his frat brothers. He and his parents were devastated. Judge Carrey's willing to expunge his record if he completes the community service by Labor Day. So you see? You get a burly college kid at your beck and call, Chris does his time, and I get to take that nasty piece of crap"—he nodded in the direction of the gun on the table—"and toss it into the box of weapons that we'll send to Traverse City for disposal. It's a win-win-win."

After a long moment, Sarah raised one brow. "What about at night? He can't be expected to be with me twenty-four-seven."

Tony's heart soared that she was warming up to the idea. "I told you, we'll go to Traverse City this afternoon and get you a decent gun. You can keep it in the nightstand until you get your carry permit. For the time being, while you're working on the shelter or out and about, Chris will be with you." He took a chance and touched her shoulder. Relief washed over him when she didn't pull away. Apparently, he hadn't blown this thing completely.

"You think I'm paranoid, don't you?" Sarah's chin lifted and she looked him straight in the eye. "You think I'm overreacting."

He fought the urge to take her in his arms and assure her that he wasn't going to let anyone hurt her. That would only frighten her more or make her less compliant, and he needed her to accept what he was offering. Otherwise, he was going to have to be Deputy Reynard.

"No, I don't think that at all," he said, tipping his head down so he could meet her fiery gaze. "I get why you're scared. That's why I'm trying to make you feel safe. However, I'm a servant of the county, so I also have to keep you legal."

CHAPTER 11

With a warm smile, Sarah accepted the cold bottle of water the young man handed her. "Chris, you're an angel."

"Thanks, but apparently I'm not or I wouldn't be doing three hundred hours of community service, now would I?" Chris's perfect teeth gleamed in the sunlight streaming through the window on the landing of the elegant staircase. He dropped onto the window seat next to her and she elbowed him gently. "We've gotten a lot done today, boss," he said after taking a long pull on his own icy beverage. "You were right about getting all the floors sanded before they put in the new furnace—the dust we're raising would destroy a new unit."

At first, she had been reluctant to accept Tony's offer of an assistant-slash-bodyguard. She wasn't sure she wanted the company of a college kid and she worried about putting Chris in harm's way. However, he was over eighteen, understood her fears, and had stepped into his new job with enthusiasm.

She and the young man had taken to one another immediately. A warm, intelligent kid, he stayed within view practically every moment they were together. He never asked any questions about her past, which she appreciated, but they talked about everything else, from where to find the best pizza in Benzie County—Mama Connie's—to music, trends, and politics.

He turned out to be great company and seemed to be devoted to the shelter project, rallying some of his local fraternity brothers to the cause of renovating the old house. Even now, the laughter and chatter of several Alpha Tau Omegas sanding the oak floors in the kitchen drifted up the stairs.

Redoing the floors had been the task she'd found most daunting, so she and Frank Law, the contractor, agreed she should start with that. Chris and his friends had jumped in with both feet, while the electricians and plumbers installed new wiring and new pipes. The new furnaces would come along next—Frank had just ordered them earlier that week after showing her half a dozen brochures.

Who knew furnaces and ductwork could be so fascinating?

Sarah glanced down at her dust-covered jeans. "I figured we may as well get all the truly grubby work out of the way up front." She brushed futilely at her T-shirt. "We can cover all the floors with tarps and paper once we get the sanding finished and then put the poly on after all the other work is done."

"I hate that I won't be here that long." Dust flew as Chris raked his fingers though his unruly mop of blond hair. "I can't believe how fast this month has gone."

"*I* can't believe how much help you've been, Chris." She laid her hand on his arm, watching powdery motes rise from the golden hair. "I don't know what I'm going to do when you leave."

He took another drink. "I'm not going anywhere for another month and a half, boss. And I've been thinking… I've always worked at Nolan's during my winter break, but I'd like to help here if you could use me. I mean, if you think you'll still be working on this old place."

She grinned. "Oh, we'll still be here and I'd love to have

you." Reaching under the bill of her cap, she used a finger to scratch her itchy scalp. "What do you do at the winery?"

"No, no, I don't work at the winery, I work at the Christmas tree farm," Chris said. "*Mr.* Nolan and his son have the tree farm part. It's *Mrs.* Nolan who owns the winery. They're up there by the lighthouse, and even though they're both under the Nolan Farms umbrella, they're like two separate businesses. Have you been up there yet?"

Scratching wasn't helping much. "Basically, I haven't gone anywhere except here and the market and the Grind since I arrived. I know Libby Nolan, but I've only been to her winery once and that was with Jules. I really need to get to know this the town, don't I?" She lifted the ball cap and reached behind her to untangle her ponytail from the hole in the back.

"You do need to get to know Willow Bay, and I can remedy that." A deep voice from the bottom of the stairs startled her so much she dropped her hand, leaving the cap dangling from her hair.

Tony was beside her in a wink, ascending the huge staircase amazingly fast for a man his size. "Here, let me help." His eyes sought permission even as he reached down to her.

Sarah nodded, warmth flooding her insides at the sight of the attractive deputy, and she was sure she was blushing. Not that it mattered, her face was all hot and sweaty anyway, so no one would suspect the effect he had.

Gently and without touching any part of her except her hair, he untangled the cap, talking casually as he pulled the strands through the hole in the back. "Why don't you start by coming to the Fishwife with me tonight? It's all-you-can-eat shrimp night."

"You should definitely go, boss," Chris admonished with a wink to Tony that he didn't even try to hide. "Best shrimp on the coast."

Tony handed her the cap with a flourish before giving Chris a mocking severe look. "Thanks, Chris, but I can get my own date. When I need a wingman, I'll call you."

"I kinda think you might need a wingman, Deputy." Chris rose and stretched, curving his back in an exaggerated motion that made Sarah envy his youth and flexibility. "You've been lurking around here damn near every day for a month and you've just now worked up the balls—um, sorry, boss—I mean the *nerve* to ask her out."

Tony gazed at Chris over the top of his glasses. "Don't you have something you need to be doing, like far, far away from here?"

She giggled and gave Chris a quick head tilt. "Why don't you go down and get the shop vac from the kitchen? You can start the cleanup in room three."

Chris glanced at Tony, one brow raised, and at the deputy's slight nod, bounded down the stairs.

Sarah rolled her shoulders and took a deep sip of her beverage. "Man, what I wouldn't give for a tenth of that boy's energy."

"Ain't that the truth?" Tony perched on the steps opposite her. "All that vigor is wasted on youth, and they have no idea how much they'll wish they had it when they get older." He squinted at her, pulling his cap around to shield his eyes from the sunlight. "So, what do you say?"

"I say I agree; vigor is wasted on youth." She was being deliberately obtuse, reluctant to get back to his invitation to dinner. Just the thought of a date with the handsome deputy made her heart beat faster—for several reasons.

She'd explored the idea of dating Tony with Dr. Benton, who, in her usual hands-off manner, had turned the question back to Sarah. Did she feel prepared to put herself in that situation? Only Sarah herself knew the answer to that one. However, the good doctor *had* encouraged her to make new friends, to participate in town events, and try to settle in. The fears would subside, she'd said, as Sarah became comfortable in Willow Bay.

Sarah thought she was doing okay. She met Julie or Carrie or Sophie or all three of them most mornings at the Daily Grind before Chris picked her up in his battered Jeep to head to the shelter. Libby joined them when responsibilities didn't keep her at the winery.

Men had suddenly become an integral part of her life as she worked in the huge old house among a platoon of electricians, plumbers, and the college kids—all men—but she never felt threatened. Julie brought new workmen in every week since the historical society had agreed to sell the place to them for a hundred dollars. How the hell she had pulled that one off still baffled Sarah—the estate had been turned over to the shelter board in record time.

The grant money and a large shot of cash from Henry Dugan got things rolling, and as chairperson of the six-member shelter board, Julie demonstrated magical powers. She'd received a commitment from the big-box home improvement store in Traverse City to donate the new bathroom and kitchen fixtures, and the lighting that was going in now; and she found electricians, carpenters, and plumbers willing to work pro bono or for a fraction of their usual fee.

Even old Frank Law, a retired contractor, had stepped up with an offer to help coordinate the whole effort—something to keep him off the streets, he'd joked. All the footwork and cajoling Jules had done prior to acquiring the house was paying off in spades as volunteers turned up every day ready to do Frank and Sarah's bidding. Julie's powers of persuasion were astounding—nearly the entire village had come together to make the project a success.

Rounding out the board were Carrie serving as treasurer, Sophie as secretary, Will as financial officer, with Perry Graham, the owner of the Daily Grind, and Margie Dixon serving as members-at-large. As a major donor, Henry had turned down a board seat, but showed up at the house regularly to pound nails, paint, or tear out old fixtures.

Julie insisted that Sarah, as shelter manager, be present at weekly board meetings. They'd already started paying her a salary, which would include a per diem once she moved into the shelter; and even though she had no voting power, Jules wanted Sarah's input on every decision.

The shelter had given Sarah the focus she needed, and Chris had clearly taken Deputy Reynard's instructions to heart. The kid stuck to her like glue, shadowing her every move throughout the vast property, even to the point of hovering outside the door of the one working bathroom when she was in there. If she needed to run personal errands, he escorted her to the market or the drugstore when he drove her back to the apartment each evening, which had kept Sarah from having to find her own vehicle, at least for the moment.

Although now and then she fought the urge to tell him to back off, Chris's presence did indeed boost her sense of safety. At home, locked doors, closed shutters, and her new Ruger LC9 gave her the security she needed. She'd found a rhythm with Chris and her work at the shelter, a soothing pattern that allowed her to sleep at night and, best of all, to breathe.

Dating? That was an entirely different story. Tony made almost daily visits to the house, seeking her out to say hello and chat for a moment after he got a job assignment from Frank. For the past two weeks, he'd been sanding and puttying woodwork around the windows and doors in preparation for painting, and had even recruited some high-school kids to pitch in.

He moved from the step to the window seat, leaving plenty of room between them. "Come on, Sarah. You need a break from this place. Have dinner with me and"—he raised one brow—"afterward, I'll take you to the shooting range out at Perkins." His eyes twinkled amber-brown in the sunlight as he made the offer and she couldn't help chuckling.

"You really know the way to a girl's heart, don't you, Deputy?" she teased. She *was* anxious to learn how to use the new gun he'd helped her buy the day he confiscated the one she'd brought from Chicago. He'd shown her the basics—enough that she could defend herself if someone broke into her house. With the shelter taking every moment of her time and having Chris at her back her fears were eased enough about being out without it, so she hadn't pushed to go out to the shooting range.

"Hey, I gotta grab my advantages where I can," Tony said. "If you told me you wanted to go shopping for lace curtains, I'd be on my phone Googling curtain stores right now." His expression softened. "I like you, Sarah. I think you know that and I believe you like me, too…just a little." That wistful smile damn near did her in.

Heat flooded her cheeks as she switched her gaze to her dusty tennis shoes. Maybe the time had come to dip her toes in the dating pool again. It had been a long time since she'd even thought about a man in her life. She'd left Ames with only one thought—*never again*—and she'd remained closed to the idea…until now.

Was this attraction part of the "Willow Bay effect" that the Posse had talked about when they'd all met for coffee one morning? Carrie had commented on how much more comfortable Sarah seemed, how focused on the shelter, even remarking delightedly that she had picked up a few pounds. She was right. Sarah *had* relaxed, due in no small part to the tranquil atmosphere in this little beach town.

The village had taken her in like an abandoned puppy and every single person she'd met had welcomed her warmly. Perry already knew she took her half-caf with two creams and that she preferred his blueberry muffins to the bran ones that Julie loved.

Margie Dixon brought her zucchini and lettuce from her big garden and, only last night, Ted at the market pointed out a new batch of Rainier cherries that had come in. He'd paid attention to the fact that she bought fresh cherries almost every time she shopped.

She was getting sucked into village life in Willow Bay with each passing day, which both pleased and worried her. She loved the helpful friendly manner of the citizens, but she worried what would happen if she was forced to flee again.

What if Paul discovered her whereabouts? What if he found out she'd gone out with Tony? What if—

"You're overthinking." His warm voice interrupted her train of thought. "Dinner? Yes or no?"

"The shooting range, too?" Sarah asked, finally meeting his intense gaze.

"You betcha." That dimpled grin made her heart stutter.

"Okay." She rose as Chris headed back upstairs toting the shop vac. "See you about seven?"

"I'll be there."

Sarah rolled her eyes as she caught the furtive thumbs-up Chris tossed Tony when he passed him on the landing.

CHAPTER 12

Tony couldn't believe he was finally sitting across the table from the woman he'd been not *pining* for, but definitely thinking about for the last two and half months.

As he watched her animated expression when she described the frat boys' latest antics, he couldn't help remembering the first time he'd met her. How her hands shook when she'd held him at bay with that nothing of a pistol, her face deadly serious. He still wasn't convinced she would've shot him, although now that he knew some of her story, he had to admit that the prospect was more likely than he first believed.

With an effort, he kept from asking her about her ex-husband and her former life in Georgia. Somehow, he simply couldn't imagine Sarah Bennett being cowed by any man, although the very thought still made his blood boil. His emotions ran the gamut, from praying Paul Prescott would never track her down in Willow Bay to wishing he *would* turn up. Tony could beat the living shit out of him and then stick him in jail for the rest of his life. Or better yet, shoot the bastard, weight his body, and drop him into the watery depths of Lake Michigan. He was fairly certain Liam, Will, and Henry would have his back on that one.

That smirking mug shot haunted Tony's dreams. More than once since Sarah had come into his life, he'd awakened in a cold sweat, trembling and furious. The crime scene pictures filled his mind every time he encountered her—those horrifying shots of her daughter's broken body and the grim photos of Sarah beaten and bloody.

Jesus, what kind of monster does—

"Don't you think so?" Sarah's voice brought him back to the Fishwife with a start.

He blinked, realizing he'd lost most of what she'd said for the past couple of minutes. Something about the frat boys... Oh hell, he couldn't come up with what and she'd know immediately if he tried to fake it.

He'd have to 'fess up. "Sorry, I was drifting." Giving her a sheepish smile, he went for broke. "You look so amazing tonight I got distracted."

Pink color stained her cheeks, disarming him completely. "Thank you," she said, lowering her eyes. "Back at you, Deputy. I think this is the first time I've ever seen you in anything except your uniform or beat-up work clothes." She chuckled and held up one hand. "Or your yachting *uniform*."

Tony grinned, enjoying how the candlelight reflected in her turquoise eyes and brought out the rare silver threads in her auburn hair. "I'm not even sure how the whole Hawaiian shirt thing got started, but an entire section of my closet is dedicated to them. I'm most comfortable in T-shirts and jeans or shorts, and I haven't put on nice pants and a button-down shirt in ages—it feels kinda good."

"I was thinking as I got dressed tonight that I need to go shopping for clothes that are more appropriate to beach town life. I don't even own a swimming suit." She leaned toward him and made the confession in a hushed tone.

He played along, faking a look of horror. "What? I can't

believe they've let you stay here."

"May I refill your glass, Ms. Bennett?" Their server arrived with a large pitcher of iced tea and poured as Sarah nodded. "Your food will be out in just a minute. Sorry it's taking so long. We're pretty packed tonight, so things are a little slow in the kitchen. I can get you some more bread if you like."

"Sure," Sarah said. "And more apple butter? It's delicious."

"You betcha." The girl topped off Tony's glass, picked up their empty salad plates, and disappeared.

"How does she know my name?" Sarah asked, her brows pinched together in a frown. "As a matter of fact, I haven't had to introduce myself to a single person in this town and, yet, everyone seems to know my name."

He chuckled. "That's village life for you."

"It's nice, if a little disconcerting." She took the last piece of bread from the basket and dipped it in the container of apple butter that had come along with it.

He was glad to see her eating with such gusto. She'd been downright skinny when she first arrived; now she was blooming like a rose. Although she was still small, her cheeks were rounder, and where she'd once been all angles and lines, now she curved quite nicely. More important, she was no longer hunched in on herself, no longer… What was the word? Cowering?

He wanted to believe that new confidence was due in no small part to him. He'd worked hard over the past few weeks to develop an easy friendship based on trust and mutual attraction. Oh yeah, he knew she was attracted to him. However, he also realized she'd never do anything about that feeling if he pushed her. So he'd stayed in the background, a steady, safe presence, keeping in her line of vision without getting into her personal space.

"Disconcerting?" he asked.

"I'm guessing it's hard to keep a secret around here."

"Well, we are a small town," he admitted. "But you know, it's not a gossipy place."

Sarah raised one brow. "Um, I've met Perry."

"Perry's harmless. The Grind is a hangout, so he hears everything. He doesn't indulge in vicious rumors or mean gossip, though. He just listens and knows what's happening." Tony rested his chin in his palm, unable to take his eyes off her. "He's a great resource for Sheriff Gibson and me because his memory is incredible."

"So I want him on my side, right?" She popped the last bite of bread into her mouth as the server arrived with another warm loaf of bread.

"You're up next," she said and picked up the empty basket.

Tony gave the girl a smile and a nod before turning back to Sarah. "We're all on your side, Sarah."

She stared at him, her face a morass of conflicting emotions. "I hope that's true."

He read the fear in her eyes and made a decision. The time had come to bring up the eight-hundred-pound gorilla that was always present when they were together. "Will you tell me about Georgia?"

Sarah had been anticipating the question for weeks, had even played out several scenarios in her mind from dumping everything at Tony's feet to refusing to speak of her past at all. Now that he'd finally asked, she was completely tongue-tied. She dropped her gaze, too aware that the wrong choice might make or break her tentative friendship with the handsome deputy.

Talking to Dr. Benton had been cathartic. Julie already knew most of the whole ugly story, and bits and pieces had come out with Carrie, Sophie, and Libby. But letting Tony in on the horrors of that time somehow made her feel vulnerable—if she revealed to him what she'd allowed for all those years, would that give him permission to treat her the same way? Was he even capable of such cruelty?

He's male, isn't he?

Immediately her conscience cried *foul* on that thought. Tony wasn't Paul. He'd never once exhibited any behavior to prove he was capable of such viciousness. She trusted him—as much as she was able to trust any man—and for what it was worth, he was the first man she'd been even faintly attracted to since Paul.

At least she assumed that attraction was what she was experiencing. Her emotions had been so stunted living with Paul that she barely recognized the flutter low in her belly when Tony came into view or the little shiver that tingled through her when he touched her, however briefly. Although the very thought of being physical with him, of having his hands and lips on her, left her nauseated and shaking with terror.

"If you aren't ready to talk to me, it's okay." Tony reached out a hand and let his fingertips brush hers across the table.

With that tentative touch, she made up her mind. "No, it's just that I–I don't talk about this easily," she said, her gaze meeting his.

"I imagine not." His eyes were so kind she almost dissolved into tears.

Thank God, their table was tucked into an intimate corner of the sprawling restaurant. The low hum of other diners' conversations, punctuated by the occasional shout of laughter, barely reached them out here on the screened porch that overlooked the bay.

Sarah swallowed hard and straightened her shoulders as Tony sat still and silent, his fingers still resting against hers. She was certain that a single word from her would give her a pass, and he'd take the conversation right back to the warm July weather or what movies were playing at the Lakeside Drive-In or whether or not two refrigerators would be enough in the new kitchen at the shelter.

Basking in the safe warmth of his gaze, she made a daring choice—she'd start at the beginning. Maybe she wouldn't seem like such a fool if he understood how it had been at first. "I was so young when I met him—only eighteen. The day after graduation, a bunch of us were at the club, lying by the pool, getting a start on our tans." She glanced down at their hands and drew enough strength to give him a cockeyed smile. "Ames, Georgia, still thinks it's nineteen sixty-four. Lots of old money, lots of privilege —think cotillions, debutantes, mint juleps, and boys in pink polo shirts and docksiders, no socks."

"I'm already picturing you at sixteen, coming down the stairs in a long dress, carrying a bouquet of what? Gardenias?" He smiled and moved his hand closer, intertwining the tips of their fingers. "Did you wear a tiara?"

She allowed the touch and her stomach unknotted ever so slightly. Her heart beat a little faster when she realized that he was trying to make this easier for her, using humor to help her take a step back from the story. "Nope, I was the rebel who wove flowers in her hair instead. Mama was crushed I didn't want to wear the tiara she and my grandmother had worn. Her only consolation was that I agreed to wear the diamond eardrops and pendant that my great-great-great grandmother had hidden from the Yankees." She let her Georgia drawl come through on the last word. Maybe, just maybe, she'd get through this without embarrassing both of them.

"Did you live on a plantation?" he asked.

"We didn't—we lived in a very upscale neighborhood that was once a plantation. Now it's mini-mansions and stables and a country club. My ancestors had a tobacco plantation, though, back before the *War of Northern Aggression.*" She kept the teasing lilt in her voice.

"Would that be the kerfuffle we Yankees refer to as the *Civil War*?" He winked and reached for a piece of bread. "I guess it's all a matter of historical perspective, right?"

"Isn't most of life?" She wrinkled her nose at him, delighted with his low rumbling chuckle at the rhetorical question.

The server appeared with their food before he could reply, and for a few minutes, Sarah focused on shrimp scampi, roasted potatoes, and sautéed green beans. Tony was right, the cuisine was delicious—well worth the wait—and they ate companionably, talking about cooking and the history of the Fishwife and what there was to see and do around Willow Bay. When he offered her a fried shrimp from his plate, she gave him some scampi in exchange. They debated the relative merits of dessert, but decided against it, opting instead for second helpings of shrimp.

Everything seemed so *normal* that continuing her personal horror story in this place felt discordant. She set her fork on her near-empty plate and met Tony's eyes over the flickering votive between them. "Could we go somewhere quieter to talk?"

He paused, the last bite of potato midway from his plate to his mouth and the look in his eyes sent a shiver down her spine. *Crap,* did he think she was flirting, trying to...to seduce him? Did that sound like an invitation?

She caught her breath, floundering. "I mean... What I meant was—"

He put the fork down, reached for her, then pulled his hand back and placed both palms on the table. "Sarah, stop. It's okay. I know what you meant." His warm gaze captured hers, affection so clear in his eyes that her stomach flipped over. "How about we finish up here and head down to the beach? We can walk out on the breakwater and watch the sunset."

Her sigh of relief was louder than she meant for it to be, but he was still smiling, so she nodded. "Sounds perfect."

S arah rarely noticed sunsets. She was always too focused on locking herself in, bolting doors, and closing window blinds or shutters against the approaching night and all the dread that came with it. Tonight though, the evening was awash with color —strokes of pink, orange, and deep red were painted over a darkening blue sky, turning the lake into a glistening pool of fire. She stopped at the edge of the beach and caught her breath at the sight of the ruby sun resting a hand's width above the horizon. "Oh, my God!"

Tony touched her shoulder. "What? What is it?"

She smiled up at him. "The sunset. It's... it's beautiful."

"I know." He led her over to a bench. "Here, take off your shoes and roll up your pant legs." He sat and yanked off his sandals and placed them under the bench.

Even his feet were handsome—not all hard and horny and rough-nailed. A startling thought considering she wasn't all that crazy about feet in general and men's feet in particular.

"Won't somebody take them?" She toed off her espadrilles and picked them up. "I can carry them."

"Nobody will touch them." He plucked the canvas shoes from her fingers and set them next to his, where they looked like a child's footwear by comparison.

"Are you sure?" She owned two pairs of nice shoes, and in Chicago, she'd never have left any belongings on a public beach, expecting to come back and retrieve them. Most of the time, she didn't even carry a purse—only her phone in a case that also held her driver's license, a credit card, and some cash tucked into her pocket as she had tonight. That and a lip gloss and her keys.

"I promise," he assured her. "It's an unspoken rule of the village."

"Okay." Sarah couldn't keep the edge of doubt from her tone as she leaned down to fold up her pant legs. "What if we forget them?"

"We won't." He stopped in the midst of rolling his own pant legs to give her a grin. "However, if we did, we'd find them in the lost-and-found box at the lifeguard station right over there, which is never locked." He pointed to a shack some fifty yards down the beach. "That's where anything left on the beach ends up. And usually, if they know whose stuff it is, one of the village kids will deliver your lost items right to your door."

Sarah shook her head. "I'm sure not in Chicago anymore, am I?"

"No, Dorothy, you're not." He extended his hand, invitation shining in his eyes. "Want to take a walk to Oz with me?"

After hesitating for a second, she slipped her hand in his, surprised that her biggest worry wasn't the intimacy of the act; rather, her fear was that her hands were coarse and not at all feminine from the work at the shelter. Even wearing gloves hadn't protected them from calluses and blisters. If he noticed her rough skin, he showed no sign as he enveloped her much smaller hand in his and started up the beach toward the rock jetty.

At the edge of the water, he stopped, pointing to the giant fiery ball settling onto the horizon. "Watch this," he murmured.

The waves *whooshed* on the shore as they stood hand-in-hand, their shoulders barely touching. The sunset took her breath away—one moment the sun rested on the surface of the lake, the next it seemed to have sunk into the water. Her hand tightened on Tony's while the whole sky became a study in crimson, and to the east, a few stars glimmered white gold above the bay. In one long hiss, she released the breath she'd been holding.

"That was... amazing," she whispered, as if speaking in a normal tone might destroy the magic of the moment.

Lacing his fingers with hers, they continued walking along the hard-packed sand. "Yeah," he said. "Gets me every time." His voice was gruff with emotion and once again Sarah was taken aback.

Who'd ever have guessed this most masculine of men would turn out also to be such a sensitive soul? So gentle? He turned any notion she'd formed about male behavior on its ear. In the short time she'd known Tony Reynard, she'd never once seen him red-faced with fury or gritting his teeth to keep his temper in check. She'd never heard him tear someone down with cold, calculated cruelty or, for that matter, even utter an unkind word. Not that she believed for a moment that he was incapable of anger—he was human after all. But incredibly, he seemed to be exactly the kind, easygoing soul he presented himself to be.

Sarah widened her stride to match his long steps and, when she did, he slowed his pace with a faint smile.

"Sorry," he said. "I sometimes forget most people's legs aren't as long as mine."

"You're fine," she said. "You're just fine."

And he was... He certainly was.

CHAPTER 13

Tony caught Sarah's elbow as she slipped on the sandy path at the top of the concrete jetty leading out to the North Breakwater lighthouse. With a superhuman effort, he resisted the urge to pull her into his arms and kiss her stupid. Kissing Sarah Bennett without her permission would be a colossal mistake, so of course, he'd never do it. However, that didn't mean he wasn't longing to.

This *thing* with Sarah, whatever it was, was entirely new to him. He'd dated plenty over the years since his divorce, although he'd never been much of a player. There'd even been a couple of longer relationships with women he thought might make good life partners. Something always stopped him from taking that final step.

At this very moment, walking the jetty with waves lapping below them and his hand firmly on the small of her back, he thanked God he'd waited, because all he wanted in the world was to spend as much time as he could with this woman.

Pictures of the two of them together played in an endless loop in his brain—he and Sarah wandering the beach, exploring the dunes, grocery shopping, hanging out with their friends, and sharing meals in their own house. His apartment in town was too small for two people, but hers above the boathouse at Dixon's had potential. Or maybe they could find a cottage somewhere close to the beach—perhaps Sophie and Henry would sell them their rental unit.

No, Sarah would want to live at the shelter and that could work, too. Having a cop onsite might be a good thing. They could claim one of the upstairs bedrooms for themselves—the master suite was certainly big enough and even included a sitting room.

Holy crap! He was ten seconds shy of tracing a huge heart in the sand with his toe and putting their initials in it. How old was he anyway? Fifteen?

His imagination continued to work overtime while his hand tingled where it rested on Sarah's spine. Emboldened by the fact that she hadn't stiffened as he guided her, he slid his hand up her back and placed his arm around her shoulders. His heart sang when after a few seconds' hesitation, she slipped her arm around his waist and settled in close to him, her head just reaching his shoulder. She fit as perfectly as he knew she would, and he checked his pace, making sure he wasn't forcing her to walk too fast to keep up.

Even though she was small, there was nothing fragile about Sarah Bennett. If he made a wrong move, a swift elbow to the gut or a kick in the balls would have him back in line in record time. Each step with her would need to be carefully considered.

"What time does the shooting range close?" Her question startled him out of his own head.

"Nine, but I have twenty-four-hour access." He slowed and moved behind her as they approached the lighthouse. A set of concrete steps on the side of the old structure would be a good spot to sit and talk.

"You do?" After he led her up the stairs, she sat on the stoop, heedless of the gritty surface. "Why?"

"Deputy privileges, plus Harry Perkins is my neighbor." Tony stood below her, resting his back against the stoop right next to her legs. "He lives in the apartment above me."

"Where do you live anyway?" Sarah tipped her head back to examine the lighthouse as she spoke. "I can't believe I haven't asked you that before."

"I knew one day I'd catch your interest." He grinned. "Lately, you've been remarkably uncurious about me. That is, given how fascinated I am by you."

"I'm sorry." Her brow furrowed.

"Don't be. I'm only teasing you." He touched her shoulder lightly. "Well, except for the part about being fascinated." When she looked away, clearly uncomfortable, he cursed inwardly and changed tacks, answering her question. "I live downstairs in the green Victorian with the maroon trim on Forest Avenue." At her puzzled look, he gestured at the village and enumerated the streets east from the bay. "Waterfront Drive, Anchor Place, Forest Avenue. The house is two blocks east of Carrie's studio."

"Oh, okay. I've been so wrapped up in the shelter, I haven't really learned my way around town yet. Chris takes me wherever I need to go and I don't pay attention. I should, I guess."

"It's not hard. Everything is pretty much within walking distance." He gazed out at the lake lapping at the rocks along the breakwater. The night was clear and more stars were beginning to appear. Soon the whole sky would be blanketed with tiny lights— a sight that still awed him. You'd never see a night sky like that in Chicago.

"This is beautiful—the lake, the dunes, the lighthouse." Sarah's sweeping gesture took in the scene before them. "I haven't spent time in a beach town before—the whole atmosphere is so, I dunno, so peaceful and laid-back. I can't imagine there'd be much crime here."

Tony shook his head with a smile. "Well, if you gotta be a

cop, this is a good place to be one. We get called out to all the same kinds of stuff the law in other places do, though, just in smaller doses. Burglaries happen here, shoplifting, DUIs—"

"Domestic violence?" The question was whispered so softly he almost missed it.

"Now and again."

She exhaled a huge breath. "He swept me off my feet. An older man—he was twenty-five and so handsome and suave and, dear God, he was charming." She shivered and thrust her arms into the sweater draped over her shoulders.

Tony turned to help her when something in her eyes stopped him, so he shoved his hands into his pockets, keeping his neutral position standing next to the stoop.

"I was the envy of every girl at the club. His family had been old guard in Ames for generations, even though his ancestors were carpetbaggers—Northerners who came down and made a fortune during Reconstruction, taking over a cotton mill and a tobacco company." She snorted a grim laugh. "By the time Paul was born, the Prescotts had reinvented themselves into wealthy Southerners. They own most of Ames, Georgia, from the IGA to the local newspaper—"

She gasped and clapped a hand over her mouth, her eyes wide.

Bewildered, Tony whirled around, scanning the beach before he pivoted toward her and placed one hand on her thigh. "Sarah, what is it?"

∼

Sarah trembled and her heart rose to her throat as realization struck her. The newspaper—*that* was how Paul had found her. The online subscription to the Ames, Georgia, *Sentinel* had been her only link to her previous life. Evenings in Chicago, she'd hunch over her laptop, reading every page of the small daily, savoring news of home and the people she'd left behind in the small town outside Atlanta, where Paul had once imprisoned her.

"God, I'm such an idiot," she said when she could finally speak.

"What are you talking about?" Fear laced Tony's tone and his hand was warm on her leg.

She wrapped her arms around her middle to control the trembling and swallowed, then swallowed again. "The newspaper is how he found me in Chicago."

"Through the newspaper?" He knit his dark brows and reached for her hand.

"His uncle owns the paper. Someone in the newspaper office must have gotten him a list of online subscribers, and then he probably went on the Web and searched on it. There can't be that many." Bile rose in her throat as she tried to regain control over the tremors that shuddered through her. "Nobody else from down there knew I was in Chicago, but how hard would it be to look at the list of online subscribers and start trying to figure out who they are? And I was so hungry for news from home I didn't even stop to think he could find me that way."

"What about your family? Could he have found out from them?"

She shook her head. "My parents have been gone for years and my brother lives in Germany. I haven't been in touch with anyone from Ames. I couldn't be—he would've found me. I haven't used my real name for anything since I left. It was just dumb luck and cold perseverance that he figured out which one was me and where I was."

"I can't believe someone at the newspaper office would do that." Skepticism edged Tony's voice. "I doubt it's even legal for them to give out information from a subscription list, even if his uncle is the publisher."

"Legal?" She rolled her eyes. "His family's owned that whole town for damn near six generations. Hell, any one of those people would give him anything he wanted."

"You make him sound like some kind of mafia boss or something."

"Let me put it this way—when he went to jail, *I* was the one who was shunned." She tugged her hand from his grip. "Julie told me once that the villagers here look after their own. Do you think it's any different in Ames?"

"Aren't you one of their own?" Tony sounded so reasonable. "Why would they shun you when you were the victim?"

"Because I wasn't paying the salaries of eighty percent of the town. The Prescotts own the glove factory, the cotton mill, the bank, the newspaper..." She shifted away from him, needing space in order to continue her story. If he touched her again, she'd lose it, and remaining in control was the way she'd get through this. "You can't imagine the power that family wields down there. He didn't spend a moment in prison because of what he did to *me*. His sentence was about what happened to...to M-Macy." Sarah choked on the word. She'd only spoken her daughter's name a handful of times in the last eight years—the pain of that day was simply too much to bear.

"Sarah." Tony placed both hands on the concrete surface of the stoop and in one smooth move, heaved his big body up to sit next to her, but not too close. "Sarah, you don't have to do this." He reached out a tentative hand and then pulled it back immediately.

"No." Scooting away, she put at least a foot between them. "I need to tell you what happened. You should know...because you're the law here and he'll come looking. He'll figure it out. He always does."

His expression was unreadable in the shadows, but he acquiesced, folding his hands in his lap. "Okay. Talk."

She'd intended to start at the very beginning and tell him everything, lay the whole mess all out coldly and without emotion. Now, her insides were roiling, and she just wanted to get through the telling as fast as possible. "We got married the December after I graduated from high school."

"What about college?"

"I told you, he swept me right off my feet." She gazed out at the lake, watching a freighter heading north. "My parents were overjoyed that a Prescott wanted their daughter. He was every Ames mother's fantasy. They didn't object in the least to me turning down the French scholarship to get married instead of going to Ole Miss with my friends. Mother couldn't wait to help me decorate whatever huge mansion Paul and I would end up in. The only person who tried to talk me out of getting married was my brother, Quint."

"You think he guessed what kind of person the guy was?" Tony asked.

Sarah shrugged. "Who knows? He moved to Germany to work for Mercedes right after the wedding. He only came back when my parents were killed and then—"

"Your parents were *killed*?" Disbelief was evident in Tony's eyes even in the dim light above the door of the lighthouse. "Holy shit, Sarah."

"When I was pregnant. A burglary. They were shot while they were sleeping. The police said the robbers probably worried they'd wake up and catch them." Sarah was aware how dull her tone was as she told the story, but she had to get through it. "Paul found them the next morning when he stopped by the house to pick up some things Mother had bought for the nursery.

"Honestly, I don't remember a lot about that time, except they were worried I'd lose the baby and I spent several weeks in bed.

He and Quint handled everything—settling the estate, selling the house, getting rid of what was left of their belongings. By the time Macy was born, they had disappeared as if they'd never existed." She was unable to stop the shudder that went through her at the memory. "Want to know something funny?"

"I can't imagine what could possibly be funny." Tony's voice cracked.

"I'm terrified of guns."

"I know." Tony extended one hand. "Sarah..."

She held up her hand, shaking her head and continued. "Daddy always had guns—he was a hunter—but they were locked up and they never scared me. After those...monsters murdered him and Mother with his own shotgun, I wasn't able to even look at a gun." She met his eyes, and the combination of horror and tenderness she saw in them nearly undid her. Then she pressed on, determined. "Now look at me. Look what he's done to me. I own a freaking Ruger. I've applied for a concealed-carry permit. Isn't that the ultimate irony?"

Tony sighed, and although Sarah could almost feel the tension vibrating in him, no way was she going to stop now. He'd asked. She was going to tell him. "The abuse started not long after my daughter was born. Before that, he'd been the ideal husband— loving, kind, supportive—all the things a man should be. Even Quint believed he was leaving me and Macy in good hands when he went back to Germany." She bit her lower lip, trying to condense seventeen nightmare years into as few sentences as she could.

"I understand that most sociopaths are excellent actors," Tony said.

"Yeah, my ex was no exception," Sarah muttered, then cleared her throat. "I tried to rationalize it—that Paul was a busy important man and if I just did things his way, everything would be fine. And they would be for a while. Sometimes for as long as a year or so, and I'd get lulled into believing he'd changed. We were text-book—he'd do something cruel and then cry and beg my forgive-ness and swear it wouldn't happen again. He was entirely different around Macy, though. He was so sweet to her and to me when she was present. She adored him."

"He never hurt her?"

"Never once in all those years. He was the perfect father." Sarah shook her head. "And when he'd hurt me, he did it when she was away from the house, like for a sleepover. Crazy as I sound, that fact gave me hope for him, for us. I saw how he doted on her, and I'd think maybe I could convince him to get some help...for Macy's sake." Tears threatened, but she swallowed them, refusing to let a single one fall.

"Didn't you ever try to tell anyone?" Tony's voice sounded far away, even though he was sitting less than two feet from her. "Wasn't there a maid or a housekeeper who knew what was going on?"

"I had a housekeeper who came in once a week to clean. Otherwise, I did the daily stuff—Paul insisted, and what else was I going to do all day? He lost his shit whenever I suggested getting a job. Besides, who would I tell?" Her stomach churned. "My friends, hell, even my parents believed he was right next door to Jesus Christ."

She stared out across the waves, unable to look at him, even though she could feel him squirming next to her. "He'd drop little hints about me being spacey or forgetful. Said with love of course —creating an image of me that almost had *me* convinced I couldn't function without him. He was brilliant and cunning and terrifying." She met Tony's eyes for a brief moment. "Don't you get it? I didn't have any cash of my own, any skills, any support from anyone. Just years of being mentally and physically beaten down."

The emotional struggle on his face was so evident Sarah

almost reached out to comfort him. However, touching him would be the end of her. She squared her shoulders instead and continued in as steady a voice as she could muster. "The last time was the first time he ever touched me in anger when Macy was at home. Back then, I would've told you I provoked him that day, but—"

"Jesus!" The word exploded into the darkness as Tony clenched and unclenched his fists.

"I know better now," she said, but it took a herculean effort to sit still and ignore the waves of anger radiating off the deputy.

Although all her common sense told her he'd never ever direct any of that rage toward her, he still scared the bejesus out of her. As subtly as she could, she put another few inches between them and glanced down to make sure she could drop to the jetty and run if she had to.

"It was a Sunday and Macy was sunbathing on a lawn chair in the driveway. She did that when the patio out back was in the shade—set her chair up in the big turnaround behind the garage. I was in the kitchen cleaning up after lunch and Paul was clearing the table. That seemed like a sign—he never helped in any way. That day he was carrying dishes and we were laughing about something that had happened at church that morning." Sarah paused, eyeing Tony, who wasn't looking at her; instead, he stared straight ahead.

"A sign of what?" he asked, still focused on the beach and the village lights in the distance.

"That maybe things were better—it had been months since he'd hurt me, except—" She was loath to bring up Paul's deviant sexual proclivities. That would only fuel Tony's anger and that part didn't matter to the story, not really. "He'd been calm and kind for almost a year, and, yes, I was always on guard, but this day had been...normal. So I mentioned talking to a therapist about his anger issues."

When Tony turned his head toward her, *had you lost your freaking mind?* was written all over his face as clearly as if he'd spoken the words out loud. He thought she was an idiot. The same look she'd gotten from the attorneys who'd come to see her in the hospital.

Great. Another self-righteous bastard.

In a wink, Sarah rose, slipped behind Tony, and down the stairs onto the jetty. "You don't know. You couldn't possibly know," she said, turning to face him, her arms folded over her belly. "I had to take my opportunities when it seemed safe."

"Obviously *not* safe that day, huh?" He set his palms on either side of his body and boosted himself off the stoop, landing, agile as a panther, onto the jetty below. "I assume he didn't take *that* suggestion well?" Was his voice seriously dripping sarcasm?

Sarah dropped her hands as frustration and hurt jolted through her.

How dare you judge me!

"Screw you, Tony." Heart pounding in her chest, she spun around and raced down the breakwater toward the beach.

CHAPTER 14

Oh, good Christ in heaven.

Tony sprinted after her, cursing himself, the sandy surface of the breakwater, and the darkness. He was an ass. His reaction had come from straight from his gut—fury at Paul Prescott overshadowing every clear thought in his head. "Sarah!" he called, not at all surprised by how swiftly she moved. "Sarah, wait!"

She didn't so much as glance over her shoulder, just kept barreling toward the beach.

He finally caught up to her when the sand slowed her pace. Grasping her elbow gently, he swung her around to face him and tried to catch his breath. She, on the other hand, wasn't even panting, even though her eyes were shooting turquoise sparks in the lights from the parking area behind the beach. "Wait, please." He puffed and swallowed. "I'm sorry. I'm so sorry."

She shook his hand away and put a couple of feet between them. She didn't bolt, simply stood there staring up at him.

He shoved his hands into his pockets. "I didn't mean... I wasn't—"

"Judging me?"

"No, I wasn't. Not at all."

"Coulda fooled me." Her eyes never left his face, and even in the dim light, he could read the pain in them.

"I *wasn't* judging you—I'd never do that. Never. I-I was…" He stumbled over the words, trying to find the right ones. "It was him. I'm so angry at *him.*"

She raised one brow, but she was still there.

He took a deep breath. "My reaction isn't about you, Sarah. I would never judge your actions that day…or any day you spent in that hell. I'm sorry if it seemed that way." He walked closer, then stopped, aware that he had to maintain space between them…and keep his hands in his pockets. "I'm just so furious. I want to strangle him with my bare hands. I want to do to him everything he did to you and then shoot him and then do it all to him again. I couldn't hold the anger in and it came out at the wrong time. Cruel and stupid and unthinking. I'm an asshole. I'm sorry."

She bit her lower lip. "You know, I've never told a man this story before, except the police officer who took my statement in the hospital and the attorneys. And they all gave me that look— that *what were you thinking?* look." Her gaze shifted until she was looking out at the lake. "The women who know—the one in my group—reacted with tears and horror and sympathy. They'd all been in that same hell. And they were new to the shelter, still shrinking into a corner whenever a man walked past them. Anger wasn't in their repertoire—it had been beaten out of them. And Julie knows enough." Her eyes came back to him, glistening with tears.

Good God, how he wanted to take her in his arms. Hold her. Protect her from everything wicked—even from himself. Instead, he stayed out of her space and let her talk.

"She was pissed, as only Jules can be, ready to collect up torches and pitchforks and head to Georgia." She inched a foot or so closer to him. "It was Julie, you know, so it was a...a sister-hood kind of angry. Not directed at me."

Tony swallowed, unable to stop another apology from bursting forth, even though his sensible brain told him to shut the hell up and let her talk. "Neither is mine. Never."

She merely nodded. "Okay."

"What about the attorneys at the trial?" He asked the question quietly, hoping he could engage her enough to keep her there. "Were they men?"

She gave a derisive bark. "There was no trial, only a hearing. He copped a plea because the neighbor saw everything and testified, as did the policemen who came. His attorney worked out a deal with the prosecutor and the sentencing judge was an old family friend. The pictures they took of me at the hospital weren't even admitted into evidence.

"My statement"—she wrapped her arms around her middle —"*my* story never entered into it, either. Interestingly, the judge gave him the maximum sentence—sixteen years—then he immediately cut the time in half. The prison they sent him to was one of those white-collar country-club places." Her face contorted before the cool mask he was accustomed to seeing slipped back into place. "Afterward, I had to get as far away as I could. I packed up, got in my car, and headed for the Orlando airport."

Tony dug his toes into the sand, his heart heavy as he imagined a defeated, grieving Sarah fleeing the home that had turned into her worst nightmare.

Dear God in heaven.

Now he'd blown it. He'd be lucky if she ever spoke to him again. She'd probably leave Willow Bay and he'd never see her after tonight. "I didn't mean to hurt you or frighten you." He hung his head. "Jesus. Those are the very words I never ever wanted to have to say to you, and here I am saying them on our first date. I like you. I like you so much and… God, I'm a jerk." He put one hand out. "Here, let me take you home."

Silence stretched between them, widening the gulf he was sure was getting bigger with every word he uttered. At last she sighed. "I believe you're not judging me, Tony. I–I'm not used to normal men, to normal male reactions." She stepped closer to him, reaching out to touch his arm before snapping her hand back. "And I'm prickly, especially when I talk about…then. I struggle everyday with the fact that I'm a victim. I hate it."

"*Were* a victim," he corrected, longing to pull her into his arms or at the very least, take her hand, but knew that touching her would be a colossal mistake. "You are a strong woman, Sarah Bennett."

"Not so much." She gave him the faintest of smiles. "I'm mostly a basket case—hopped up on mood-enhancing drugs and just trying to make it through each day without screaming like a banshee."

Encouraged by the smile, however faint, Tony extended his arms toward the sky. Time to bring in some levity. If *he* was emotionally exhausted, poor Sarah had to be drained. "You feeling the need to scream right now? I've been told I can sometimes incite that urge. Hey, we can stand here and howl at that puny-ass moon if you want." He threw his head back and let out a low coyote yowl, side-eyeing Sarah the entire time and praying he hadn't ruined their tentative friendship.

～

Sarah stared in disbelief as Tony took a deep breath and let out another howl that echoed over the bay. The silver threads in his salt-and-pepper hair shone in the lights the lined the sidewalk to the beach and she clenched her fists to keep from stroking the strands that curled over his shirt collar. Inanely, the thought occurred to her that he could use a haircut. Dimples bracketed his grin when he glanced over at her and nodded.

Dammit, he was handsome. Not suave, sophisticated handsome, but good-looking in a rugged, plaid-flannel-and-denim kind of way. He exuded gentleness. Even though he was a cop, she couldn't picture him ever deliberately hurting a living soul. She realized that now as she studied him standing there at the edge of the water yipping at the moon. Tony Reynard was the kind of man you instinctively trusted even if you were a woman who'd never consider trusting any man again. Ever.

"Come on, join in," he said. "It's very cathartic and kinda fun."

"Um, I'm not all that much of a howler," she said, even though the idea was intriguing. How many times in her life had she wished she could let go and wail? She'd never done it—not once in all the years of her marriage…or after.

Maintaining an iron clamp on her emotions was what kept her sane. If she let herself howl, she might not ever be able to stop, and then they'd surely lock her up in a rubber room forever. "Besides, there are people down there." With a little jerk of her head, she indicated a group gathered around a beach fire in the distance.

"Nobody cares. Hell, I'm surprised they haven't already joined in." The words were barely out of his mouth when a yowl that sounded like a wounded hyena, followed by laughter, came from the direction of the bonfire.

He chuckled. "See?" He howled again, grinning as several of the beach partiers responded in kind.

"I seriously wonder about this town." Ambling closer to Tony, she put her head back and let out quiet yelp. She sounded pretty pitiful, so she took a deep breath, opened her arms, and gave it another try. This one came out more like an owl's hoot. However, her effort got an answering cheer from the group in the distance, most of whom were on their feet, dancing, yowling, and whooping. When she glanced at Tony, he was beaming at her like a proud father whose kid had just hit a home run in the little league championship game. She faced him, turning her palms up in a self-conscious shrug. "I imagine I'll learn to howl better."

"You howl just fine, Sarah Bennett." Tony extended his hand. "Come on, wanna go shoot some bad guys?"

~

Sarah pushed the button to bring the paper silhouette of a man up to the booth. She'd hit his heart twice and even managed to put one right between his eyes. Not bad for only an hour of practice. She glanced at Tony, who was leaning against the wall behind her, his neon green earmuffs glowing in the semi-darkness of the shooting range. A poster with a likeness of Thomas Jefferson and the words...*the right of the people to keep and bear arms*...was tacked up beside him. The words gave her pause— she'd been so anti-gun since her parents died, yet here she was firing a Ruger and doing a damn fine job of hitting her target. Most surprising of all was how good the weapon felt in her hands —how empowering.

"Nice job, dead-eye." Lowering his muffs so they sat around his neck, he came forward to examine the target. "Where's the gun go?"

Sarah set the safety on the pistol, released the magazine, and laid both pieces on the counter before removing the muffs he'd presented her with when they'd arrived at the shooting range. They were neon pink and matched the frames of the safety glasses that were also in the box, along with pink foam earplugs. She kept those in place and pushed the glasses up on her head. "Thanks again for the ear and eye protection. I didn't think of that." She hoped she wasn't talking too loudly—the earplugs made it hard to tell.

A smile bloomed on his handsome face. "You're welcome. Sorry about the cutesy pink. You're so little, I knew they needed to be smaller, so my extra pair wasn't going to work well, and this hot pink kit was all Harry had in stock this afternoon." His deep voice came through the foam loud and clear.

"I kinda like the pink," she said and touched one finger to the muffs around his neck. "Yours are pretty snazzy. I had no idea there was so much gear involved."

"Safety's number one when you're shooting. Noise reduction, too, especially indoors where the gunfire can hurt your ears; that's why we use both earplugs and the muffs." He tilted his head toward the target. "You did well. He's dead."

Sarah scrutinized the target, proud of her effort, but not convinced she wanted to shoot to kill. "What if I don't want to kill an intruder, only stop him?"

"Asks the woman who had a gun pointed directly at my heart the first time I ever met her." Tony's lips twitched and his eyes gleamed amber in the light above their heads as he stepped into the booth with her.

Sarah chuckled. "You should've knocked."

"Next time." He nodded, dimpling when he allowed the smile he'd been hiding to show.

Her heart sped up. This attraction was unsettling as hell, mostly because she wasn't sure she would ever be able to do anything about it. The very thought of intimacy with any man filled her with dread, yet pangs and zips of heat sparked through her at Tony's merest touch.

She'd been worried that he'd want to stand behind her while she was shooting, perhaps put his arms around her to guide her hands. But he hadn't. Instead, he demonstrated the proper stance and arm positions, explaining how most women instinctively want to lean back, away from the recoil of the gun and away from the target.

She found he was right—at the moment her whole body ached from the conscious effort of leaning in, keeping her weight forward, and unlocking her knees to maintain the correct position. "So where do I aim to maim, not kill?"

"Look, deadly force is deadly force under the law." Tony took off his glasses and pinched the bridge of his nose. "It doesn't matter where you shoot someone, you could potentially kill him or cripple him for life. If you aren't prepared to kill someone who's threatening your life, you shouldn't have that gun." Pausing, he quirked one dark eyebrow. "Here's the thing, if he comes after you, adrenaline is going to kick in. Your hands will shake and your focus will be off. Besides, he's not going to be standing perfectly still like that target there—he's going to be moving erratically and doing unexpected things. And I think it's safe to say that *your* ex-husband will be playing mind games with you."

Suddenly chilly in the air-conditioned metal building, Sarah wrapped her arms around her waist. He was right about the mind games—that was how Paul had always cowed her before any actual physical abuse had started. He was the master of the crushing reply and had the uncanny ability to find just the right words to turn her into a sniveling mess. She stared at her shoes as Tony continued.

"During a shooting, an officer may only hit the target a small percentage of the time. They're aiming at someone who's fleeing or lurking in a poorly lit place where the suspect may or may not be returning fire. And these are trained cops who've practiced for hours. They have mere seconds to react. You're going to be in the same boat in the remote possibility he shows up out of the blue. Chances are good you won't even have your gun handy."

Her head up snapped up. "Are you *trying* to scare the crap out of me?"

"Of course not." His voice was quiet.

"You think this gun is a terrible idea."

"I think all guns are a terrible idea." Tony covered her Ruger with one big hand. "If having this thing makes you feel safe, I can't stop you from carrying it. I'm just trying to make sure you know how to use it and that you're in reality. Frankly, I'd rather be like the police officers in England who don't carry a gun on patrol."

"That's kinda radical thinking for a cop in this country, Deputy Reynard." Sarah's reaction to Tony's big warm body so close to hers in the confines of the booth bewildered her. She was dying to smooth back the lock of hair that flopped over his brow, run her fingers over the slight stubble on his cheek. Part of her longed for him to gather her close against his muscled chest, while at the same time, the certainty that he could break her neck with his strong hands made her stomach roil.

God, would she ever be normal again? Or had the possibility of a loving relationship with a man been beaten out of her?

"Yeah, that's me." Tony grinned. "Always been one of those radical peace-and-love hippie types."

Sarah couldn't help picturing him all beardy in a tie-dyed T-shirt and torn jeans—a look that would work for him way better than the sheriff's uniform. "I can totally see that." She gazed up at him, her heart beating a little faster at his tender expression.

"Sarah..." He raised one hand toward her, but when she flinched reflexively, he rotated his wrist to look at his watch, disappointment clear in his eyes. "Hey, it's getting late, and I've got an early court appearance tomorrow."

Dammit. The reaction was pure instinct, even though he was awakening an ache inside her that she hadn't experienced in almost thirty years. "Tony, I-I..." She looked away.

"Hey, don't." He shoved his hands in his pockets, and his smile was warm. "We're good." After dropping a quick kiss on the top of her head, he became all business. "Pack up and don't put the magazine back in. Pull the slide back and if there's a bullet in the chamber, it should eject."

Sensation fluttered through Sarah as he turned away, and once again she fought the urge to stroke the thick hair curling over his collar.

CHAPTER 15

"Sarah, it's Home Depot, not the White House." Julie's voice carried up the stairs. "What the hell are you doing up there?"

"I'm coming." Sarah scowled at her reflection in the bathroom mirror. Was the taupe eye shadow too much? The peachy lipstick too glossy? Makeup was something she hadn't messed with in years—not since she'd left Georgia. In Chicago, a quick brush of blush across her cheeks and a dash of mascara to color her auburn lashes and she was good to go. Women in the shelter wore makeup to hide bruises, not to look attractive, and Sarah had simply gotten out of the habit.

Today, she wanted to look good and she wasn't fooling herself about why. Instead of a quick ponytail, she'd coaxed her unruly hair into a softer, more feminine knot at the base of her skull, letting a few strands curl around her face, and she'd popped a flowy flowered blouse over her tank top and jeans, lending a much more feminine appearance to her usual workaday outfit. She shook her head. Was she seriously prettying herself up for a man?

Her shiny lips twisted into a grimace. Yup. That's exactly

what she was doing. Heat suffused her cheeks as she recalled how she'd shivered at Tony's light touch on her spine when he walked her to her door the night before. He'd dropped his hand when they reached the door, standing still as a soldier as she worked the two locks. A single move from her and she'd have been in his arms, but she couldn't muster the courage, so she thanked him for a lovely evening, trying to put into those few words what she couldn't make herself demonstrate with a goodnight kiss. His smile was so warm and friendly when he stepped away she'd almost called him back.

But she didn't.

When she'd peeked between the slats of the shutters, watching as Tony ambled down the dock to check on the *Allegro* before he headed up the hill to town, her heart ached. She'd lain awake for several hours after she'd made her final pass through the apartment, testing doors and windows. Her fantasies never got past a few passionate kisses, though. The rest was…unthinkable. This morning, the ache had turned into a quiver of anticipation at the idea of seeing the sexy deputy.

With a nod to the redhead in the mirror, she hurried down the stairs to the kitchen where Julie had helped herself to coffee and one of Margie Dixon's blueberry scones.

"Well, look at you!" Jules exclaimed around a mouthful of pastry. "You clean up nice, kiddo."

"It's just a little makeup." Sarah poured herself a second cup of coffee.

"And a very pretty blouse and, um, hey, I like what you did with your hair. I'm sure I'm not the only one who'll appreciate the extra effort." Julie's eyes held a teasing glint, which Sarah pointedly ignored.

"I have a list on my phone." Pulling the device out of her jeans pocket, she tapped the screen awake. "We need at least two towel racks for each bathroom plus some for the kitchen and the mudroom, toilet paper racks, and I'm thinking a couple of paper towel holders for the kitchen since it's such a big room. Like one by the main double sink and then one by that smaller prep sink? Also one in the mudroom above the laundry tub. Man, I'm so glad we decided to give each bedroom its own bathroom. It took out some closet space and meant jockeying things somewhat, but I like that each family will have a private bath, don't you?"

"Sure." Julie grinned over the rim of her coffee cup as Sarah scanned the list, mentally going through each room of the big house. "Come on, Sarah, dish!"

"Oh, I'm going to add those big hook things for the backs of the bathroom doors—you know, like for robes?" Sarah concentrated on the list. At last she looked up, and the goofy expression on her friend's face was irresistible. Pocketing her phone with a sigh, Sarah poured another cup of coffee and sat down on the other tall stool by the kitchen bar. "We had a nice time. We went to the Fishwife for supper, took a walk on the jetty to watch the sun set, and then went to Perkins to shoot."

"Okay"—Julie's blue eyes sparkled with curiosity—"cop date, but the sunset has potential. Was it, you know, romantic?"

"It was a first date, Jules." Sarah reached for a scone and a napkin. "Very casual." Heat rose to her cheeks, so she took a bite to avoid talking.

"Sarah, talk to me."

Sarah chewed and swallowed. "He's a great guy."

"I've always thought Tony was kinda hot." Julie mused. "That intellectual lumberjack vibe totally works."

"He was… He was very kind."

"Hmm, not exactly a ringing first-date endorsement. I'm going to ignore that for the moment, because this morning you're wearing eyeshadow and lip gloss." Julie quirked one brow. "That tells me you liked him enough to want him to ask you out again."

Sarah sighed. Julie was relentless and, besides, a little post-game rehash might calm the butterflies in her stomach. "I told him about Georgia—not the details because they don't matter. I talked about that last day and Macy."

"Did you tell him what happened in Chicago?"

"No, did you?" Sarah's heart rose to her throat. As far as she knew, there was no police report about that night. She couldn't imagine that Paul had turned her in. Besides, the network had simply wiped her existence from the shelter.

"No, all he knows about that night is that the bastard turned up and you ran." Julie's gaze drilled into Sarah's. "Don't keep secrets from him. He's a good guy and he's already falling for you, Sarah. I can see it on his face every time he looks at you. If you're going to let things progress, he deserves the whole truth. And your trust."

Shaking her head, Sarah felt sadness welling up inside her. "Maybe I'd better stop now before things go too far. I'm a mess. He doesn't need a woman like me. He's got a great life here and he's too much of a gentleman to end things if they get to a point where he can't handle all my stupid baggage."

"Why don't you let Tony decide what he needs?" Julie's voice was gentle. "Do you like him?"

Sarah hesitated before she answered, pondering the question as she chewed another bite of scone. "Yes. Dear God, yes. I like him." She twirled sideways on her stool and leaned against the granite countertop. "It's the first time in over twenty-five years that I've had the…the *feeling*. You know the one? That unsettled, sorta tingly sensation right *here*." She put her hand over her lower belly.

Nodding, Julie chuckled. "Yep—the one I get every single time Will comes into view."

"Seriously? Still?"

"Of course, still. I'm crazy about him. The same thing

happened with Charlie the whole time we were married." She touched Sarah's arm. "That's attraction, sweets. It's a good thing."

Heat suffused Sarah's cheeks and she gazed at her coffee cup. "I don't even recognize this, Jules. I haven't felt it in ages. It disappeared the first time Paul shoved me to the floor, grabbed me by the hair, and forced me to—" Glancing up, she pressed her lips together at the tears welling in Julie's eyes.

Julie blinked. "Oh, babe..."

"It doesn't matter." Sarah forced a small smile. "The point is, it's been so long and here it is again."

"That's wonderful, isn't it?" Julie asked, obviously seeing the confusion etched on Sarah's face.

"Not if I can't ever do anything about it."

"What do you mean?"

Sarah sighed. "He's a normal guy, Jules. He's going to eventually want...you know"—she opened her eyes wide at Julie's bewilderment—"sex," she finally managed. "He's going to want to have sex and I can't even imagine ever letting a man touch me that way again."

For once, Julie had no snappy reply. She simply stared at Sarah with a puzzled look on her beautiful face. No matter how hard her dear friend tried to understand, she never would.

Sarah sipped her coffee and toyed with her scone, giving Julie time to figure out why making love with Tony—hell, making love with *anyone*—was impossible. After a moment, she whispered, "The attraction doesn't mean I want him to touch me, Jules. Just the thought of *that* nearly turns my stomach."

Setting her cup on the bar, Julie slid off her stool to wander to the huge window overlooking Willow Bay. When she finally turned around, she wore the same determined expression she'd had the night Sarah had appeared on her and Will's doorstep after Paul had turned up. Clearly, she was ready to do battle with whatever demons might be holding Sarah hostage. "Have you talked to Dr. Benton about this?"

Sarah's heart overflowed at her friend's let's-get-this-fixed-and-move-on outlook. How she wished life was that easy—a few sessions with the therapist and she'd no longer flinch when Tony raised his hand toward her. She searched for the words to explain how torn she'd been last night each time he touched her—longing for his touch and yet dreading it at the same time. How she was hungry for his kiss, yet terrified at what might come next. When he'd offered his hand down on the beach, the most natural thing in the world was to lace her fingers with his. But the very idea of his big body over hers, smothering her, pounding into her...

Dear Lord.

A long agonized shiver ran through her.

"Jesus, Sarah!" Julie rushed over to peer into her face, hesitating for a moment before gathering her close in a sympathetic embrace. "I–I'm an idiot. I had no idea."

Swallowing hard, Sarah returned the hug, grateful once again for the gift of this friendship where she felt safe and protected. She sniffed and leaned back. "No tears. I'm not redoing this damn mascara, Jules."

Julie plopped back down on her stool and offered a fresh napkin from the basket on the counter. "Honey, I really think you need to bring this up with Dr. Benton. It's part of the crap that you have to get rid of. All the bullshit has to go. *All* of it. You deserve a new life, and frankly, I hope Tony can be in it. But whether it's him or someone else, you can't just shut down that part of you." Blue eyes glittering, she pressed her lips into a thin line. "That bastard wins if you do."

Sarah dabbed at her cheeks, careful not to smudge her makeup, before giving Julie a tremulous smile. "I love you, Jules," she said around the lump in her throat before straightening her shoulders and taking a deep breath. "It's not that I don't want a normal life—hell, look at me! I'm wearing makeup for God's sake. I spent fifteen minutes accomplishing this carefully careless hairstyle." She gave a little self-deprecating shrug. "If I've got a chance at normal at all, it's here in this beautiful place with you and Carrie and Sophie and Libby. Here where there's important work for me to do, where I can make a difference for women who've been in the same hell I lived through for too many years. Right now, that's my focus. Maybe Tony's a part of it too, but—"

"He should be." Julie's voice was urgent. "Tony's perfect for you."

"Ah, that may well be." Sarah nodded sadly. "The more significant question is, am I perfect for him?"

"I happen to think you are," Julie replied firmly. "Promise me you'll talk to Dr. Benton about the sex. She'll help you through it. Look how much better you are already."

"You know, a man isn't the answer to every problem." Sarah rose, rinsed out their cups, and tucked the foil back around the plate of scones. "I've done fine and dandy for the last eight years without a man in my life. I haven't missed it one bit."

"That's because the only men you've been around for the last eight years have been sweet old Mack and those jackasses who came looking for the women they beat the crap out of. You built up this sturdy armor around your emotions and became tough-chick Sarah." Julie tipped her blonde head to look into her eyes across the bar. "You don't have to be tough here. We've got your back. Me and Carrie and the rest of the MP and Tony too, if you'll let him."

Sarah bit her lower lip to keep back the threatening tears. Hell's bells, she'd cried more since arriving in Willow Bay than she had in the last twenty-eight years. In Ames, she couldn't afford the luxury of tears—crying only encouraged Paul's viciousness. And if she stopped to indulge her sorrow over Macy since escaping Georgia, she knew she'd never stop weeping. That pain was tucked in the furthest recesses of her heart, something never to be taken out and examined if she was to remain sane.

"Don't close your mind and heart to new possibilities, babes," Julie said. "You're too young. There's too much of life ahead."

A spasm twisted through Sarah's heart. How did she deserve a new wonderful life when Macy never had a chance at a life at all?

CHAPTER 16

Dusk darkened the sky by the time Tony finally managed to get out to the huge old mansion. His long stride took him swiftly past Chris's beat-up Jeep, which was the only vehicle left in the parking lot. He'd been itchy all day, anxious to see Sarah after their "first date."

God, wasn't he beyond all this high-school crush nonsense? He was a damn grandfather, not some overly hormonal teenager. Apparently not, or why was his stomach juddering as he opened the front door? Why were his knees weak at the sight of her adorable behind stuck in the air as she... What exactly was she doing up there anyway?

"Sarah?" Tony approached the staircase where she was using a putty knife to scrape at something on the newly sanded landing.

She dropped the tool and jerked around with a gasp.

He made it up the steps just in time to catch her as she lost her balance. "I've got you," he said, pivoting her around to face him while she flailed, finally settling her hands on his shoulders.

"You scared the crap out of me." The obvious delight in her eyes curbed the accusatory tone of her voice.

Her hair, pulling out of the knot in the back, fell in curly tendrils around her face. Her flowered blouse was tied under her breasts over a snug yellow tank top that had come untucked from her jeans, revealing an expanse of taut white stomach, and she had a smudge of dirt across one cheek.

Adorable.

Tony's reaction was as instinctive as racing up the stairs to catch her. He bent his head and captured her lips in a kiss.

Sarah slipped one hand up his shoulder to the nape of his neck, where her fingers slid into the hair curling over his collar. She tilted her head and leaned into the kiss. Without breaking contact, he tightened his grip on her hips and tugged her up off the steps to a safer position on the landing.

The kiss, gentle and yet somehow full of passion, lasted for a long moment. When he finally lifted his head, he realized his hold had left her toes dangling above the sanded surface. He eased her back down onto her feet, his hands still firmly on her waist. Letting her hands fall to her sides, she rested her forehead on his chest.

They were both breathing heavily, and suddenly, Tony wasn't at all sure what to do with his own hands. Should he release her? Had he scared her? Maybe not—she was still there. She hadn't bolted. His heart pounded so hard he was surprised her head wasn't bouncing as he waited for her to say or do something.

Finally, she stepped back a few inches, staring up at him with wide eyes, a hint of a smile on her full lips. Was there anything sexier than a woman who'd just been thoroughly kissed? "Well, hullo there, Deputy," she said, her voice soft and breathy.

Relief coursed through him. "Hi." Resisting the urge to go in for another kiss, he reached for her hand instead and laced their fingers together as he led her to the window seat. "You're here late. Where's Chris?"

"Up in the master bath caulking around the tub." When she

didn't pull away after they sat, Tony was thrilled beyond words. "Did you come to lend a hand?"

"Nope. I actually came to see if you wanted to go get a pizza, but I'm happy to help out. What needs doing?" Her hand was so small in his. Hell, *she* was so small. He wanted to tug her onto his lap and hold her. Given the current state of his lap, that would probably be a tactical error. Moving slow was key in this relationship. He knew because for several nights, he'd read into the wee hours about the PTSD suffered by abuse victims.

In particular, he'd Googled information about sexual abuse. Julie hadn't given him any personal details and he hadn't asked. Sarah's inclination to flinch at almost any affectionate touch, his own cop instincts and Paul Prescott's smirking mug shot were what had convinced him she'd probably been terrorized in every possible way by the bastard. One day, she might confide in him, but whether she did or not, he would progress gently no matter how desperately he wanted her.

Right now, victory was sweet as she gazed up at him, her fingers twined with his and a tiny pulse fluttering above her collarbone. "I was trying to scrape grout off the landing." She indicated the putty knife with a brief nod. "I think someone had it on the bottom of their shoe. I've already done four steps and I can see a little more on the lower steps. I guess I should've taped the staircase with paper after we sanded."

"We can do that. I think there's a roll of paper down in the dining room. Unless you think it's too late to bother."

"It is. I need to get this stuff scraped off tonight because the guys are coming tomorrow to start sealing the floors. Chris and I are going to run the shop vacs over all the hardwood in the place and then damp mop everything before we leave." Her voice was calm even though her hand trembled as she curled her fingers in his.

He bent down and dropped a kiss on her tousled hair. "Why

don't I order a pizza and pitch in? Three of us working will get stuff done quicker."

"You don't have to—"

Tony cut short her protest with a quick touch of his lips to hers. "I want to," he said simply as he dropped her hand and pulled his phone out of his pocket.

≈

"God, I'm beat." Chris stuffed a painter's cloth into the huge box by the front door before dropping onto the bottom step, his head sagging against the newly painted wall. "It's after midnight," he said with a glance at his watch.

"Get your filthy head off that wall," Sarah scolded good-naturedly before frowning. "Maybe it was mistake to have the painters in first. Everything looks amazing, but what if the floor guys scuff up the paint?"

"And what if the painters had spattered paint all over the newly poly-ed floors?" Chris sat up straight and grinned. "Look, you had to pick one or the other. Frankly, I'd rather touch up scuffed walls than scrape and sand these floors again."

Sarah chewed her lower lip as she turned a complete circle in the high-ceilinged foyer that gleamed with fresh paint the color of buttermilk. She'd chosen the soft pale color for all the walls in the house and a slightly darker shade called Oats and Honey for the woodwork, which they'd chosen to paint instead of refinish. Julie and Carrie had agreed that washable paint would be easier to maintain, plus the lighter surfaces lent an airy ambiance to the whole house. They weren't trying to register with historic land-marks, so keeping the hardwood floors was true enough to the era of the house. Color would come in with whatever they could find the way of art, rugs, furniture, and accessories.

"Okay, this is the last of them." Tony sauntered in with

another huge box of drop cloths and set it by the front door. "Shop vacs are stowed in the mudroom and Chris here has volunteered to empty the buckets and rinse and wring out the mops and hang them up." He stared pointedly at the young man, who rose with a weary sigh and saluted.

"I'm going, I'm going." Chris headed for the kitchen.

"Make sure the back door is locked and that you get all the dirt out of the laundry tub." Tony called after him.

Sarah's heart swelled at the sight of her deputy, clad in a faded Led Zeppelin T-shirt over slightly baggy jeans and sporting a backward baseball cap over his salt-and-pepper hair. Ordinarily, she'd be the first to tell any male over fifteen to spin the damn cap around right. However, on Tony, the look was all him—natural and easy. Nothing at all like the men she'd known in Georgia, who were always immaculately dressed in designer suits or expensive casual golf or tennis togs.

Wait. *My deputy?* When had she started taking ownership of Tony Reynard in her mind? That was dangerous territory, although watching him fold the flaps on the boxes of drop cloths made her heart speed up at the memory of his warm lips on hers earlier. That kiss was every bit as delicious as she'd fantasized it would be. She wanted more, but the thought of *more* made her stomach clench and an acid taste rise in her throat.

"We should probably take that leftover pizza with us," Tony said, stretching like a big lazy cat when he finished with the boxes. "Once Greg starts the floors, we'll be banned for a few days while they dry. Did they say how long we'd have to stay away?"

Sarah turned away to stop herself from staring at his brawny form. "Why do you wear your hat backward?"

"Huh?"

"Why do you wear your baseball cap backward like a kid?" The question came out snippier than she intended, but she needed to get her mind off his hands and his lips and how much she wanted them on her again. Back in some measure of control, she faced him and said in a gentler tone. "I'm curious."

His brow furrowed. "It's a seeing thing," he said, pulling the hat off and running his fingers through his thick hair before replacing it correctly. "The brim shadows the floors in here and I wanted to make sure I mopped up all the dust. And when I drive the boat, I need to be able to see the water and everything around me."

A frisson of disappointment shot through Sarah as the hat hid Tony's eyes. Without a second thought, she crossed to him and reached up to switch the cap back-to-front again. "Leave it. I like to see your face. It's a nice old face." The last words came out in a whisper.

Tony's smile lit up his toast-brown eyes and he brought one hand up between them slowly, cautiously. "Yours is just fine too," he said, his voice husky as he stroked her cheek with one finger. "Even all covered in sanding dust."

She needed to explain. Before things went too far between them, she had to tell him why they could never... "Tony, I need to tell you—"

"Shh." He touched her lips for a brief second and shook his head. "Not right now."

"But—"

"We're good, okay?" He dropped his hand and pressed his lips to her forehead as Chris called from the dining room.

"Hey, you want me to bring the pizza from the fridge? Greg said we aren't gonna be able to get back in here for at least a week."

Tony stepped back and gave her a grin. "And there's the answer I was seeking." He headed for the dining room. "Yeah, find a grocery sack and let's take anything that might not last for a week."

Sarah stood still for a moment, savoring the memory of Tony's lips warm on her skin. Wishing she could take her imagination beyond kisses without feeling physically ill or unbearably sad or being terrified of where every touch might lead.

Maybe Jules was right. Perhaps she *should* bring the sex thing up with Dr. Benton.

What a hideous thought. Nonetheless, the idea niggled at the back of her mind because, dammit, she wanted Tony. There was no question about that. Yet, every time she thought of making love with him or making a life with him, despair washed over her. Overwhelming sadness made her cringe at his touch.

This morning, she'd had what Julie would call an "ah-ha moment"—one that she needed to face, because if she didn't, she'd never know another moment of happiness. Damn. Damn. *Damn.* Her heart pounded and her mind raced. Okay, this was *not* the time to take that crap out and examine it.

"Hey lady, get in here and tell us what you want from the fridge." Tony's deep voice hailed her from the butler's pantry, rescuing her from her own train of thought.

Shaking her head, she scurried to the kitchen. "Guys, we need to make sure we take the trash bag out, too. Otherwise, it's going to stink to high heaven when we do get back in here."

Tony met her at the door of the pantry with the kitchen trash bag, already tied up and ready to go, clutched in his hand. "Great minds," he said with a grin that set her pulse racing.

You have no idea, my friend. No idea at all, Sarah thought, deciding right then and there what her next session with the therapist would entail.

CHAPTER 17

C hewing her lower lip, Sarah slouched on the sofa in Dr. Benton's office, watching rain drip down the window that overlooked Grand Traverse Bay. The therapist didn't say a word as she sat patiently in the armchair across from the couch, legs crossed and a notebook and pen on her lap. Over the weeks, Sarah had come to genuinely like Dr. Benton with her designer pantsuits and her blonde-going-to-gray hair cut in a cute bob. Today's suit was the color of ripe peaches and she wore it with a breezy peach-and-lime scarf tied in an intricate knot around her neck.

Her quiet smile engendered trust, something that was in short supply for Sarah. That fact alone made borrowing a car from Carrie to drive up here once a week a little bit easier. As they sat in silence, Sarah speculated idly if psychiatrists took a class to learn that inscrutable smile. The therapist at the shelter in Chicago had mastered it as well.

"I'm going to have to buy a car," Sarah said, then frowned, realizing that she was wasting her time today. Cars were not at all what she'd prepared to discuss. She hated unproductive sessions, not only for herself, but for Dr. Benton, too, although the good doctor never seemed to mind when she couldn't open up.

"You haven't done that yet?" Dr. Benton uncrossed her legs and then re-crossed them the other direction.

"No, I haven't really needed one in the village. I have Chris and everything is pretty much within walking distance."

"Chris is the young man hired to be your"—she quirked one brow—"escort? Chauffeur? Bodyguard?"

"All those things."

"And who hired him again? The local deputy?"

Sarah nodded. "Still, I should have my own car. I can't keep borrowing Carrie's or asking Chris to drive me places that aren't related to the shelter. Do you know somewhere to get a good used car?"

"There are several places here in the city. My Prius came from the Toyota dealership on Garfield." Dr. Benton flipped a few pages in the notebook and perused her notes.

"Do you have a separate notebook for every patient?" Toeing off her canvas espadrilles, Sarah tucked her legs up under her on the sofa, and scowled again. *Dammit.* She couldn't seem to get down to business, which surprised her. Normally, she made a point of getting her money's worth out of her visits by coming prepared with an issue she wanted to discuss. Sarah was nothing if not practical, and she'd decided up front that if she was going to pay a shrink, it was going to be for more than a prescription for antidepressants. Besides, from the first visit, she'd been mostly comfortable talking to Dr. Benton. Usually after her sessions, she left the office feeling a little less burdened. But today, the words simply wouldn't come forward.

"Yup, everybody gets a notebook."

"Then what? After the appointments, you transcribe everything to an electronic file?"

Dr. Benton nodded. "That's pretty much it."

"Why don't you use a tape recorder?"

"I used a digital recorder for a while. However, it intimidated some patients. Besides, the notebook and pen give me something to do with my hands." Dr. Benton chuckled.

"Nice for you." Sarah scoffed and stretched her hands out in front of her. "I have to sit here staring at my fingernails and wondering if I'll ever get them clean again."

"I can give you a notebook if you want one," the doctor offered. "Although that might distract you from talking to me, which *is* why you're here."

"What's the most notebooks you've ever filled with one patient?"

Dr. Benton tucked the pen into the black-and-white marbled composition book, closed it, and folded her hands. "We've got a lot of avoidance going on here today. What's up, Sarah?"

Sarah sighed, started to speak, then closed her lips tight. Finally, she said, "Have you ever noticed how one thing in life may seem to be completely separate from something else, then somehow it turns out they're actually connected?" That came out way more convoluted than she intended, but she was fairly certain Dr. Benton would unravel it. Otherwise, why was she here?

"Yes, I have." That therapist smile appeared and Dr. Benton's gray eyes twinkled. "Would you like to expand on that?"

Suddenly, Sarah's heart rose to her throat. She swallowed as tears pricked her eyes. "It's sex," she choked out and heat flushed her cheeks. "Oh, dammit."

"Okay. And what's the other thing?" Dr. Benton asked quietly. "The unrelated thing?"

"I–I'm not sure." Sarah reached for the tissue box on the table beside the sofa as tears rolled down her cheeks. "But I think it might be…Macy."

"Your daughter?"

"Yes." Sarah buried her face in her hands and gave into the tears, weeping and gulping great deep breaths. Her heart ached— literally. Pain sat on her chest like huge stone, and once again as the master of compartmentalization, she wondered whether she might be having a heart attack. Rocking back and forth, she crossed her arms over her breasts as if the gesture might hold the agony at bay. It didn't. She continued to rock and sob while Dr. Benton sat still as a mouse, watching and waiting.

When she could finally breathe again, she met the psychiatrist's concerned gaze. "Jesus. I really am a goner, aren't I?" She swiped at her cheeks with a fresh tissue, tossed it into the wastebasket next to the sofa, and reached for another.

"Oh, I'm fairly sure there's hope for you," Dr. Benton said. "Make the connection for me, Sarah."

"You've probably figured it out."

"Maybe. I need to know that *you* have." Dr. Benton opened her notebook. "*Are* you having sex with someone?"

Sarah barked a short laugh. "Not hardly. Not when I want to puke damn near every time he touches me."

Dr. Benton simply raised one perfectly plucked brow.

"I thought…I truly thought I was ruined by"—she took a deep shuddering breath—"by all the sick, sadistic crap that Paul did to me. When I left Georgia, I couldn't imagine ever wanting any man again. Not ever. I haven't dated in over eight years. Haven't even had the desire."

"So now, you found someone you want to date and possibly have sex with?"

"I think so." Sarah turned the tissue box over in her hands, staring at the design on it. *Huh. Paisley. Why bother to put this much work into packaging something people blew their noses into?*

Focus, you idiot.

She blinked. "I–I mean, I've met this really great guy and he makes me feel, you know…all tingly again. God, I barely recognize that stupid I-want-to-be-in-love feeling. I'm not even sure that's what this is. I dunno. I think I want him, but I freaking flinch almost every time he gets close to me."

"And how does he react?" Dr. Benton asked.

"He's kind and not at all pushy." Heat rose from Sarah's neck to her cheeks and she raked her fingers through her hair, irritated at the tendrils that stuck to her damp face. "He's a smart guy. He knows enough of my history to figure out that intimacy is going to be hard." She moved to the edge of the sofa. "Here's the thing, then I'll shut up and get out of here because I know my time is almost up."

"We can take as much time as you need, Sarah." Dr. Benton sat forward in her chair. "What's the *thing*? Tell me the connection between sex with this new guy and Macy."

A lump rose in Sarah's throat again and she swallowed hard against another storm of tears. The words wouldn't come. If she could only get this out, maybe she could relax with Tony. Look at how much better she was since she started seeing Dr. Benton. Wasn't this just one more issue to take out, examine, and clear away from her messed-up mind? Why couldn't she speak? She lost the battle with the tears and flopped onto the cushion next to her, wailing helplessly into a handful of tissues.

"Sarah, did your ex-husband molest your daughter?" Dr. Benton's firm voice came through the tempest of weeping.

Sarah popped up, trembling with the shock of the question. "No! Jesus!" she cried. "No, no. I-I mean, not that I—" Her breath caught in her throat, and she clamped her lips tight together before continuing slowly. "No, not at all." She shook her head. "No, he never did. She was…she was too happy a child. So open and sweet-natured. And I do believe that as much as he was capable of loving anyone at all, Paul loved Macy. He wouldn't have hurt her like that. *I* was the one he wanted to control." She plucked more tissues from the box. "Besides, he was never alone with her. I made sure of that."

"Then you protected her. You kept her safe."

Tears rolled down Sarah's cheeks as she shook her head. "I didn't. She died." Sarah bent over, her arms wrapped around her aching middle, crying and chanting uncontrollably. "She died. She's dead. My baby's dead. My baby…"

Suddenly, Dr. Benton was beside her on the couch, her strong arm around her. "Tell me what happened that day."

E very muscle in Sarah's body ached as she ended her story in a monotone. "He got the maximum sentence of sixteen years because the prosecutor proved reckless conduct. He was so enraged that day he didn't bother to look behind him. The guy next door was trimming the hedge between us and saw the whole thing." She sighed. "I don't remember any of it. I spent ten days in the hospital before I…I buried her. He wasn't there, thank God. He didn't get bail because, by the grace of God, the judge that arraigned him happened to be the only woman on the bench at the time."

"Did you go to the trial?" Dr. Benton moved back to her chair and resumed her relentless note-taking.

Sarah glanced around at the mess of tissues scattered around her on the floor and on the sofa. "There was no trial. He pleaded guilty, and I didn't press charges for the battery. There was a chance I'd be called as a witness, though. The prosecutor had a subpoena ready."

"Why didn't they call you?"

"Apparently, between the neighbor's testimony and the cops from the scene, they had him. It was quick. There was only the judge. I think Paul knew a jury trial would mean that I would testify and he didn't want that."

"Why didn't you press charges for what he did to you?" Dr.

Benton's fancy pen flew over the page.

"I couldn't handle it. I just wanted to go. I wanted it to be over." Sarah started picking up tissues and tossing them in the wastebasket. "I packed up, drove to Orlando, and got on a plane. Hell, my car may still be in the long-term parking lot there." She laughed grimly.

"I doubt it." Dr. Benton chuckled. "I imagine it was towed long ago and has probably been sold at auction by now."

"Yeah, no doubt." Sarah leaned back and closed her eyes. "I went to Denver first, hooked up with a shelter there, and got my new ID. Did you know that Sarah isn't my real name?"

"No, but I suspected it."

"Susannah." Sarah whispered. "I'm Susannah Elizabeth Boatwright." A pang spasmed through her as she said the name she'd blocked from her memory for the last eight years. "It was my great-great-great grandmother's name. She was a teenager during the Civil War and she worked in the tobacco fields side by side with the slaves who stayed after the Emancipation. She was a Boone, then she married a Boatwright after the war. The Boatwright plantation was destroyed when Sherman marched on Atlanta and they never rebuilt. I was the first girl born in generations and my grandfather insisted I be named for her. God, it's been years since I've thought of that."

"Come back around, Sarah." Dr. Benton stared over the top of her half-glasses and made a circling gesture with her pen.

"If...if I make love with Tony, I'm claiming happiness as a possibility. How do I deserve a happy life when Macy never had a life at all?" Sarah managed the words through clenched teeth.

"You aren't responsible for her death." Dr. Benton's voice was quiet.

"If he hadn't been so angry with me, he wouldn't have stormed out."

"What could you have done to keep him from getting mad?"

Sarah contemplated her answer, debating which answer would be the least painful, although at this point, she was beyond feeling anything at all.

"Sarah?"

"I could've kept my mouth shut that day." Sarah twisted the tissue she clutched. "I was an idiot to bring up anger management therapy." She met Dr. Benton's steady gaze. "I knew how he'd react, but I took the chance and when he turned on me…" Shuddering, she swallowed and rubbed her face.

"So this"—Dr. Benton's face was impossible to read as she indicated Sarah's bedraggled state with a small gesture—"is all about your simple suggestion that he consider therapy? Not saying that one thing would've changed everything, and you and Macy and Paul would've lived happily ever after?"

Sarah glared. She was about three seconds from splintering into a thousand pieces. Her head ached and her heart hurt. Jerking the clip out of her falling-down hair, she pushed up off the sofa and stomped to the window. She stared out at the gloomy sky and then down at the people in the street struggling with umbrellas in the stiff breeze. Rage boiled over and even though she knew it wasn't the psychiatrist she was furious with, she still shouted, "No, godammit!" Her hair flew in all directions, tangling across her wet cheeks when she whirled around. "Do you think I'm an idiot?"

"Of course I don't think that."

Jesus! Did the woman ever use any other tone of voice? She probably spoke in the same controlled way when she was in throes of passion with Mr. Doctor Benton. Sarah bit back the sudden urge to giggle at the mental picture of her staid therapist— perfectly still and calm—in bed under a humping faceless man.

God, she truly was going 'round the bend. It was inevitable. How the hell would she get Carrie's car back to her if Dr. Benton had her taken away in a straightjacket?

Longing to bolt, she turned back to the window, folded her arms across her belly, and laid her forehead against the cool glass. "I should have left," she murmured.

"I'm sorry. I didn't catch that."

Sarah squared her shoulders and padded slowly back to the couch. She shoved a pile of used tissues aside and dropped to the cushions before she met the doctor's warm gaze. "I should have left the very first time he grabbed me. The first time he hit me or at least the first time he...he forced me." She shrugged. "I should have taken Macy and gotten as far away as I could. But I didn't. I stayed."

"Why did you stay?"

Sarah shook her head. "So many reasons. Looking back, none of them were very smart." She smoothed the wrinkled khaki of her shorts. "He was always so sorry. I loved him. So much of the time, he wasn't a monster, and I thought I could see the good in him. I was sure I could help him. Later, long after Mother and Daddy were gone, I didn't know where I'd go. He controlled everything. I guess I was more afraid of what he'd do if I left and he caught me than I was of the bad times."

The list came out so calmly, Sarah honestly wasn't even sure she was the one talking. She snorted a small laugh. "I sound like every other battered woman I've ever heard. I hate this—I hate being a victim. But I'm still afraid. He's out there and he's looking for me."

"You're not a victim anymore, Sarah," Dr. Benton insisted. "You are *not* a victim. You're an independent woman who's been through hell and come out the other side stronger and wiser." She set the notebook aside and leaned forward as if to emphasize her words. "You are no longer a victim." She put both hands on Sarah's knees. "And you, as much as anyone else on this planet, deserve to be happy."

CHAPTER 18

"I've got an idea." Shoving aside the box of clothing she'd been going through, Sarah wiped her brow and surveyed the organized chaos before her. Bags and cartons filled nearly half the space in the center of the huge room above Carrie's garage, while the walls were lined with clear plastic bins.

When they'd put out a call for new and gently used clothes and shoes and household items, the Reillys had offered their garage as a landing zone for donations while renovations were taking place at the shelter. The villagers had responded with their usual generosity, and the Posse had spent the better part of the morning sorting items into the bins that Carrie had labeled according to size and gender.

"Oh my God, look at this!" Julie held up a powder-blue polyester leisure suit jacket and burst out laughing. "I'm pretty sure this can go in the theater bag, don't you agree?" She glanced at Sarah, expectation in her blue eyes. "Sorry, sweets, what's your idea?"

"Let's go shopping for real." Sarah dropped into the folding chair next to her box. "How about we clean up and find a mall?"

"There's Grand Traverse Mall in the city." After Sophie

folded a shirt, she dropped it into the bin marked WOMEN'S SIZE 14. "It's got all the big department stores and tons of other shops."

"I need some new summer clothes and that kind of stuff is bound to be on sale racks by now," Sarah said. "I've only got these shorts and two other pairs and my tops are embarrassing. I want to buy a dress to wear to Libby's fundraiser on Saturday, and I want some sandals to go with it. Plus, I need new underwear and I'm tired of sleeping in just a tank top and yoga shorts. I want some real jammies. Something feminine and pretty. Is there a Victoria's Secret up there?"

Julie looked up from her spot on the floor where she was sorting men's golf shirts. "Victoria's Secret?" Her eyes narrowed. "Sexy lingerie? You're looking for sexy lingerie? You got something you want to share with the group?"

Sarah gave her a brief scowl. "I just told you. I need new clothes."

"Yeah, but *lingerie*? And a dress and stiletto sandals? That all points to one thing." She wagged her finger at Sarah then winked. "Our girl's embracing her feminine side, and I'll bet I know the reason." Her voice rose in a lilt.

"I didn't say a word about stilettos," Sarah denied, struggling to keep from grinning. "Or *sexy* lingerie. I said underwear and pajamas."

"It was implied when you asked for a Victoria's Secret. Underwear and pajamas say Target. However, you specifically asked about VS—that's *lingerie*." Julie waved her away airily. "And I saw you and Tony at the Fishwife night before last, remember? You looked pretty…cozy."

"We were eating dinner, nothing more." Warmth flooded Sarah's cheeks. She'd seen a lot of Tony since her gut-wrenching session with Dr. Benton a few days earlier because they'd both been working with a crew of volunteers to clean up the shelter grounds. Grabbing a bite to eat together after a hard day's raking and digging just seemed natural.

While she'd worked in the gardens around the old place, pulling weeds and transplanting perennials, he'd trimmed the lilac bushes by the carriage house and took his turn on the lawn tractors. She had to confess to sneaking peeks at him one day when he'd removed his shirt under the noon sun, and his nicely furred chest gleamed with exertion. He might be a grandpa, but he still made her heart beat faster in his low-slung jeans, backward baseball cap, and the scruff of a couple days' beard. She'd ended up moving to the front yard to keep from staring and, yes, possibly even drooling.

Thanks to the tireless volunteers like Tony, the shelter property was starting to look quite presentable with all the brush gone, and sporting newly planted gardens and lush green lawns. She was anxious for tomorrow when the men in the village were going to start building the elaborate play-scape swing set that Julie had begged from the wholesale club in Traverse City. Somehow, she'd also conned the store into donating last year's floor sample outdoor furniture for the flagstone patio that some dedicated volunteers had uncovered behind the house.

Sarah was beyond grateful for Julie's unyielding nudging and prodding of local businesses, so she couldn't work up much of a pique over her friend's teasing. And maybe there was more than a germ of truth to Julie's insinuations. Instead she simply offered her an eye roll and a middle finger. "Let's bag this chore and hit the mall, okay?"

"Sure." Julie winked. "We'd love to help you pick out something lacy and enticing."

"Jules, leave the poor woman alone." Carrie blew a sigh into her bangs, fell back onto a pile of jeans—girls' sizes six through ten—and closed her eyes. "I, for one, would love an afternoon out after sorting these clothes for three days." She stretched, twisting her back one way and then the other before she sat up. "Shopping for Sarah will be much more fun."

"I'm in," added Sophie, laying a stack of carefully folded T-shirts into the WOMEN'S SIZE M bin. "Let's go get cleaned up and meet at Sarah's in an hour. I'll drive."

"Wow." Tony blinked when Sarah greeted him at the door on Saturday night. "Just...wow."

"Thank you, kind sir." She looked amazing in a soft-green print sundress, strappy sandals that added at least three inches to her height, and her hair pulled up in a messy-chic bun. The skirt belled as she twirled around for him to get the full effect, and did he ever get it. The crisscross straps revealed more of her lovely freckled back than they covered and clearly, she was braless... unless the dress had one of those built-in things. Her hair was pulled up, but auburn tendrils framed her face. She was wearing makeup that brought out those blue eyes and made her luscious lips even more delectable.

"You went shopping." He let the screen door close behind him. "You're going to be the belle of the ball tonight."

"Well, the fundraiser isn't exactly a ball, although Libby said there would be dancing. She hired an oldies cover band for tonight, which thrills me no end. The music is a little before my time, but I remember my mom's records from the sixties."

"Yeah, *that* was music—the Stones, the Beatles, the Who, and anything at all from Motown," Tony added.

"Oh, I love the Drifters!" Sarah cruised the apartment shutting windows while Tony stood by the door. Biting her lower lip, she paused at the thermostat. "I've never used the AC before, but the temperature isn't supposed to go below seventy-five tonight, so maybe I'll turn it on now. Then the place'll be cool when we get back." She adjusted the temperature, switched on a couple of lamps, and grabbed a filmy shawl that matched her dress and a small bag that Tony noted was too tiny to hold the damn Ruger.

Thank God.

"You've *never* used the air conditioner?" He held his hand out to help her on with the shawl, but she shook her head.

"I think I'll carry it for now, thanks." She led the way and then turned to secure both locks and drop her keys into her bag. "And, no, I don't use the AC. It makes too much noise."

"You should tell Noah—" He closed his lips on the words when she gave him a sideways glance and realization blossomed. Of course, the unit was fine, but she wouldn't be able to hear over the sound of the fan blowing cool air. Another safety precaution that hadn't occurred to him. He'd figure them all out eventually. For tonight, he simply nodded and followed her down the steps.

The lot at Nolan Farms Winery was packed and cars were already parked along the road to the lighthouse. Tony found a spot closer to the lighthouse than the winery, and he caught the look of skepticism on Sarah's face when he opened the door of his truck to help her out. Her shoes weren't made for walking any distance.

After a deep breath, she squared her shoulders, obviously prepared to go for it, so he kept his concern to himself. She stumbled once or twice along the gravel road before he touched her shoulder. "Oh man, those shoes aren't going to make this jaunt, are they? I can drive you up to the winery or"—he offered what he hoped was a guileless smile—"I can carry you."

Her eyes widened, but just as he prepared to swing her up into his arms, a golf cart slid noiselessly to a stop beside them. A grinning Will Brody was behind the wheel.

"Um, Julie sent me to fetch you." He glanced from Tony to Sarah and back again before the grin shifted to a smirk. "I can always say I couldn't find you," he offered, clearly holding back laughter.

Tony dropped his arms and rolled his eyes. "Nice timing, dude."

Sarah's cheeks reddened as she gave Tony a pointed glance before slipping around him and into the front seat of the cart next to Will. "No, this is great. Thanks, Will."

Tony narrowed his eyes at his friend and hopped onto the back of the cart, wrapping one hand around the post behind Sarah's head as they spun gravel on the turnaround and zipped back toward the party.

No matter. There would be plenty of time to hold her in his arms when they danced.

As if she'd read his mind, Sarah chuckled. "If the poor guy carried me all the way to the winery, he wouldn't be fit to dance later."

"Sarah!" Libby squealed as they climbed the steps to the crowded deck at the front of the winery. "You look amazing. Love your dress." She pulled Sarah into a hug, before turning to Tony. "And check you out, Deputy Tony. You clean up nice."

The winery was hopping—all three decks surrounding the barn were filled with people enjoying Libby's delicious wines and food. Sarah caught the tantalizing scent of pepperoni pizza as a breeze ruffled the tendrils of hair on her neck. "Libby, you've done an incredible job. Look at this crowd!"

"Our daughter, Tess, did the promo." Libby gazed out over the lawn below where tables were set up under a giant white canopy. "She hit the campgrounds and resorts with flyers, so a lot of these folks are tourists just looking for a good time, but most of the locals are here too." Libby fairly bubbled with excitement. "Come on in and get a glass of wine and then head downstairs for pizza or a cheese and fruit plate. The band's going to start pretty soon.

Eli and Daniel and Henry built us a dance floor off the patio. Except for weddings, this is my first dancing event."

"Eli?" Sarah glanced at Tony over her shoulder as he herded her into the winery.

"Libby's son—he runs the Christmas tree part of the farm with Daniel, his dad."

"Ah, okay. I knew she had a son. I didn't remember his name."

The winery was packed. Familiar faces greeted her from every corner with nods and smiles and hellos. Overwhelmed, she halted her steps so suddenly that Tony bumped into her. "My God, the whole town's here." She tossed a general wave to Bertie from the yarn shop, Mel from the bookstore, Gary, the pharmacist at the corner drugstore, and Noah and Margie Dixon. Even Perry from the Daily Grind offered a salute and a grin from the corner where he sat downing pizza with a very attractive brunette. "Is that Perry's wife?"

"Yup. That's Carla." Tony set a hand on her shoulder and guided her through the clutch of people at the tasting bar.

A lump rose in her throat. These lovely, lovely people. Damn near every villager had shown up to show their support for the shelter.

"You okay?" He peered down into her eyes, concern etching his face.

She swallowed hard. "I–I'm stunned at this turnout."

"This town loves an event. And a good cause even more." He led her down the steps at the back of the cavernous barn and out to a booth on the patio where he bought a chilled bottle of Libby's Riesling and two huge slices of pizza while Sarah hovered nearby.

"Sarah!" A familiar voice called from an umbrella-covered table near the dance floor. Julie waved furiously. Sitting with her were Henry, Carrie, and Liam.

Tony tilted his chin in their direction, handed Sarah the wine and the glasses, and followed her as she threaded her way through the crowd. Her stomach tightened as a hint of familiar cologne wafted by and she cast her eyes around, searching, watching for... something out of place. Someone who didn't belong. But it was nothing—just someone wearing Paul's cologne. The clench of fear was habit. One she would probably carry with her forever. It had kept her safe for eight long years until it didn't and she ran to this place, hoping for a reprieve. Shaking her head, she thrust those grim thoughts aside and smiled at the group seated at the table. "Where's Sophie?"

"We sent her for brownies and another bottle of zin." Henry rose and pulled out a chair next to Carrie for Sarah. "A seat of honor for the lovely Sarah." He unfolded another lawn chair and squeezed it in beside Sarah. "And here you go, Tony."

"I don't know wine all that well," Sarah confessed as Tony set her pizza and an empty glass in front of her. "What does zin taste like?"

"Zinfandel is a rich dry red," Liam explained. "Great with chocolate, which is why we sent Soph for brownies. What've you got there, Deputy?" He took the frosty bottle from Tony and read the label. "Great choice, but don't pour any of that yet." He grabbed a near-empty bottle from the center of the table. "Try this first." He poured a taste of deep ruby wine in both empty glasses while Tony settled into his chair.

Will sauntered up carrying a stack of paper-plated pizza. "Hope you guys are still hungry. They brought out the margherita pizzas and that's Jules's favorite." He set one plate in front of Julie and the others in the center of the table. "Here you go, babe."

"My hero." Fluttering her lashes, Julie fake-swooned as Will scooched his chair in next to hers.

"This is delicious!" Sarah exclaimed, holding up her glass.

The zin was rich and full-bodied and she was sure it would go great with the pepperoni pizza sitting before her.

The band, which covered mostly songs from the sixties, opened with a rollicking version of "Good Vibrations," and then rolled right into "Under the Boardwalk." The music took her back to her childhood and rainy Saturdays in her parents' basement, listening to her mom's records and dancing with her friends. As the group chattered and noshed, chowing down on pizza and brownies, she relaxed, basking in the camaraderie of good friends, good music, and good wine.

The band geared down to "Hungry Eyes"—one of her favorites. Lounging, she bumped Tony's warm arm, resting on the back of her chair. A shiver raised goose bumps on her neck when he leaned down to whisper, "Dance?"

CHAPTER 19

"Will you stop looking at me like that?" Tony's dimples showed as he put the truck in Park and switched off the ignition.

Chuckling, Sarah gave him wide innocent eyes. "Like what?" Releasing her seatbelt, she waited as he sauntered around the front of the vehicle to open her door. Her heart stuttered at the sight of his brawny frame silhouetted against the parking lot's sodium-vapor lights. Dear Lord, how was she ever going to resist the urge to throw herself at him? The ache low in her belly only increased when he grinned at her as he held open her door.

"Like a zoologist who's just caught sight of a weird and obscure species of mammal," he said, handing her out of the high seat and twining their fingers together as they headed for the docks.

She snickered. "I think I have."

He glanced at her over the top of his glasses. "The elusive dancing bear?"

"My God, Tony! You never said a word!" Releasing his hand, she leaned down to yank off her stiletto sandals while he supported her elbow. Her feet were done—she couldn't take another step in the unfamiliar shoes. They might be sexy, but they definitely weren't made for comfort—or hours of dancing. "You were amazing out there! I had to fight every other woman present just for a chance to dance with my own date."

He shrugged as he led her up the steps to her apartment. "You never asked if I could dance. You just assumed that because I'm not some lithe ballet-dancer type that I didn't have any moves." He held out his hand. "Keys?"

"Unquestionably, you have got moves, my friend." Still shaking her head, Sarah handed him her keys, then stepped inside, fully expecting Tony to follow. When he didn't, she turned to gaze at him. "Are you coming in?"

"Am I?" His amber eyes widened slightly, his expression eager, but not insistent. "It's late."

"Please." She nodded, tossing her shawl, clutch, and shoes on the chair by the door. When he hesitated, she gave him her best inviting smile. "I want you to."

"Lock up?" he asked as he pulled the door shut behind him, his hand hovering over the deadbolt.

"Well, I do have a cop here with me, but, yeah, go ahead." She switched on the pendant lights above the tall counter. "Coffee?"

"No, I'm good, thanks." He paced between the living room and the kitchen, jingling his own keys in the pocket of his khaki pants. Somehow the fact that he was clearly nervous made her feel a little less so. "When will Tessa have a final tally on what we made for the shelter tonight?"

"Probably Monday, but if the crowd's any indication, I think we did great." Sarah fidgeted with her necklace, suddenly shy.

Inviting him in was purely a reaction to desire. She wanted this—wanted him. She'd even prepared for it, but what if she couldn't go through with it? She hadn't had sex, real loving sex, since her honeymoon. After Macy was born, Paul had turned intimacy into an evil, terrifying power game that she lost every time. Even though she was certain that Tony would be loving and kind and gentle, the knot in her stomach got tighter.

Tony removed his glasses, tucking them into his shirt pocket as he perused the CDs some previous tenant had left in the bookcase under the stairs. He held up one that she didn't recognize. "Do you know her? Skyler Hiatt?"

Sarah shook her head.

"She's a local torch singer. Incredible voice. She sometimes performs at the hotel lounge in Traverse City where Carrie plays piano." After pushing a few buttons on the dated receiver and CD player that Noah had on top of the bookcase, he popped the CD in. "This one's a few years old, but she sings standards, so it doesn't matter."

Her heart sped up as Skyler's rich contralto filled the high-ceilinged space—"The Nearness of You"—an old Ella Fitzgerald song she recognized from her mother's record collection.

When Tony toed off his shoes and quirked one brow in question, a shiver quivered through her. "I'm pretty sure I owe you at least a couple of dances after you kept getting cut in on all night." He held out his hand, one finger crooked in a come-hither gesture that was impossible to resist.

She didn't even try.

He walked toward her, big and sexy and smiling. She met him halfway, slipping into his arms and resting her head on his shoulder. They danced, his hand warm on her back, raising goose bumps where the crisscrossed straps left her skin bare. As he guided her to the gentle rhythm of the music, his breath stirred the hair over her ear. When he sang softly, tremors of delicious sensation zipped right to her core.

Longing trumped fear as Tony's fingers traced her spine and then slid lower—below the small of her back to tug her closer. The dance became merely swaying when he released her left hand

and nudged it up to his shoulder. When his lips found that ultra-sensitive spot behind her ear, Sarah turned her head, yearning for more, seeking his mouth with hers.

For the first time in too many years, she wanted heat and desire and most especially *this* man's hands on her. The kiss that had started with a gentle touch of lips turned hungry as she met his tongue with her own, and they gave up all pretense of dancing. Sarah surged her body to his, coming up on her toes to deepen their kiss. When his erection pressed against her belly, for one fleeting moment, she clutched, and her heart rose to her throat. She almost pushed him away.

No! This was Tony—kind, gentle Tony—and, dear God, how she wanted him.

Shoving aside the fear, she pushed into his hands as they curved around her behind. His lips moved to her throat, dropping little nibbling kisses from her chin to her ear. His fingers gripped her, urgent and tender all at the same time. She licked his neck before reaching for the buttons on his shirt, kissing each patch of newly exposed skin as she released them.

His chest was warm, lightly furred, and inviting as she slid her hands over his tanned torso. He leaned back to grant her access and when his rock-hard shaft pressed into her, that twinge of anxiety slithered through her mind. Once again, she forced it away. Resting her head on his chest, she breathed in the scents of woodsy soap and male musk and desire.

Tony bent his head to hers. "Sarah?" he whispered, and she detected wine and chocolate on his breath.

For one inane moment her mind compartmentalized, and she thought of how much the sense of smell played into making love —his body, his breath, hers. Did the touches of the clean scent she'd dabbed behind her ears and on her throat still linger?

Focus! This isn't Paul. You don't have to go someplace else. Stay right here—in this moment.

He lifted her chin, gently insistent that she look at him. Desire glowed deep brown and amber in his eyes. "I want you," he said, his voice husky with need. "I want you so bad I ache, but... I don't know how to... tell me what to..." His teeth caught his lower lip and he tipped his head back. He sighed. "I can't *take* you. Sarah."

God, how she loved this man.

I love this man.

Suddenly, it was easy and so clear. All the fear and doubt dissolved into desire. She kissed down the column of his neck. "Then let me take *you*," she murmured without even a second's hesitation.

Tony nearly stopped breathing when Sarah stepped away and headed for the stairs. His breath did stop when she turned on the first step, offering her hand and a smile that suggested more than any words could ever express.

Following her up the stairs, he halted at the open French doors that separated the bedroom from the loft, watching as she slipped the straps of her dress down over her shoulders, baring her beautiful back. The dress bunched at her waist and his groin tightened.

Should he go to her? Take her in his arms? Shrug out of his clothes? Fifty-two years old, and yet he was as shy and terrified as a teenager in his parents' basement on prom night.

Dear God, don't let me screw this up.

When she glanced over her shoulder at him, the moon shining through the skylight above the bed gave her skin an ethereal glow. A slight hitch of her chin brought him to her side, and she swiveled, placing her arms around his chest, under his open shirt. He slid his hands over her back as she tugged the shirt off his shoulders and kissed his chest.

Her tongue touched his nipple, sending sparks of heat surging throughout his whole body. He brought one hand around to cup her breast, the slight weight of it filling his palm. She shivered when he brushed the hardening tip with his thumb. Sliding her fingers in his hair, she astounded him when she leaned back and tugged his head down.

He bent down and took her nipple between his lips, then lowered himself to his knees before her as she increased the pressure on the back of his head. Caressing her breasts, he suckled first one tightened bud and then other, hot hunger rising in him when she moaned. He longed to touch her everywhere, kiss every secret place, and worship her with his body. "Sarah," he whispered against the heated skin of her belly. "You're so beautiful... so incredibly beautiful."

He kissed and nibbled his way down to where the dress had dropped to her hips. He touched his tongue to her navel, amazed at the softness of her skin. She quivered as he moved his mouth lower, shoving the dress fabric with his chin.

"Tony." His name—spoken so softly he wasn't sure she'd actually said anything until she raked her fingers through his hair. When he lifted his head, she was gazing down at him, her expression so full of emotion that, at first, he wasn't sure of what he saw there. Then she chuckled, a gorgeous delighted laugh that brought him to his feet to sweep her into his arms and fall sideways onto the bed with her.

"What?" he asked belatedly between long lingering kisses.

"What?" She slipped her hands into the tight space between them and worked at the buckle of his belt.

"You said *Tony*." He touched his lips to her nose and then each cheek and then rested his forehead against hers, looking into her blue eyes.

"I did?" A dreamy smile lit her face. "I don't know. I think I just wanted to say your name out loud. Tony..." She kissed him and her brow furrowed slightly as she struggled with his belt.

"Would you like some help down there?" His own hand was busy pushing the dress over her delectable behind. Truth was it was probably better for him to remove his own clothes. At this point, he was so aroused, he'd probably lose it at the first touch of her hand.

"What kind of belt is this anyway?" She scooched back to frown at the recalcitrant buckle. "It's like a freaking chastity belt."

Tony couldn't stand her fingers brushing his erection another second. "How about we both just strip down?" He sat up, bringing her with him and pulling her to her feet. "Unless you want me to teach you how to open this thing. It *is* weird." His voice trembled and he grimaced, certain he'd broken the mood with the offer to show her how the damn buckle worked.

God, what an idiot.

But Sarah only grinned and slowly slithered the dress down her body revealing the sexiest pair of lacy light-green hip-hugging underpants Tony had ever seen. "Your turn, Deputy."

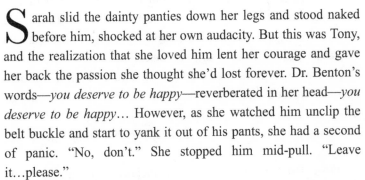

Sarah slid the dainty panties down her legs and stood naked before him, shocked at her own audacity. But this was Tony, and the realization that she loved him lent her courage and gave her back the passion she thought she'd lost forever. Dr. Benton's words—*you deserve to be happy*—reverberated in her head—*you deserve to be happy...* However, as she watched him unclip the belt buckle and start to yank it out of his pants, she had a second of panic. "No, don't." She stopped him mid-pull. "Leave it...please."

Bewildered, he simply stared at her for a moment, before his face fell and he closed his eyes in horror. "Oh, Jesus, Sarah. I'm so sor—"

She put one hand to his lips. "Let me." Stepping closer, she brushed her nipples against his chest, savoring the ticklish touch of the dusting of hair there. He had the perfect amount of chest hair, just enough to be sexy. Following the line of fur to his khakis, she opened the button and zipper and shoved his pants down.

He stepped out of them, taking his socks along and kicking everything aside. "I didn't think. I'm sorry," he whispered as he wrapped his arms around her. "Please forgive me." He was shaking when she slid her arms around his neck and pressed as close to him as she could. The erection that had been so evident earlier had softened slightly.

"It's okay." Sarah kissed his throat, then strung nibbling kisses upward to his ear. "I'm okay," she breathed. "Just love me." Pulling back slightly, she gazed into his eyes, love for his tender heart welling up inside her. Hooking her fingers in the waistband of his knit boxers, she tugged them down, capturing him in her fingers, stroking and caressing him. "Let me love you."

Her words were like gasoline on a bonfire. Tony stepped out the boxers, scooped her up, and landed on the bed with her, covering her face, her neck, her collarbone with kisses. He stroked his big hands down her body, sending pinwheels and flames though her veins with every touch.

Reaching for him, she couldn't help smiling at how fast he'd become aroused again and she caressed him to the point he groaned aloud.

"Sarah, you're driving me insane," he murmured against her breast.

"I'm glad," she said, skating her fingers over his thighs before grasping him again and tugging him gently closer to her.

He pushed up on one elbow, clearly uncertain if he should

swing his body over hers. A look of dismay came over his face and he dropped back on the bed. "I'm not prepared for this. I don't have any protection," he said on a frustrated breath.

She quirked one brow and gave him as sexy a smile as she could muster. "I do." Sitting up, she reached over him and yanked open the drawer in the bedside table. Now he was going to know she'd planned this, but at this point, she was beyond caring. All she wanted was Tony, big and hard inside her, a thought that surprised her as much as her behavior tonight was probably surprising him.

"Oh, really?" Grinning, he accepted the strip of condoms, tearing one off and tossing the rest back in the drawer. "How do you happen to have these so handy? Please don't tell me they're left over from a previous tenant."

"I bought them myself," she replied saucily, taking the packet from his fingers, tearing it open, and rolling the condom over his rock-hard erection. "Stop asking questions, Deputy. I need you. Now, please."

"Oh, God." His breath hitched when her fingers slid the condom down. He gasped when she kissed across his chest and then swung one leg over his thighs. His eyes widened when she leaned over to brush her breast on his chest, delighting in how his nipples tightened into little pebbles at the touch of hers. Slipping his hands under her, he grasped her hips. "Sarah, Sarah. What you do to me..."

She ran her fingers through his hair and pressed her lips to his, showing him with her tongue what she wanted. In one swift move, he rolled them both over, and with a single gentle push, he was inside her. She opened her eyes to meet his smoldering gaze, so full of passion, and her heart nearly burst. Tightening her muscles around him, she basked in the long-forgotten pleasure of being filled to overflowing with love.

He slid his hand between them, touching between her legs as

he moved slowly within her, triggering a tsunami of sensations—intoxicating heat, hunger, electricity, joy, and then...*ahhh*...white-hot mindless rapture.

Gasping for breath, she lifted her hips to meet Tony's thrusts as another tremor shook her body. She clutched his shoulders and his mouth was on hers, kissing her frantically. Slipping one hand behind her thigh, he raised her hips and drove deeper, faster.

"My love," he whispered as his body shuddered, and they came together in a shattering climax.

CHAPTER 20

The second time they made love was slower—long moments of touching and discovering ways to pleasure one another. Afterward, Sarah was starving, so she threw Tony's shirt over her flushed, naked body and headed downstairs to find a snack. Tony pulled on his boxers and followed her to open the bottle of zinfandel he'd bought at the winery.

"Thank you," Sarah whispered as they sat on the rumpled bed with crackers, cheese, strawberries, and chocolate on a tray between them.

"For what?" Tony dipped a strawberry in the dish of warmed chocolate and popped it in his mouth.

"For this. For"—she ducked her head, suddenly shy—"being patient. For showing me how…how good things can be. I dunno. For being okay with eating crackers in bed." Closing her eyes, she blew a breath into her bangs, certain he'd expect her to explain the cracker comment, but he didn't.

Instead, he took a sip of wine, then leaned over and kissed her forehead. "First of all, this is your bed, not mine. But if you want to crunch up this package of saltines, scatter it across the sheets, and roll in it together, baby, that's what we'll do."

Relief washed over her at the touch of his lips. God, how she loved him. And dear Lord, how delicious his touch had been—the feel of him against her skin. She glanced down at her thighs, reddened from the rasp of the stubble on his cheeks above the perfectly trimmed beard. She'd forgotten that sex could be making love. For so long, it had been terror and pain and ritual humiliation. She dropped her head back, shuddering at the memory.

"Hey?" Tony ran one finger down her throat to the V of his shirt where it buttoned over her breasts. "Wherever you just went, come back."

"Sorry." Shaking her head, Sarah met his eyes for a moment before hiding behind her wine glass.

"No." He set the tray aside and scooted closer to her. "Don't apologize." His hands on her thighs were warm and firm. "Talk to me. I mean, if you want to. I'm here. I'll always listen. Only don't go away, okay?"

"I'm here." Sarah cupped his cheek with her free hand. "Why do you think I'm not here?"

"Sometimes you get a look—a sad, sort of closed-up expression—that tells me you're back in the"—he gazed at the framed photos on the wall above her head—"blackness. I know it happens and may always happen now and again, but let me help you stay in the light." His white teeth gleamed in the low lights of the bedside lamps as he bit his lower lip, clearly weighing his words. "I know I can't fix your past with this." Pointing to his crotch, he gave her a rueful smile, then set one hand over his heart. "But I hope I can with *this*."

Sarah's breath caught in her throat. "Oh, Tony, I—"

He put his fingers to her lips. "No, you don't have to respond. I'm not asking you for anything at all. I just want you to know I'm in." He replaced his fingers with his lips—a gentle lingering kiss that turned Sarah's insides to mush.

"You make me very happy, Deputy," she said when he pulled away. Although she was longing to, she couldn't say the words that were simmering in her heart.

I love you.

It was too soon. Although she was healing, she was still too broken, and Paul was still out there, searching for her. Until she was completely free from him and from the past, she couldn't drag Tony into her mess of a life. But this—what they had right now, right here—was so good. Setting her glass on the bedside table, she reached down between his legs to caress him through his boxers. "And for the record, you did some damned impressive fixing here tonight."

He gave her a long look and a smile that told a much more serious story than his next words. "It's what I'm famous for, baby." Swinging his legs over the side of the bed, he replaced his own wine on the night table and shoved the tray to the far side of the wide bed. Like a snake shedding its skin, he slithered out of the boxers as he stood up and turned to face her with a lascivious grin. Striking a pose like a male model, he stood by the bed suggestively rotating his hips.

She rolled her eyes. "I know. Your prowess was the talk of the winery tonight. " Her fingers skated over his belly and moved down from there. Amazed at her own daring, she tugged gently, bringing him toward her. A shiver raced through her.

God, he's delicious. And naked. We're naked.

How did we get this comfortable? How did I?

Tony sucked in his breath, caught her fingers in his, and plopped back down on the bed. "We are still talking about dancing, right?" He slipped his arm around her, drawing her against his warm body. "I mean, everybody in town knows I'm a wicked combination of Fred Astaire, John Travolta, and Ryan Gosling on the dance floor. How'd you miss that memo?"

"Somehow that never came up over coffee at the Grind. I

certainly saw it tonight, though." Sarah snuggled once more against his heat, unable to keep her hands or eyes off him. "And exactly what other hidden talents do you have?"

"Several others actually." He pressed her onto her back, leaning over her, his too-long salt-and-pepper hair falling into his eyes. "How about a demonstration?"

"Okay," Sarah agreed, the hot desire in his eyes sending a surge of heat right to her center. "Show me."

Planting tiny nibbling kisses on her neck and face, he reached for the buttons of his shirt, slipping them open with a speed that amazed her. "What do you think they are?" he whispered, licking her ear and biting the lobe gently. "What do you want me to do?" He cupped one breast, stroking the hardened nipple with his thumb. "Talk to me, Sarah. Tell me how to love you."

"Oh, God." She moaned when he ran his fingers across her ribcage, tickling her softly, then following the same path with his lips. She smoothed her hands across his broad back, moving downward to his hips before sliding one around to grasp his hardening erection.

Swiftly he sat back on his heels, capturing her fingers before she reached her goal. "Nope," he said with a wicked grin. "This is about you. *Your* pleasure." He released her hand. His eyes pinned her to the bed as he dipped his finger in the chocolate on the tray next to them. Bringing it to his mouth, he sucked the sweet liquid off slowly, sensuously. "Stop me if something isn't okay." He eyed her, clearly watching for some kind of signal.

Spellbound, she nodded, watching as he took another fingerful of warm chocolate. With one hand, he pushed the shirt apart and painted the chocolate between her breasts and over her stomach, following her flat belly to the thatch of hair at the juncture of her thighs.

She lay perfectly still, hands clenched at her sides as he leaned down and leisurely, erotically lapped at the chocolate with warm swipes of his tongue.

"Tony…" His name came out on a groan.

He slid his hands up over her breasts, squeezing the flesh, rolling her taut nipples between his finger and thumb. Delicious sensation after sensation swept over her. His hands sent tremors through her. Then he moved down between her legs. Gripping the quilt, she closed her eyes.

"Do you know how hungry you make me?" he murmured, his breath hot on her belly. "Do you have any idea?" Dipping his finger into the chocolate once again, he painted another line down the soft skin of her inner thigh. "Is this okay?"

"Yes," she moaned as he kissed and licked the sauce away. "Yes!"

"And this?" He ran his chocolate-coated fingertip down her heated center, following it with his tongue. Grasping her hand, he brought it down to his mouth and pressed a kiss into her palm. "Sarah, look at me."

She lifted her head to gaze into his smoldering eyes. Electricity sizzled between them.

"Tell me what pleases you," he whispered.

She thrust her hands into his hair, guiding him back to her body. "You, always you." Her voice came out husky with need. "*You* please me."

The sound of the shower woke her, and Sarah rolled over to blink at the clock. Seven thirty. It was morning. She'd slept for a solid six hours without waking once. A miracle! She never went to sleep after Paul was done with her. Pain and fear kept her wide-eyed, terrified that he'd roll over and brutalize her again.

But this time she'd drifted off in Tony's arms, sated and safe, and now he was in her shower.

She stretched luxuriously, feeling sore in muscles she never even knew existed. A good kind of sore.

What a night!

The wine bottle and tray still sat on the bedside table, the chocolate hardened now and pulling away from the side of the dish.

Oh God, the chocolate.

Heat rose in her cheeks just thinking about what he'd done with that sweet treat. Maybe it time for a little reciprocation. She hesitated, biting her lip. Could she do this? Just go with her desires? Sitting up, she tossed back the covers and climbed out of bed. Sure she could.

Grabbing his shirt from the floor where it had landed, she plucked a condom from the bedside drawer, and tiptoed into the bathroom.

Tony stood under the shower, water pouring over his head, his lanky frame shadowed by the glass door.

After dropping the shirt in the sink, she opened the door and slipped in behind him. Sliding her arms around his waist, she pressed her lips to his broad back and felt rather than saw his smile.

"Good morning, Deputy." She hoped she had the right touch of sultry in her voice. Tensing under the warm spray, he started to turn around, but she kept her place behind him, holding him still. "I didn't get a chance to show you any of my secret talents last night."

"*Your* secret talents?" He reached back to touch her hips. "I'm intrigued."

She swiveled away from him as best she could in the cramped space. "Care for a demonstration?" Smoothing her hands down his belly, she let her finger follow the arrow of hair that grew there. He shook with laughter, even though he didn't make a sound as her hands moved lower.

"I am longing for you to"—he gasped as she found her goal —"show me your hidden talents." As she took the weight of him in her hands, his voice roughened. "Already I can see that you're quite adept."

"Are you sure you're not too tired after last night?" she asked, rubbing her breasts against his dripping back.

"I'm not too tired," he replied in strangled voice. He reached behind him again, but she grabbed his hands and brought them back around, and down. Then farther down. She placed his fingers on his burgeoning erection. Resting his head against the shower wall, he gazed down at their hands on him.

"Adept?" Sarah whispered, pressing her lips to his shoulder, licking the water droplets. "I could be even more adept if you show me how. What pleasures *you*? What's your fantasy?"

He took her hand, wrapped her fingers around him, and moved them for her, stroking, slowly. Up and down. "You, my love. Only you."

His hip muscles tightened. His breath came faster as she caressed him. Desire flamed low in her core as her sensitive nipples nudged his back. Touching him like this was beyond erotic. She experimented. More pressure. A little less. Then more again as the water poured over them. Her own arousal grew to an almost unbearable level as she used her hands to pleasure him. She'd never known she could become so stimulated simply touching a man this way.

"Sarah, I'm...losin' it...here," Tony growled. He caught her fingers in his. Turning around, his eyes widened when she handed him the condom that she put on the shelf behind her. In seconds, he was sheathed and he pulled her up on her toes. Knees bent, he cupped her bottom and lifted her to thrust into her heated core.

She was more than ready for him. Wrapping her legs around his waist and her arms around his neck, she held on for dear life.

Driving her back against the shower wall, he took her, his tongue emulating the thrusting of his hips as they moved together hungrily. Their coupling was hot and swift and wordless. When it was done, they leaned against one another, panting under the now-lukewarm shower.

Enfolding her in his arms, he held her next to his wet skin, his lips on her forehead. As he stroked her hair, she raised her face to him, to the spray. He claimed her mouth with a sweet gentleness that countered the unrestrained ferocity of their lovemaking.

"How did we ever accomplish that remarkable bit of gymnastics?" Sarah's voice was full of wonder when he lifted his head.

"Lust!" Tony replied. "Lust and adrenaline! Plus it helps that you're little and I'm big." He tugged her back for another kiss.

"No doubt," she agreed. Pivoting in his arms, she let the water hit her back as she reached behind him for shampoo. With more kisses and touches, they finished showering.

"What's on your agenda today?" he asked as they dried off.

"It's Sunday, so nothing's happening at the shelter. I thought maybe I'd go over and check on the floors." She tucked a towel tighter around her damp body.

Naked, Tony borrowed her comb, running it through his damp hair as he stood behind her at the vanity mirror. He put his arms around her and pulled her back against him. "I'm starving. What are we making for breakfast?" His lips touched the back of her neck.

She shivered as she met his eyes in the mirror. "I like how you said *we.*"

"We're in this together, baby." Releasing her, he headed toward the bedroom. "I'll be right back. I'm gonna run down to the boat and change. I've got some clothes in my cabin." He pulled his khakis over his naked, glorious behind and tossed on his shirt, leaving it open. Gathering up his socks and boxers, he peered around the bathroom door. "Okay if I take your keys so I can lock up behind me?"

Nodding assent, Sarah wanted him all over again, not only because he was delectable in his unbuttoned shirt and bare feet, but also because he acknowledged that he needed to lock up, even though he was only going a few hundred yards away.

She dried her hair and dressed slowly, still feeling his hands and mouth on her, causing the now-familiar tingling between her legs.

Lord, I'm insatiable. How long can this last?

Reality had to set in eventually. A chill developed in the pit of her stomach when she thought about Paul showing up in Willow Bay, which he was bound to do. No way would he give up his search. Inevitably, someone in Chicago would give him some seemingly insignificant piece of information and he'd be hot on her trail. The internet made disappearing damn near impossible. She didn't have a doubt he'd track her down, and she didn't have a clue what she would do when he did. Her stomach tightened at the thought as she heard Tony's step on the deck.

Stop it, she told herself. *Just enjoy the moment.*

CHAPTER 21

"Why are we meeting at the shelter instead of at town hall?" Sarah grumbled, scurrying to keep up with Julie, whose long legs carried her along Waterfront Street much faster than Sarah's shorter ones.

They were on the way to the weekly meeting of the shelter's board of directors; however, they were *walking* this evening. Ever since they'd consumed two entire plates of brownies, untold slices of pizza, and several bottles of wine at Libby's fundraiser a couple of weeks ago, Julie had gotten a bee up her butt about all of them needing more exercise. Little did she know, Sarah was getting plenty of exercise—in her bed, in Tony's bed, in his cabin on the *Allegro*. Dear God, even in the cab of his pickup one late night in the shelter parking lot. Hot and heavy sex with Tony burned calories by the hundreds.

"Because I found an awesome dining room table that seats like sixteen and I want you to see it." Julie's words nearly got carried off on the breeze from the harbor.

"I was there this morning. I didn't see any table." Picking up speed, Sarah caught up to her friend. "Besides, there's no rug in the dining room yet. We need a rug under the table and chairs, otherwise the floor's going to get all scratched up."

"Stop worrying." Turning west up Ninth Street, Julie waved away her concern. "It's all handled, I promise."

"Did you *buy* a rug?"

"Actually, I found a rug. Will and I went to our storage place and raided the stuff from my old house. A lot of it went to auction when I sold the house, but I hung onto some things I thought I might want later. I've only used a couple of pieces since I bought the condo, though, so I figured why not see what would work in the shelter?" Thankfully, she slowed her pace as they neared Eastern Avenue. Sarah had been taking two steps for every one of Julie's. "I had a huge Persian area rug that fit under the table, and it looks amazing."

They took the last few hundred yards to the shelter at a more reasonable pace. Sarah couldn't help stopping at the end of the long curved driveway to admire their handiwork. The wrought-iron fence was gone, as were the big gates and brick posts that had separated the old place from the rest of the town. Several discussions about whether or not to replace the fencing had ensued at board meetings, with Sarah vacillating between wanting to be locked in and not wanting to draw attention to the place with a high enclosure.

Ultimately, dollars won out. The cost of replacing that much wrought iron was simply prohibitive, and any other kind of fence would look tacky or wouldn't serve the purpose. She didn't really mind. The house was securely alarmed and much more unobtrusive without a tall fancy barricade.

As they rounded the curve in the driveway, she caught her breath at what had been added after she'd left that morning. A white picket fence now surrounded the yard directly in front of the house, with an arched latticework arbor over the sidewalk leading to the porch.

Opening the gate in the arbor, Julie stepped aside and let Sarah pass through first. Some enterprising soul had tilled garden space along the fence row, and the air was redolent with the scent of freshly turned earth. For now, pots of golden mums stood sentry on either side of the arbor. Sarah pivoted, taking in the lovely addition, already picturing lavender and daisies and other perennials making a colorful border inside the picket fence.

"Oh, dear Lord, how perfect!" she exclaimed just as she noticed the entire board standing shoulder to shoulder on the top two steps, as well as Henry, Liam, Libby, and Noah. Towering over all of them on the porch stood Tony, looking delicious in a light-blue button-down shirt.

Sarah's heart sped up when his dimples showed. "Did you guys do all this after I left this morning?"

"Yup," said Will with a grin. "We thought you'd never leave. Weren't you even a little suspicious that Julie was practically yanking you out the door?"

"No kidding," added Perry from his spot between Carrie and Margie. "We were all hiding in the carriage house waiting for you to get the heck out so we could start work."

Carrie came down the steps. "It's not a six-foot wrought-iron fence or razor wire, but it's one more small barrier. A little extra protection since you'll be living here. We thought it worked well with the house and the porch. Plus"—she ran to the gate and when she closed it, it squeaked loudly—"I asked Henry not to oil the hinges, so you'll hear it when someone opens the gate."

Tears pricked at Sarah's eyes. Swallowing the lump in her throat, she caught Tony's eye, and he gave her a wink and a barely perceptible nod. "It's amazing. Thank you—all of you. And the squeak—what a gift!"

Julie put an arm around her shoulders. "There's more."

Stopping a few feet from the bottom of the stairs, Sarah looked askance at the group of friends grinning down at her, then turned to Julie, who was clearly bursting with news. "What else are you guys up to?"

Head cocked, Julie took a deep breath. "Well, here's the thing. We decided the shelter needs a name. Something that speaks to what we're doing here and, more importantly, *why* we're doing it."

"Okay." Sarah crossed her arms. "A name is good idea."

"Glad you think so. We got together last week and talked about it—and frankly, sister, *your* name kept coming up." Julie offered the endearing smile that experience had taught Sarah meant she was up to something. "You are the reason we're all here. You inspired me to do this, to be a part of the network in Michigan, and to ask the village to participate."

"Huh-uh. No way." Sarah held up one hand, her heart in her throat at the thought of the Sarah Bennett Women's Center. *Ye Gods.* "Please don't tell me you're naming this shelter after me."

"We're not." Carrie stepped forward, a huge smile on her face. "We wanted to honor you, though, your courage and your commitment to the cause of battered and abused women. This place is beautiful—and it's you who inspired all of it. Even more significant is that you are the one who's going to be serving the women who show up here, giving them a piece of your courage to help them on their way."

"And although not everyone knows your story," Julie cut in, "that's yours to share when and if you choose, *I* knew the one way we could honor you and the work you'll be doing here. We all agreed the shelter name needed to be not only hope, but also remembrance." She and Carrie led her up the steps as the group parted like the Red Sea at the touch of Moses's staff.

"Julie... What—" Sarah clamped her lips shut at the sight of the discreet bronze plaque next to the front door. A rectangle with a curved top and bottom, embossed with a design of elegant woven flowers and vines that surrounded three words: MACY'S GARDEN GATE.

"Garden because gardens are happy and beautiful places," Carrie explained quietly. "And Gate because this shelter is a gate to a new future for the women who will pass through here. Not a place to stay, but a safe haven while they regroup for a new life of freedom."

"And Macy because she's the reason you found the courage to leave your abusive situation and begin again," Julie added.

Sarah pressed her fingers to her lips to keep from bursting into tears, unable to speak as she gazed at the bronze sign. She closed her eyes for moment, thinking how blessed she was in this little town with these dear, dear people. How could they possibly have known that choosing this name was the perfect way to remember her daughter, to always have Macy close to her heart? She wanted to say something, but if she opened her mouth, she'd only weep at this point and possibly send the wrong message to her friends who waited in tense silence for her reaction.

A warm hand on her elbow tugged her back against a firm chest and Tony leaned down to whisper, "Is this okay? If it's too much for you, we'll take it right down and start over."

Galvanized by his words, she gave him a tremulous smile before turning to the folks gathered around her. "It's more than okay. It's exactly"—she took a deep breath, no longer trying to keep the tears from running down her cheeks—"exactly the right name for the shelter. I couldn't have chosen better myself." Gripping Tony's hand, she gazed around, meeting each and every person's eyes. "Thank you all so much for this"—she touched the plaque with trembling fingers—"for *everything*. You all mean the world to me."

Margie gathered Sarah close in a hug. "You're sure, honey? It was a risk, but it felt so right to us." When she leaned back, tears glistened in her eyes.

"It *is* right. Perfect and so right," Sarah said, smiling through her tears as Margie passed her to Libby for an embrace, then to Perry, and on down the line until she'd been thoroughly hugged and stood beside Tony again.

He tucked her close against his side and kissed her forehead. "I'm so proud of you." His soft words were for her ears only and she touched her lips to his stubbled cheek. "Now, you have to cut the ribbon for the official opening of Macy's Garden Gate," he announced in a normal voice.

A wide yellow satin ribbon hung across the intricate wooden screen door that Henry and Liam had painstakingly sanded and repainted to match the porch. Julie stepped up with a pair of scissors. "We didn't invite the whole town, even though the grand opening of Macy's Garden Gate is a reason to celebrate, because it's probably time to start downplaying the attention we're getting. We didn't think the newspapers needed to be here, so this is our own private celebration." Handing the shears to Sarah with a smile, she added. "Go ahead. Cut the ribbon. There's so much to show you inside."

~

Exhausted and exhilarated, Sarah dropped onto a high-backed stool at the newly installed gathering table in the center of the shelter's roomy kitchen. Around the table sat Carrie and Liam, Henry and Sophie, Julie and Will, and, of course, Tony. She couldn't stop the satisfied little sigh that escaped.

"You okay?" Sophie asked, patting her knee before helping herself to the bottle of wine that was making its way around the table.

Sarah smiled and nodded, her heart so full that she couldn't find words to express her gratitude and love for her friends.

They'd stayed to clean up after a delightful grand opening

celebration that included music cranked up on a stereo donated by Bertie from the yarn shop, tours of the facility, and food—sandwiches, fresh fruit, a plate full of crudités with dip, chips and salsa, and two of Carrie's delicious three-layer orange-coconut cakes. The eight of them had put in the last load of dishes and, except for the wine they were finishing, all the leftovers were in the refrigerator or sent home with the other board members.

"The dishwashers got a pretty good inauguration," Carrie observed as the machine hummed quietly in the background. "I'm glad we installed two. Maybe we should've gone with paper plates, but I wanted you to see the stuff Drew and Holly from the Fishwife donated. They're in the process of updating the dishes and cutlery, so we've got service for thirty-six here in the kitchen, the butler's pantry is full, and there are several more boxes downstairs in storage. I love the white pottery with the embossed border. It's pretty and sturdy, and to tell the truth, it's where we got the idea for the design on the name plaque."

Swallowing a sip of wine over the lump in her throat, Sarah shook her head in amazement. "I can't believe how generous this town is. Drew and Holly could've traded those in at the restaurant supply place. And Perry and Carla's leather furniture looks fantastic in the front parlor. They said they were in the market for new sofas and chairs anyway, but who knows?" She swiped at her cheek after a tear leaked out. "And the bedrooms—I can't believe you guys hauled all that stuff in here so quick."

"Everything's just stuck in the rooms right now. Nothing's in place and there's still plenty to do what with hanging blinds and digging through boxes for curtains and towels and stuff. Plus there's art to hang," Carrie said.

"Uh oh, hanging blinds, curtains, and art." Liam chuckled. "She didn't say my name or yours"—he gestured around the table at the other men—"but she may as well have."

"Ouch!" Will groaned, although Sarah could tell it was good-natured. "Hanging the art in Julie's condo almost caused me to get a divorce...*if* I were married, that is." He gave Julie a pointed stare.

She simply fluttered her lashes at him. "I'm yours, baby. Who needs a piece of paper?"

"I do." Will gave her puppy dog eyes. "Marry me, Julianne. Make an honest man out of me."

But Julie only kissed him and turned to Carrie. "Is there any cake left?"

"Jeez, Jules, how can you possibly be hungry again?" Sophie asked, but then Henry agreed more cake was definitely in order.

He rose to get the cake out of the fridge, even as the others laughed and ribbed him mercilessly about his notorious sweet tooth. In spite of the teasing, they all fell on the rest of the dessert with gusto, dirtying more plates and forks. Henry passed around generous slices while Julie dabbed a fingerful of orange-coconut frosting on Will's lips and kissed it away, and Liam fed Carrie a bite of the delicious treat from his own fork.

Sarah savored the clamor of chatter and merriment. She'd missed so much during her first marriage. Dinner parties at the Prescotts had been staid formal affairs—elegant with candlelight and expensive china and crystal. People around the table spoke quietly, dividing their time equally between the person on their right or left. Joking, laughing out loud, sharing food—that kind of silliness was simply not acceptable.

A dollop of frosting dropped from her fork to her round-neck knit shirt, landing right below her collarbone. Before she could dab it with her napkin, Tony swiped it away and popped his finger in his mouth while his eyes twinkled. "I think I've found a whole new way to enjoy Carrie's cake," he said, dimples bracketing a devilish smile.

Heat suffused Sarah's cheeks as she leaned away from his seeking fingers. "You are incorrigible, my friend."

He managed an affronted expression for about five seconds. "Excuse me? I'm not the one licking icing off her significant other's lips." He grinned fiendishly at Julie and Will while Liam and Sophie yawned in unison.

"I think we're all getting punchy," Carrie declared, rising from her stool to rinse off the cake plate. "Come on, Maestro, I'm taking you home."

"Looks like I need to tuck Sophie in too." Henry stacked plates as people scraped the last of the cake onto their forks. "We'll take the trash to the dumpster on our way out since we're all parked in back anyway."

Suddenly, a thought occurred to Sarah. "Guys, I want to do something for all the volunteers who helped. I was thinking maybe a fall picnic here in the yard, but then I realized I don't want to do social stuff here. It'll draw attention to us. Do you think we could do it in the harbor park? Or maybe a big bonfire down at the beach?"

"I'd love a beach fire. We haven't done a single one yet this year and summer's practically over." Sophie carried plates and forks to the sink to give them a quick rinse. "Let's do it on our beach. Henry's collected a bunch of driftwood down there."

"Sure," Henry agreed. "We've got plenty of parking in the lot across the road from our place, plus I think everybody on Beach Road volunteered here this summer, so there are five driveways."

"A lot of folks will walk up the beach from town anyway," Tony put in as he tied up trash bags and set them by the mudroom door.

Carrie pulled the ever-present notebook from her capacious purse that hung on the back of her chair. This pad had bejeweled dragonflies on it. "I'll start a list of stuff we'll need—hot dogs, buns, chips." She wrote furiously.

"Don't forget stuff for s'mores," Will said, and Carrie jotted more in her tidy script.

She glanced up expectantly. "Sarah, you and I can go into the city and grab everything from Costco. What's a good day? How about"—she pulled her phone out of her pocket—"two weeks from Saturday? That gets the start of school out of the way."

When everyone immediately reached for their phones to check calendars, Sarah's heart swelled again and she blinked to keep the tears at bay.

This town, dear God, this town.

A simple request became a beach party in seconds. It was as if all she had to do was make a wish and Willow Bay made it happen. All of Paul Prescott's money and prestige back in Georgia couldn't even begin to buy the huge hearts of the people in this little village. She bit her lip and then spoke. "Hey?" Raising her voice to be heard over the cacophony of voices comparing dates and times, she said, "Carrie?"

Carrie glanced up from tapping the screen on her phone. "What?"

"This is on me, okay?" Sarah held out her hand. "Give me the list. I want your help, absolutely, but *I'm* paying for this."

The room hushed so that the only sound was the hum of the dishwashers as seven pairs of eyes turned toward her. "I love you all for hopping onboard at my every little desire, but you have to promise to let me start pulling my own weight. At least let me pay for this party."

"Sarah, we can—" Carrie snapped her mouth shut at Sarah's quirked brow.

"Please, it's important to me. I've saved almost all the money I earned at the Chicago shelter, so I can handle it, plus you're paying me a good salary. I want to thank everyone who's supported me and taken me in without any questions because"— she took a deep breath—"I'm going away soon. I'm staying long enough to get the shelter going and help you hire a good manager, but then I'm leaving Willow Bay."

CHAPTER 22

Sarah could see that her announcement had stunned everyone, particularly Tony, who dropped a trash bag and stared at her, curiosity and dismay evident in his eyes. "Come on, everybody sit for a second." She circled her hand to encompass the whole group.

Sophie turned off the water and dried her hands on a tea towel as the others settled back into their chairs around the table. "Sarah, what are you talking about?" She tossed the towel on the counter and plopped onto the stool next to Henry's. "You're finally settled and happy. Why would you leave?"

Sarah folded her hands in front of her. "I have to go. You all have become my dearest friends and"—she met Tony's hard stare —"*that's* why I have to leave. Paul Prescott is going to show up here one day and I can't risk him hurting one of you…or anyone in the village." She held up one hand at the chorus of protestations.

"You don't know that he'll find you." Carrie's brow furrowed. "And we *do* know how awful he is."

"You *think* you know." With an effort, Sarah tore her gaze from Tony and glanced around the table. "He wants me, that's true enough, but he's so determined to have what he believes is rightfully his, he would rather see me dead than happy with anyone else. And he'll go right through anyone to get to me."

Julie gasped. "Oh, Sarah! Do you truly believe that?"

Sarah nodded vehemently. "Absolutely, I believe it. I realize now that I panicked after he was convicted, and I ran when I should have stayed there and figured out my life, planned my escape better. I probably would've ended up with more than the cash I found stashed in his desk. Who knows what the hell he had in the safe in his office, but I had no way to get into it. He was in jail and he couldn't get to me, but he had people on the outside who would do his bidding and *that* scared the crap out of me.

"He was taking kickbacks and bribes from contractors and companies who wanted favors from the bank his family owned. They owned practically the whole town, and even though he already had more money than he could ever spend in one lifetime, he still wanted more. It was a control thing, you know—making people pay him under the table because they were afraid of him. He's a thug. A gangster like Al Capone, without the double-breasted suits and spats." She hoped her grim chuckle would lighten the moment just a little; however, everyone else simply gaped at her. "And he's vicious. He'd have no compunction about getting rid of anyone who got in the way of what he believes is his property."

Julie's jaw dropped. "*You* aren't his property, Sarah Jane Bennett. Don't ever refer to yourself that way."

Sarah's heart ached. She didn't want to hurt these dear, dear people, but once that bastard figured out where she was, he'd stop at nothing to get to her. And before he took her, he'd hurt her most effectively by destroying the lives of her friends. Oh, nothing as dramatic as a bloodbath at the Daily Grind. She shuddered, remembering the nightmare that had yanked her from peaceful sleep the previous night. No, he'd never come with guns blazing. He was too clever and subtle for that. Little accidents would start happening in town. Liam's boat might mysteriously catch fire or Bertie would be hit by a speeding car as she rode her bike to the yarn shop one morning. "Thanks to all of you, I've learned that I'm not anyone's property. I'm much stronger now, which is why I have to go. I have to make sure he can never hurt anyone I love—not ever again."

"So, what? You're just going to run for the rest of your life?" Tony asked, a muscle working in his jaw. He dropped into the stool he'd been standing behind, straight and stiff as an arrow.

She took a deep breath, unwilling to meet his eyes because the pain in those brown depths was killing her. "I don't know. Maybe. I was actually thinking about Europe. My brother's in Germany and he would help me find a safe place over there. Not near his family, of course, I'd never agree to that, but somewhere." She gave them all a sad little smile. "I thought I'd found a safe place in Chicago, but Paul found me, and he'll find me again. This time it's different. You all have empowered me, given me back myself, and I don't know how I'll ever repay you." She hesitated, gazing at the faces of her friends. "So you see? That's why I have to go."

"I don't think he can track you *here*." Doubt filled Henry's tone as Tony simply sat gaping at her. "How could he?"

She gave a snort of grim laughter. "He'll find me, Henry. Who knows how? I'd guess he's probably hired a private detective by now or he's using online search apps." Sarah glanced down at her whitening knuckles. With an effort, she unclenched her hands and stretched her fingers. "When he turned up in Chicago in April, I wasn't even surprised really. It was inevitable he'd find me. So I grabbed the first thing within reach—the stupid skillet—and I hit him. Then I ran...again." Dropping her head back, she closed her eyes and released a huge sigh. "He's cunning and he's smart and he's evil"—she opened her eyes and looked directly at Tony —"and he doesn't ever lose."

"Sarah, you've got a new name now and you're miles from Chicago and even farther from Georgia. I know the internet makes it hard for people to hide, but I truly think you're safe here." Julie dismissed her fear with a wave of her hand, but her blue eyes were huge.

"I'll never understand why someone would want to be with a person who didn't want them," Sophie said.

Will nodded in agreement. "Me, either. Surely he's figured out you're done. You don't want to be with him anymore. He needs to move on."

"I wish he could do that, but he won't. I know him." Sarah clenched her fist again and tapped the table with it. "He's relentless. He won't give up until he finds me and beats me. And I don't mean literally, although I'm sure he'll do that, too, if he has the chance. I mean, he's a narcissist of the first order, a true sociopath, and he *has* to win. You guys, this town, you all can't spend your lives watching *my* back. The best thing I can do is make a careful plan and leave."

Henry thrust his fingers through his salt-and-pepper hair and raised one finger. "But, Sarah, if you leave, aren't you just giving him control again? Letting your fear of his actions keep you from being happy?"

Sarah eyed him from across the table. He had a point, but he didn't know Paul Prescott.

Liam crossed his arms over his broad chest. "Well, okay, that settles it. You won't be spending a single night *here* alone."

"No, she won't." Tony's quiet deep voice and the look of determination on his face when she finally met his eyes again sent a shiver through her. "I'll be here with her. I'll move in too."

Sarah gave him a faint smile. "My own personal cop?" She touched his stubbled cheek with one finger. "I adore you for suggesting it and nothing would make me happier than to live with you, Deputy, but that would put you in so much danger. I couldn't bear anything happening to you."

An expression Sarah had never seen before crossed Tony's face and, without taking his eyes off her, he said, "Guys, could we have the room, please?"

~

Tony didn't believe he'd seen his friends vacate a room that fast or that quietly before—ever—but mere seconds later, all six of them were out the door, taking the trash bags with them. Sarah still sat with one hand pressed to her chest, gazing into his eyes. He'd never seen such sadness on anyone's face and his heart tore a little. When she didn't speak, he glanced away. "Were you planning on discussing this with me before you booked a flight?" He didn't even try to keep the bitterness out of his tone. This was so not the conversation he'd planned to have with her tonight— not by a long shot.

She sighed. "Yes. Of course. I'm sorry. It just came out—"

"Sarah, for God's sake. I thought we had something special going here." He shook his head, trying to clear his brain, desperately trying to understand what she was thinking. She was safe here; surely, she knew that by now.

"We do." Her breath hitched. "Tony, I–I'm in love with you." She whispered the words he'd been longing to hear. Yet, somehow, they weren't warming his heart the way he'd expected.

"I'm in love with you too." When he gently lifted her chin, her lip quivered. "That's a good thing, right?"

"I've never been happier in my life, but it's because I love you that I have to go." She raised both hands, palms up, in defeat. "Don't you see? You're not safe with me. If he knew we were together, he'd kill you and then me and then anyone else who ever knew and supported us."

"Honey, he's just one man. I know you see him as a monster, but I can protect you. I promise I—" He stopped when she put one finger against his lips.

"He *is* a monster," she said firmly. "And he won't stop hunting me down. I know him. He's cold and ruthless and calculating."

"Listen to me, please." Tony grasped her hand and pressed a gentle kiss into her palm before he knit their fingers together. "Do you want to leave?" He held his breath.

"No." She shook her head firmly, then repeated. "No. I love it here. I love this town and the villagers and the Posse, but most of all I love you. I'm excited about what we've accomplished this summer and, if I could, I'd stay here forever."

"Okay." He sighed. "Next question. Do you trust me?"

"Yes," she replied without a moment's hesitation. "I trust you implicitly. But Tony, he won't give—"

This time he put one finger against her soft mouth. "Then marry me."

Sarah simply gaped at him.

"Please…if you'll have me, I want us to get married," he repeated, tugging her off the stool and placing his hands on her shoulders. "I'll get down on one knee right now if you want all the sappy stuff, Sarah. We'll do this however you like. The simple facts are I love you and I want to spend the rest of my life with you. I'm getting grayer by the minute, sweetheart, and I don't want to wait another second to start our life together."

"Tony, I-I…" Sarah floundered, too astounded to speak. Dear God, had he really asked her to *marry* him? But how could she endanger him—this beautiful man who'd helped her turn her life right side up with his patience and kindness and love?

"Hey, you want romance? I can do sappy better than most." With his dimples in full bloom and warm honey lights in his eyes, Tony knelt before her. "Susannah Elizabeth Boatwright, will you marry me and grant me the honor of sharing the remainder of life's joys and sorrows with you?"

After his astonishing use of her birth name, Sarah didn't think he could shock her further, but when he reached into his pocket and pulled out a small red leather box, her heart damn near stopped. Opening it, he revealed a simple pear-cut ruby set in old-fashioned gold filigree—the most beautiful ring she'd ever seen—nestled in gray velvet. With a gasp, she clutched her hands to her chest, unable to tear her eyes from Tony's handsome, earnest face.

Good God, he's serious. He's been planning this.

"I actually meant to do this after we'd had a little more time together—you know, like over a romantic dinner. But I just picked up the ring from the bank this afternoon, so I'm hoping it's fate that it's in my pocket." Tony shot her that disarming smile. "This ring was my grandmother's. Grand-père bought it for her in Paris right before they immigrated to the States. He chose a ruby because she had red hair and a fiery spirit like you, and the stone made him think of her." Tony reached out and set the box in her palm. Her fingers closed around it automatically. "I knew from the moment you pulled a gun on me that you were the woman who was meant to wear it next."

Dazed beyond words, Sarah gulped. She should speak—say something intelligent. Somehow her vocabulary had suddenly gone missing. Perhaps it was possible to marry him, stay in Willow Bay, and make a life with him, helping other abused women. A wave of strength surged through her as she stared into Tony's dark amber eyes. Together, they could face anything—even a monster… Couldn't they?

Still on one knee, Tony gazed up at her, love shining in his face. "Sarah, say something."

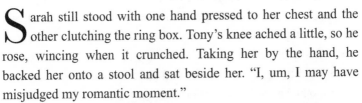

Sarah still stood with one hand pressed to her chest and the other clutching the ring box. Tony's knee ached a little, so he rose, wincing when it crunched. Taking her by the hand, he backed her onto a stool and sat beside her. "I, um, I may have misjudged my romantic moment."

Sarah opened her fingers, stared at the box, and blinked as a tear crept from the corner of her eye. "No," she whispered, then cleared her throat and said more loudly, "No, you didn't. You just...floored me."

"In a good way?" Tony realized how inane that sounded as soon as the words came out, but his heart was bouncing between his socks and his throat. Had he blown this thing completely?

The smile he'd been waiting—hoping for—finally appeared. It was gorgeous, even through tears. "In a very good way." She leaned over to press a soft, salty kiss on his lips.

Instinct told him to let *her* take charge now, so even though he was longing to pull her into his arms and kiss her stupid, he kept his hands in his lap. The gentle kiss deepened as, with tears still running down her face, she put her hand on his thigh, tilted her head, and thrust her tongue between his lips. His body reacted immediately, her touch sending pangs and zings of heat through him. After a moment, he pulled away. "You're killin' me here, Susannah."

She smiled tremulously. "How'd you find out my real name? I thought I never wanted to hear anyone call me that again, but oh, Tony—when you say it, it's a...a caress."

"Yeah?" Delight coursed through him when she didn't flinch as he stroked his thumb through the tears on her cheek. He was always careful touching her face, usually giving her some unspoken signal that he was going to raise his hand; this time, she leaned into his touch with a contented sigh. *God, how I love her.*

"I hope you don't think I've been invading your privacy, but I found it on your marriage license when I was researching what happened in Georgia. I had to know what happened, what I was dealing with, you know?" When she nodded slightly, he continued. "It's a beautiful name. It's how I've thought of you ever since. My little Southern belle—soft as cotton and tough as nails." He smoothed a wayward curl off her wet face. "I love you, Susannah. Please marry me."

She gazed into his eyes. "I love you, too, I do…"

"I hear a *but* coming."

"*But,* I'm such an unholy mess," she moaned. "I come with more baggage than an Air France flight to Paris, and the specter of Paul Prescott will always hang over us. You can't possibly want that in your life, in your family's life."

"I want *you* in *my* life," he replied firmly. "My family will adore you because I adore you. And we'll worry about your ex if and when we need to. He's not a specter; he's an annoyance. If he shows up—"

"*When* he shows up," Sarah corrected.

"Okay, *when* he shows up, we'll swat him away like the tiresome bug he is." Tony rested his forehead against hers. "My Susannah, you are a strong, bold woman who isn't going to let anyone intimidate her ever again. I'm so proud of you. We can't spend our lives worrying about that jackass. Stop hiding, please? Marry me and let's get this place up and running—together."

Sarah closed her eyes, tipped her head back, and sighed a huge breath, almost as though she were releasing a lifetime of despair. When she met his gaze, there was that amazing sweet smile again. "It is an awfully pretty ring," she said with a twinkle in her eyes.

"That it is," he agreed solemnly and took the jewel from its velvet-lined box. "Let's see if it fits. As I recall, Grand-mère had little fingers like yours." He slid the ring onto her left hand. It was a perfect fit. "Ah, just like it was made for you." Raising her hand, he kissed her fingers, then turned her hand over and pressed his lips to her palm.

"You are the most beautiful man, Tony Reynard—inside and out," she whispered. "Becoming your wife sounds like heaven on Earth to me."

Sarah's fingers in his hair brought his head up and he tugged her off the chair and into his arms. "So that's a yes then?" He let his hand wander across her back and down to pull her hips against his.

"It's a yes." She nodded, tears glistening in her blue eyes. "Only if you promise to always call me Susannah in that incredibly sexy way." She touched her lips to his. "Tony, can it please be just ours—that name? For our most intimate times? I need to be Sarah everywhere else."

"Just ours." He agreed and stopped fighting the urge to make love to her right then and there. Picking her up, he boosted her onto the table, and pulled down the straps of her tank top, exposing her shoulders to his seeking mouth. Her gasp at the touch of his tongue on her skin sent an arrow of desire straight through him. This woman was his destiny, his future, his world, and he would defend her to the death.

She touched his cheek as he dropped kisses along her bare collarbone. "Take me home, Deputy. I can't have sex on this table and then feed my clients on it. I've got a nice soft bed."

CHAPTER 23

Sarah barely got seated on the sofa in the Posse's usual corner at the Daily Grind before Julie grabbed her left hand. "Well, look at you, sporting a new piece of jewelry. He proposed, didn't he? You're staying!"

Sarah couldn't resist tweaking her just a little. "What if Tony's decided to travel to Europe with me?"

"Has he?" Carrie's brown eyes widened.

"No," Sarah admitted. "I'm staying and we're getting married."

Julie let out a whoop that turned heads in the coffee shop. "Baby, we are all delighted. This is so right." She held Sarah's hand up to the sunlight coming through the window beside them, turning it first one way and then another. The ruby winked and sparkled.

From her chair, Libby leaned over and squeezed Sarah's knee. "I miss everything because I work all the damn time. I've gotta release some of the winery responsibilities to Tess, 'cause I hate being out of the loop. I'm so happy for you, Sarah. Let me see that ring."

Pulling her hand from Julie's grip, Sarah held the ring out for the women to admire, grateful the place was nearly empty. She'd deliberately arrived late this morning, knowing her friends would be all over her about her announcement the previous night. She was thrilled to share her good news with her best pals, but she still glanced over her shoulder to check out the rest of the customers. She recognized the villagers who came through every morning and she'd learned how to identify tourists, but when a stranger came through, she clutched. Perhaps wary was her new normal, but wary beat the hell out of terrified and cowering. She had Tony, the Posse, and the entire village of Willow Bay to thank for that.

Everyone looked familiar. She waved to Bertie from the yarn shop, tossed a nod to a tableful of the harbor crewmen, and acknowledged two moms clad in running gear with three-wheeled strollers beside them. She'd already checked out the people sitting outside—nobody suspicious. If he'd found her and was stalking her, he was damn subtle about it. Sarah turned back to her friends.

"You and Tony are perfect together." Carrie touched the ring with one finger. "He's one of the best men I know and you deserve the best."

Sarah glanced away, suddenly shy. "Thanks. He *is* the best, isn't he? How did you know?" She shivered involuntarily, then smiled. "I've never felt this way before. Ever."

"Julie ran into him at the bank when he was picking up the ring, and she spilled the beans, although we had no idea he was planning on doing it last night. Great feeling, huh?" Sophie grinned, clearly thinking of her Henry. As Sarah cast her glance around the group, Libby, Carrie, and Julie also wore those faraway it's-fabulous-to-be-in-love expressions.

So this is what it's like to be a part of a circle of women whose relationships work.

Henry, Liam, and Will were all kind, good-hearted men. Sarah had discovered that as they'd pitched in renovating the shelter.

She'd only met Daniel Nolan once out at the winery, but he was a jolly sort, and his pride in his wife's accomplishments shone in his eyes. And Tony?

Well, Tony was gift she intended to spend the rest of her life cherishing.

Carrie nudged her out of her reverie. "So you're definitely not leaving then?" Curiosity gleamed in her dark brown eyes.

"No." Sarah saw no reason to be coy. "And, Soph, it was Henry who really made me think clearly when he said that if I left, I was giving control back to Paul. That made so much sense."

"That's my darling geek. The quiet ones always surprise you with their depth, don't they?" Sophie sipped her coffee before nabbing a piece of bran muffin from Julie's plate.

"Henry's a smart guy." Julie flashed a bogus hard stare at Sophie before moving her plate a few inches away. "Get your own, dammit. This also means you're staying on as manager of Macy's Garden Gate, right?"

Sarah nodded, unable to keep from grinning at Sophie and Julie's customary ritual—Julie bought the muffin, Sophie snitched bites. "Yup, that's exactly what it means. And Tony is going to move in when I do. I just pray that bastard doesn't find me."

"We need to find a nickname for that creepy ex of yours so we don't have to acknowledge him by actually using his name." Libby gave a fiendish grimace. "Something suitably evil."

"How about we call him Hans—for the villain in the *Die Hard* movies?" Sophie's eyes lit up, but Julie shook her head vehemently.

"No, no way! He was played by Alan Rickman and even if the character was evil, still…Alan Rickman."

"Excellent point. We shouldn't besmirch darling Alan's memory." Sophie chuckled. "What about Lord Voldemort from Harry Potter?"

"Too easy." When Julie waved away that suggestion, Sophie stuck out her tongue and swiped another piece of the bran muffin.

"Gargamel? From the Smurfs?" Carrie offered, one brow quirked.

"Cripes, you've been hanging out with your kindergartner too much, Caro." Julie guffawed. The others burst into gales of laughter as Carrie raised her hands in supplication. Everyone loved Isabella, Carrie and Liam's precocious and adorable adopted daughter.

Settling into the leather sofa, Sarah drank her coffee and basked in the warm glow of her friends' silliness. They threw several more names out before she suddenly snapped her fingers. "How about Iago? From *Othello*? He destroyed a lot of people's lives—seems appropriate."

"Perfect!" Julie clapped. "And it has the added panache of being very literary. Villainy with a touch of class. I love it! Iago it is. So that's our code name for the bastard, ladies." She shook one finger around the group. "Don't forget it."

"Okay, now that we have *that* out of the way, let's talk weddings." Carrie pulled out her ubiquitous notebook and pen. "First, do you have a date? Then we need to talk venues."

"Tony says ASAP." Sarah's cheeks burned as she remembered all the other things he'd said the previous night, as well as all the sexy things they'd done. "And I agree—the sooner the better."

Julie slapped a hand on the arm of the sofa. "Beach wedding. Yours was gorgeous, Carrie."

"It's October." Sophie brushed off Julie's suggestion with a backward wave. "Even if we started planning right this second, we don't have time to put together a whole wedding before the weather gets too chilly for the beach."

"What about doing it at the winery? I love hosting weddings." Libby grinned, revealing a tiny space between her front teeth that reminded Sarah of some model or actress, but she couldn't remember who. It was adorable.

"Oh, yes!" Carrie began writing. "A December wedding in the evening with a fire in the fireplace and mulled wine. How romantic!"

Julie warmed up to the idea immediately. "With a Christmas tree and Sarah in a cream-colored velvet gown? We can do the decorations in Christmas colors, red and green and gold."

Sophie was also onboard. "I love Christmas weddings!"

"So do I!" Kelly, the barista, eavesdropped unashamedly from the counter behind them. "Oh, Sarah, you and Tony? Perry's been predicting this for weeks! Congratulations!"

"Kel, it's bad luck to congratulate the bride," Julie scolded with a smile.

"Really?" Kelly stopped wiping down one of Perry's huge espresso machines and cocked her head.

Julie nodded vigorously. "Yup, you congratulate the groom. You say *best wishes* to the bride."

"Oh, well then best wishes, Sarah." Kelly waved her dishrag in Sarah's direction. "I'm thrilled for you. Tony's hot." She glanced at Julie. "It's okay to say the groom is hot, right?"

Sarah chuckled. "It's definitely okay, Kelly, thank you. And yeah, Tony *is* hot."

"So Christmas wedding then?" Carrie wrote something in her perfect script, and Julie nodded before Sarah could even respond.

"Um, guys? Remember me? The bride? *I* like Christmas and *I'm* crazy about romantic." She set her cup on the table beside her. "Libby, you're a doll to offer the winery, but it might be a good idea for me to talk to Tony before we start making plans. He may want some input. It is his wedding, too."

Julie scrunched her nose. "Oh, please. Tony is so nuts about you he'd get married on the moon if you asked him. Let's make plans and just tell him and the other guys when and where to show up."

"We can talk about this all you like, Jules, but Tony gets a say." Sarah kept her tone firm, even though in her heart she knew Julie was right. Tony would agree to anything if it meant getting married as soon as humanly possible. "He and I are a democracy."

"Of course he gets a say," Carrie soothed. "But we have to have something to present to him."

Ideas for dresses, flowers, food, and decorations flew as the group chattered and brainstormed eagerly. There in the sunny warmth of the Daily Grind surrounded by her friends, Sarah almost believed she could finally be safe and happy for the first time since she left her parents' home at the tender age of eighteen.

Afternoon sun shone through the newly washed windows of Macy's Garden Gate as Sarah stood back to admire her handiwork. Liam, Will, and Henry had spent the day installing plantation blinds, following behind Sarah and Julie as they washed each window in the house. The men had left, taking the empty blinds boxes and their tools with them, Julie was in the kitchen cleaning up from lunch and taking trash to the dumpster, and Sarah had just put up the shirred panels at the sidelight windows on either side of the heavy front door, which stood partially open. The soundtrack to *Dirty Dancing* played in the background, thanks to Julie's phone attached to the donated stereo in the dining room. The whole downstairs was filled with music. Swinging her hips, Sarah sang along with The Ronettes' version of "Be My Baby."

A cool October breeze came in through the ornate screen door lifting the curls off her neck as she smoothed and evened the gossamer fabric at the top and bottom rods. They'd debated whether or not to cover the sidelights, but Sarah decided it would be best if people couldn't easily see in from the porch, and Julie agreed, particularly since double-rod curtains were true to the period of the house.

A creaking sound outside stopped her short and sent a frisson of fear through her. Someone was coming through the arbor gate. She peered through the sheer material, but could only see the gate banging in the early autumn breeze. Nobody was there. The guys must not have gotten it closed tight.

But then heavy footsteps clumped on the porch and she smiled as she glanced around the huge foyer. That weighty gait could only be Henry. *Good grief, what has he forgotten this time?* Their absent-minded novelist was notorious for leaving at least one tool behind.

"What're you missing?" she called as she headed to unlock the screen door. A waft of October wind brought a horrifyingly familiar scent through the mesh. Then she gasped.

"My wife." Her ex-husband yanked the door open, breaking latch, then shoved her aside, and let it bang shut behind him. Pieces of the door latch clattered on the wooden porch floor.

A shiver ran down Sarah's spine, but somehow, she kept the neutral expression in place as she backed away from him. She'd learned long ago never to show him fear. It only encouraged the violence. "Hello, Paul." The words were shaky, but she got them out without choking. She'd already managed to put the length of the foyer between them. How had he gotten this far without her seeing him on the porch?

Sarah was amazed that, although she wasn't in the least surprised he'd finally showed up, she also wasn't as terrified as she'd expected to be.

"Isn't this quite the endeavor, my dear?" Paul's eyes swept the foyer and the broad curving staircase, a sneer on his handsome face. "Bringing your cause to small-town America now?"

"Apparently, small-town America needs advocates for abused women. Aren't I proof of that?" Proud that her voice sounded clear and strong, she slid sideways toward the dining room, visualizing the Ruger in her back pocket and praying she wouldn't have to use it. She'd gotten her carry permit a couple of weeks earlier, but she hadn't been to the shooting range for a while. Her phone was in her purse in the butler's pantry, doing her absolutely no good. If she had to, she could yell for Julie, but she'd rather not expose her dearest friend to the son of a bitch. She was fairly certain Paul believed she was alone —and she preferred to keep it that way. "Why are you here, Paul?"

Keep him talking; that was the key. He loved the sound of his own voice.

"I think you know." Paul still lounged, too casually, by the front door, hands in his pockets. He hadn't changed much in eight years. A little gray at the temples and a few more lines around his eyes only gave his handsome face a more distinguished look. He was trim and fit, more muscular—probably from lifting weights in the penitentiary yard. That would be the kind of thing Paul would do in prison. Rehabilitation to him would mean getting buff. And planning payback.

A trendy golf shirt, obviously new khakis, and a pair of unscuffed Topsiders had replaced the dated Armani suit she'd last seen him in when he'd found her in April. Obviously, he was trying to blend in, because when she glanced out the door behind him, the car in the driveway was a generic rental sedan, not the sleek black limo he'd had in Chicago. He ambled farther into the house, filling the space, causing her to back more toward the dining room. He wasn't a particularly big man—average height and weight—but he'd always managed to intimidate her with that look of derision. The scornful gaze that told her how insignificant she was in his eyes. An insect he could crush under his heel if he so chose.

Well, screw that.

Sarah straightened her shoulders, contempt surging through her. "You need to leave. Now."

His lids lowered lazily as he gazed at her, but he didn't come after her. Instead, he merely shook his head. "Come on, Susannah, we're going home."

"I *am* home." Sarah unclenched her fists, unaware of exactly when her fingers had curled inward. "We're divorced. You signed the papers." She swallowed hard trying to keep her voice steady. "I'm not going anywhere with you. Get out of my house."

"I signed under duress. That divorce isn't legal. You're still my wife."

"It's perfectly legal." Sarah had reached the opening to the dining room. She leaned against the arched doorjamb, trying to appear relaxed. "Don't make me call the police."

Tony was the only thing that kept that threat from being empty as Satan's heart since Paul hadn't actually done anything illegal yet, nor had it occurred to her to swear out a restraining order against him when she'd arrived here in Benzie County. Damnit, Tony had talked to her about it just last week and she simply hadn't made the time to do it. *Well, it's a little late now.*

"You're not going to call the police." The more pleasant his tone, the sweeter his smile, the more brutal the attack would be when it came. There was no doubt where this was headed, because she had no intention of going anywhere with Paul Prescott.

"Paul, I'm only asking one more time. Leave. Now." Her eyes didn't waver from his as she watched for signs that he was losing his grip. First, his eyes grew darker and then, his lips thinned. The space between his brows furrowed as his stance firmed.

"I'm not leaving without you, Susannah. You know that." His

voice was quiet and sounded reasonable, but when she dropped
her eyes to his hands, she saw his fingers stretch, clench, and then
stretch again. He was winding up. Nothing had changed.

Faster than she thought possible, he grabbed a pottery figurine
of a sitting woman from the three-legged table in the foyer and
hurled it in her direction. "Get your shit, bitch, you're coming
with me."

Sarah ducked, cringing as the piece shattered against the tiles
of the fireplace behind her. Ah, just as she suspected—he thought
he could cow her with words. She took a deep breath and stood
her ground.

"No." She shook her head and slid one arm behind her back.
"Give it up, Paul. We're done. I tolerated your violence and your
abuse for too many years. But no more. Never again." She softened her voice as she wrapped her fingers around the grip of the
Ruger. "I want to believe you suffered over Macy's death. I can't
imagine how it must feel to know that your uncontrolled anger
caused your own daughter's death. Get some help. Go back to
Georgia and make some kind of life for yourself. Just leave me
be, okay?"

"Macy's death was an accident, pure and simple, and you
damn well know it." His voice hardened as he slammed a fist on
the table, making the spindly legs shudder. "You've had your fun
—while I spent eight years in hell, living with the scum of the
Earth. Not a word in my defense, bitch. Then you disappeared as
if you'd never taken marriage vows. Not a single visit or letter or
even a fucking phone call in eight years."

She raised one brow and somehow managed to keep her voice
even in spite of her weak knees. "Seriously? You didn't actually
believe I'd hang around for freaking *conjugal* visits?"

Heart pounding, she watched him warily. Time was growing
short. He'd stooped to using profanity, which meant that he was
getting close to exploding.

"You're my wife." Dull red color crept up from his collar and stained his cheeks. Another bad sign.

"I am *not* your wife." She glanced over her shoulder as she heard the back door open and then close. Oh, good God, Julie had come back in from the dumpster. Sliding the gun from her back pocket, she brought it up in front of her, holding it at arms' length, both hands around the grip.

"What the fuck are you doing?" Paul crossed to within three feet of her. "A gun, Sarah? Seriously?"

She had to warn Julie.

"Not another inch, you bastard." She turned her head so her voice would carry through the butler's pantry and into the kitchen. "Iago!" The she backed up another foot toward the butler's pantry as Paul eyed her, a small smile playing on his lips.

"You wouldn't dare shoot me, you stupid fucking bitch." He said the words in a tone so conversational that Sarah wasn't even sure she heard correctly, but fear showed clearly in his eyes. Something she'd never seen before today. Her sense of empowerment increased tenfold.

"I wouldn't test her on that if I were you, asshole." Julie sauntered in from the butler's pantry, shoving a chair in with her hip as she passed the table, a grim smile on her face. When she stood next to Sarah, she held up the cell phone, shook her head in obvious disgust, and hit the Emergency button. "We've got an intruder out here at 923 Eastern Avenue."

Paul's expression changed in a heartbeat and suddenly he was once again the charmer who'd fooled Sarah all those years ago. "Come on, baby, don't do this. Your friend doesn't need to call the cops. Let's you and I go somewhere and talk."

"I have nothing more to say to you." Sarah basked in her newfound confidence, relishing how easily she held the gun, unwavering, pointing right at his chest. "Except maybe goodbye. Get out, Paul."

"You owe me." The ugly expression returned, Paul's eyes turned stormy and, once more, Sarah was still astounded at how quickly his mood could change. She wasn't sure what was more disturbing—his mood swings or his anger. Either way, she wanted him gone.

He blinked at her. "You'll never pull that trigger. We both know that." His face was flushed and his eyes belied the bluster in his tone.

"You really wanna try me?" Sarah held the weapon firmly with both hands, leaning forward slightly just as Tony had showed her. "I don't owe you shit. One more word and I'll put a bullet right through your black heart. I've got a witness here who'll swear it was self-defense."

"Earl's on his way." Julie tucked the phone into Sarah's hip pocket. "Yup, it surely would be self-defense. No question."

"Get out, Paul." She gestured with the gun toward the banging screen door. "Just go. If you move your ass, you just might beat the sheriff."

"Goddamn you to hell, Susannah! We're not done!" Red-faced and panting, Paul turned and fled, his heavy tread thumping on the steps.

Storming to the door, Sarah and Julie watched as he revved his engine and took off down the drive in a cloud of dust. Julie put one bracing arm around Sarah and tugged her close.

Laying her head on Julie's shoulder, Sarah heaved a huge sigh. "Oh no, Iago, you couldn't be more wrong! We *are* done."

CHAPTER 24

Tony had spent most of the morning cleaning up paperwork —citation follow-ups, case files, a couple of warrants he needed to serve—then trying to figure out what happened to the pound of weed that Earl had locked up in the evidence closet earlier in the week. The damn stuff had gone missing, and although he considered making a list of possible suspects, he was fairly sure the cleaning crew had figured out how to jimmy the lock. Which meant investigating and arresting one of those dumb kids, and probably finding a new cleaning crew. *Crap.* Some days he really wasn't all that crazy about being deputy sheriff.

"Tony?" The dispatcher stuck her head around the doorjamb. "We just got a call about a possible intruder out at the new shelter. Earl's on his way, but I thought you might want to know."

His heart dropped to his socks, then immediately rose to his throat at Marlene's words. "An intruder?" Leaping to his feet, he reached into his bottom desk drawer for his weapon, buckling the heavy leather holster around his hips and then grasping his hat. "Who called? Was it Sarah? What'd she say?"

"Nope, it was Julie Miles. She just said they had an intruder."

She backed away when he charged toward the door. "Easy, Deputy. When I asked her if anyone was hurt, she said no, but to send someone out."

Tony scowled, his heart racing, blood pounding at his temples. "Dammit, Marlene, you should've kept her on the line."

Marlene grabbed his shirt sleeve. "Hey, dude. Chill. It's Deputy Reynard answering this call, not Tony, the fiancé." He'd announced the engagement over coffee in Earl's office that morning, and the three of them had celebrated his new status with Perry's breakfast blend and chocolate croissants.

Jesus, he hadn't meant to bark. "They're both the same guy, Marlene; I dunno how to separate them." He patted her hand on his sleeve. "Sorry for jumping on you."

She gave him a rueful smile. "No sweat. But you'd better learn to separate them if you're going to keep this job. This may be our first, but it won't be our last call out to that shelter."

"I know. I know." Heart pounding, he straightened his shoulders, giving her a quick nod before heading out the door.

He hurried the few blocks through town with his siren and lights going, careful to avoid tourists and villagers, some of whom stopped mid-step to watch his flashing lights as he passed. Earl taught him early in the game to avoid using his lights and siren if at all possible. In a tourist town, that kind of attention always stirred up trouble. But this was Sarah, and he itched to get to her as soon as humanly possible.

The shelter seemed quiet when he pulled in and shut off the noise. Earl's car was nowhere to be seen, and he spotted Sarah and Julie huddled together on the wide veranda.

"Sarah?" He flung the gate open, unreasonably grateful for the look of relief on her sweet face as she ran down the steps and straight into his arms. "Where is he? Where'd he go?"

"We chased him off, Deputy!" Julie offered a huge wave as

she swaggered down the steps. "Sarah did a stellar Dirty Harry impression, while I dialed 9-1-1. Asshole fled like a scared rabbit."

Sarah trembled against him, her arms wrapped around his neck. "I could've shot him, Tony." She pressed her cheek against his chest, her tears dampening his shirt. "I wanted to put a bullet right through him. I *wanted* to hurt him." When she looked up, her expression was so stricken, it tore at his heart. "That's not me. That's not *me*."

"I know, baby. I know." He stroked the tears from her cheek with his thumb. "Prescott, right?" He gazed over Sarah's head at Julie who nodded in assent.

"She shouted the code word as I was coming in from the dumpster, so I grabbed her phone from her purse. He damn near had her backed up against the wall in the dining room, but she had her gun at the ready and scared the shit out of him." Julie patted Sarah's shoulder. "She done ya proud, Deputy."

Sarah's quaking calmed slightly, but she shook her head. "No more guns, Tony." She pushed the Ruger into his chest. "Take this damn thing."

"Sarah, what the hell? Here, give me that." Julie reached over Sarah's shoulder, took the gun from her shaky fingers, and double-checked the safety. "Honey, you did great. Not a moment of fear. That asshole didn't have a single doubt you were serious."

"Not the point, Jules." Sarah shuddered as she surrendered the weapon, making no secret of how affected she'd been by her first encounter using the Ruger.

In a way, Tony was grateful Prescott was the one who'd been at the business end of the damn pistol. At least if she would have shot him, she wouldn't be suffering all that much guilt over having pulled the trigger on someone she didn't know for sure was pure evil. "Where's Prescott? And where's Earl?"

"Earl flew by, but when Marlene said you were on the way, he took off after Prescott."

"He can't arrest him. He didn't do anything but show up." Sarah pressed her face against Tony's shirt before straightening and stepping away from his arms.

He released her reluctantly. "Tell me what happened. What'd he say? Did he threaten you? We can go after him if he threatened you."

Sarah shrugged. "He wants me back and he wasn't taking no for an answer. I'm not sure if he got scared by the idea that I might really shoot him or by the threat of the cops, but he's gone, thank God."

He led her to the porch, where they all sat down—Tony and Sarah side by side on the wicker settee and Julie bouncing from the armchair to the swing and back again. She was clearly wired, but Tony wanted the story from the beginning. It was the only way he'd be able to determine if this jackass was going to be a perpetual problem. "Right off, you have a *code word*?"

"Yeah. This morning, we came up with a word in case that bastard showed up." Julie grinned, setting the Ruger on the table next to Tony, out of Sarah's line of sight. "Who knew we'd use it the very first day?" She glanced over at her friend, who'd laid her head back against the settee and closed her eyes. "Iago—we all liked it. Seemed appropriate."

Tony shook his head. "Yeah, that's pretty clever." As Julie chattered, he gazed at Sarah for a moment, watching as she made a conscious effort to calm down. Her breasts rose and fell as she took deep breaths. He gave her a few minutes before finally touching her cheek. "Honey, you okay?"

"Yeah. I'm okay." She opened her eyes and gave him a small smile. "He found me. I knew he would."

"We're going to fix this." Tony had no doubt about that. No

way was Paul Prescott going to haunt their lives, not as long as he was a sheriff in this town. The bastard was resourceful; he had to give him that. It took some research to figure out where Sarah had landed. Probably some money exchanged hands in Chicago or threats were made.

"I heard the gate squeak." Sarah lifted her hair and rubbed the back of her neck. For a moment, she seemed smaller, drawn in on herself, but then she straightened. "I was surprised I heard it because I had the music blasting."

"Speaking of music"—Julie's grin widened—"only you could have the perfect soundtrack to squashing your bastard ex."

Sarah raised one quizzical brow as Julie burst into laughter.

"The song that was playing when I came into the dining room was 'You Don't Own Me.' You couldn't have done that better if you'd planned it for weeks." She chortled.

Sarah finally managed a weak smile, then a bigger one that warmed Tony's heart. "You're kidding." She chuckled and Tony heaved an inner sigh of relief. She was going to be okay. "I didn't even hear the music after he yanked the door latch off. We're going to have to install a stronger one, by the way. All I could hear was the blood rushing in my ears."

"You're not moving in here until we figure out what to do about Prescott." Tony leveled a hard stare at her. "We'll move in together after we get married, but for now, you probably need to stay at Noah's, okay? I'll come and live with you there until the wedding." He knew he was pulling rank, but he couldn't think of any other way to keep her safe.

"I can handle him." Sarah grimaced, then set her jaw. "I handled him today."

"We can all handle that little pischer." Julie cut the air with her hand, clearly still in Dirty Harry mode. "He ran like a wuss when Sarah and I threatened him. Honestly, I don't think he'll be back, but if he does show his face, Sarah's got her gun. She can handle him until you guys arrive."

"He'll be back." Sarah rose and paced the porch. "He's determined to have what he believes to be rightfully his. Surprisingly, I'm not really worried. He won't come with a weapon or anything. He's too cool for that. He thinks he can cow me with words and intimidation, but—"

Static from the radio on Tony's belt interrupted her, and Earl's voice came through loud and clear. "Tony, I'm out here on 115. There's been a wreck. Pretty bad. I think I've got a fatality on my hands and we need to shut down the road. If things are stable there, why don't you head out here?"

Sirens wailed down Forest Avenue as Tony pressed the button on the radio. "On my way." Shoving up from the settee, he reached for Sarah as she passed him in her pacing. "Babe, I gotta go, but I'll be back after we get this mess cleaned up."

"Go, I'm fine." Sarah met his gaze, a small smile curving the corners of her mouth. "I'm okay. Truly."

Hesitating, he placed both hands on her shoulders. "If he comes back, call me immediately."

"You're number one on my speed dial." She touched his cheek. "Go. We're under control here."

With the imprint of his kiss still warm on her lips, Sarah watched as Tony sped away, lights flashing, siren wailing. She shot an arrow of prayer heavenward for the victims of the crash before she plopped back into the settee.

"Man, excitement overload tonight." Julie had finally settled into the swing, but she pushed the wicker seat back and forth with one foot against the wood floor of the porch.

"I could do without it." Sarah shook her head. "Gotta tell you,

Jules, that gun and I are never gonna be friends. I've been so cocky—no pun intended—about learning to shoot. Going out to the range and hitting that freaking target, believing I could shoot that bastard and never feel a thing." She shrugged. "But the reality is completely different."

Julie gave a short bark of laughter. "I knew you'd never pull the trigger, kiddo, but *he* sure as hell didn't." She stretched one arm across the back of the swing, finally relaxing into the seat. "And maybe that's the key, you think? Having the gun is like insurance. The dudes who are gonna come through here looking for wives or girlfriends don't know you or me. They have no idea if we'll cower in a corner or shoot them straight through the heart. As long as they don't know for sure, we've always got the upper hand."

"That's one way to look at it." Sarah couldn't deny Julie's logic, but she still quivered inside thinking about how close she came to pulling the trigger. When the reality of actually needing the pistol occurred, she found out that having it wasn't the huge comfort she'd thought it would be—a disconcerting discovery given how hard over she'd been about owning the damn thing. "I think there's more of the pacifist than the vengeful victim in me, Jules."

"That's not a bad thing."

"What happens if some guy comes in with a bigger, badder gun?" Sarah couldn't stop the thoughts tumbling through her head. Funnily enough, even though she'd gone through a shooting mess at the Chicago shelter, where Julie's Will had been shot by an angry ex-husband, it still hadn't occurred to her to get a gun until Paul returned. Then finding one became such a priority that she'd gone out into the night to purchase one illegally. "Fear makes us stupid." The statement came out louder than she meant for it to, causing Julie to rear back in the swing, a doubtful expression on her beautiful face. "Guns aren't the answer."

She stared at Sarah for a moment. "So, what? You want to get rid of the gun after everything you've gone through to have it? The licensing? All the lessons and practice?" She shook her head. "*I* think you need one here. Even if it's just in a locked desk drawer in your office. Or in your nightstand by your bed."

"I'm going to keep the damn gun." Sarah dropped her head. "I just don't want to depend on it, you know? It'll be different here because I'll have Tony, but also because now that I've faced Paul, I see what a small, insignificant little jerk he really is. That's the case with all these abusers. They're just bullies. And how do you handle a bully? You don't let him push you around. You stand up. You don't take his crap."

Julie nodded. "You're absolutely right."

"Killing Paul won't bring Macy back." Sarah swallowed hard, not even fighting the tears that stung her eyelids. "Hating Paul won't do that, either, although I confess to truly hating him. But he didn't *murder* her. It was an accident caused by his anger and inattention. He deserved the prison time for what he did, but I have to believe"—she choked, swiping at her cheeks with her palms—"I *have* to believe his heart is broken too. He's broken."

Julie leaped up and snuggled next to Sarah on the settee, one arm around her shoulders. Murmuring little comforts, she rubbed Sarah's back and offered a crumpled tissue from her shorts pocket.

With a frown at the slightly shredded hanky, Sarah wiped her eyes and took a deep breath. "I need to forgive him for what happened to Macy. I *have* to do it for me and for Macy, so I can move on. If I'm going to make room in my heart for Tony's family, I've got to forgive him for Macy."

"Can you do that?" Julie tipped her head to give Sarah an encouraging smile.

"Yup." Sarah said with a nod. "I can. Right now as a matter of fact. He doesn't have to be here for it, right?" She rose, walked to the porch railing, and threw her hands into the air. "I forgive you, Paul Prescott!" Her voice echoed over the garden trellis. "I'm releasing all my pain to the universe and I'm moving on with my life. Macy will always, always live in my heart. I hope she'll live in yours too, and that you'll find some peace in your soul one day." She gazed out at the sunset coloring the sky all shades of pink and purple and orange. The intense beauty of it felt like an affirmation. "Do you hear me, Paul? I forgive you."

When she closed her eyes, her entire being lightened as if a suit of heavy armor had been removed from her chest and shoulders. Arms spread wide, she basked in the sensation of weightlessness, in the release, in the sense of pure joy.

"Hey, here comes Tony." Julie popped out of the settee to stand beside Sarah. They watched as he pulled his lanky body out of the squad car and stood for a few seconds talking on his radio. "He looks grim. Must've been a bad one. God rest the soul of the victim."

Sarah fought the urge to race down the walk to meet him, instead waiting for him to approach the porch.

He clomped up the stairs, his tread heavy. "Sarah, the accident... It was your ex."

Sarah's heart rose to her throat. "Is he hurt? Did he hurt someone else?"

Tony reached for her hand and knit his fingers with hers. "He's dead. Witnesses at the scene said he ignored the STOP sign at the crossing and just blasted through the intersection. A semi T-boned him."

"Is the driver of the semi hurt?"

"Not a scratch, but he's heartsick."

"Anyone else hurt?"

"Nope. Only Prescott. Died instantly as far as we can tell." Tony pulled her into his chest and Sarah's arms went around him. "I hate being the one bringing you this news, sweetheart."

"One of life's little ironies that it was his own anger and not mine that killed him," Sarah whispered, looking up into Tony's dear face. "It's okay, my love. I'm okay. As a matter of fact, I'm better than okay. I'm sorry he died, but I'm not sorry he's gone." She pressed a kiss to Tony's cheek and then kissed him full on the lips. "Time for us to move on. You and me…together."

CHAPTER 25

December 22

     Sarah leaned into the lighted mirror on Libby's desk, moving aside a stray auburn curl as she put the finishing touches on her makeup. She was alone for a few precious minutes since Julie, Carrie, Sophie, and Libby had left the bridal preparation room to check on last-minute details for the service and the reception. Everything was already perfect, but the Posse never rested.

"Miss Sarah?" The door opened a slit and Emma, Tony's four-year-old granddaughter, peered into the room.

"Hi, sweetie." Sarah spun around in the office chair and held out her arms. "Come on in."

Little Emma had captured her heart from the first moment she'd met the child when Tony took her to Chicago for Thanksgiving dinner at the home of his newly pregnant daughter, Olivia, and her family. As it turned out, she'd also met Tony's ex-wife, Shannon, and her partner, Francie, both of whom had charmed her almost as much as Emma. The couple was so thrilled Tony had finally found someone that she invited them to the wedding. They were out in the winery right now, ready to party.

Shannon had pulled her aside last night at the bachelor/bachelorette combo party Carrie and Liam had hosted at the Fishwife. "I knew he'd find someone perfect one day," she'd said, looking remarkably like Judy Collins with her long silvery hair, gypsy skirt, and handmade hemp sweater. "Love him with everything you've got, girl. He deserves it. He's got the biggest heart in the Midwest."

"Oh, I intend to." Sarah's own heart had swelled when she'd glanced over at Tony, who was deep in a conversation with Henry at the bar. In that moment, utter contentment had washed over her.

Tony had brought family to their marriage—unusual family in some respects, but family nonetheless—something Sarah had been hungry for since her parents died, and even more so after Macy's passing. Olivia, Brian, and Emma had accepted her without question. If Dad loved her, so did they, and apparently, Shannon and Francie were following suit, which warmed Sarah's heart no end since grandchildren meant sharing, divorced or not.

Now, Emma stared up at her, a serious expression in her golden-brown eyes, the same color as her grandfather's. "Mommy says you'll be my grandma after you marry Poppy tonight. Will you?"

Sarah gathered her close and kissed her dark silky hair. "I sure will. Is that okay with you?"

"Well, I already have three grandmas 'cause there's Granny and G-maw Francie and also Grandma Moe in Indiana."

"You think one more might be too many?"

Emma considered this, her big eyes serious as she chewed her lower lip. "Grandmas are awful nice. I think you should have as many as you can."

Sarah laughed and hugged the little girl. "I agree. I'm very excited about being your new grandma."

"Do I still have to call you Miss Sarah after you and Poppy are married?"

"What do you want to call me?"

"Um…" Emma toyed with the ivory satin ribbon trimming the lapels of Sarah's silk suit. "I could call you Grammy; that's what Jacob calls his grandma."

"Who's Jacob?"

"A boy at school. On Grandparents Day, he had *six* grandmas and grandpas there." Emma leaned in to sniff Sarah's hair. "You smell good."

"Thank you." Sarah gave her another little squeeze. "I like Grammy Sarah. Why don't we try that one on and see what we think?"

"Okay." Emma grinned and planted a big kiss on Sarah's cheek just as Olivia opened the door.

"Emma! There you are." She hurried over to grab her daughter. "Honey, don't mess up Sarah's outfit."

"She's fine, Olivia, truly." Sarah rose and smoothed her floor-length skirt.

"You look gorgeous, Sarah." Olivia smiled, gazing at her. "Dad's going to be bowled over."

"I sure hope so." Sarah had opted for the formal suit, rather than the velvet dress that Julie had campaigned for. It was a beautiful dress, but the elegant ivory silk skirt and peplum jacket suited Sarah's simple tastes. Her bouquet of red roses and baby's breath looked stunning against the creamy silk, while the baby's breath and mistletoe tiara in her hair added just the perfect touch of whimsy. She wore her mother's gold locket on a fine gold chain around her neck. The locket, containing pictures of her parents and Macy, rested next to her heart, while Tony's ruby glowed on her right hand, waiting to be fitted over the plain gold band they'd chosen as wedding rings.

Emma tugged on her mother's skirt. "Mommy, Miss Sarah and I 'cided I should call her Grammy Sarah, okay?"

"If it's okay with Miss Sarah, it's fine with me." Olivia ran her fingers through Emma's dark hair and straightened her flower tiara.

"I love it." Sarah gave the pair an affectionate smile. "Thank you so much for welcoming me so warmly."

Olivia stepped forward and pulled Sarah into an embrace. "Thank *you*. I've never seen Dad so happy."

"He makes me pretty happy too." Sarah returned the hug, fighting tears. "Don't make me cry. I finally got my makeup perfect."

"Okay, no crying 'til later." Olivia touched Sarah's cheek, then leaned down to Emma. "Kidlet, it's time to get you ready to walk down the aisle. Where's your basket of flower petals?"

"I put it on the chair in the back row so I wouldn't lose it." Emma marched to the door, letting in the murmur of voices of the people gathering for the ceremony—a crowd that included everyone from the village who could make it and even the three women who were currently residents of Macy's Garden Gate. Perry's booming guffaw and Bertie's high-pitched answering giggle floated over the other voices, and Sarah couldn't help smiling. This town had captured her heart. She was finally home.

As Olivia and Emma left, Julie, Carrie, and Sophie spilled into the room, laughing and oohing and ahhing over Emma's dark green velvet dress and flower headpiece. Her friends were all dressed alike in deep forest green street-length dresses that they'd fashioned after the velvet cocktail dress Rosemary Clooney had worn in *White Christmas*. Sarah had fallen in love with the idea, as that was one of her favorite holiday movies, and the gowns had turned out fabulous. "You guys look so amazing!"

"So do the menfolk," Carrie said. The guys had chosen black tuxes with dark green brocade vests and bow ties. Their boutonnieres were red roses with holly leaves, adding to the holiday theme of the wedding. "Everybody is Christmasy and gorgeous."

"I can't believe Libby pulled this whole thing off in just two months." When Sarah shook her head, another tendril of hair slipped from the elegant knot at the base of her neck. "Dammit, my hair keeps pulling out of the bun."

"It's adorable; don't touch it," Julie commanded. "Libby says everything's on target. You ready to do this thing?"

"I am ready." Sarah picked up her bouquet and turned to face her friends. She took a deep breath. "I know this is a moment when I should have something profound to say about dear friends and unwavering support and how much you all mean to me." She blinked. "But you know me. If I start talking, I won't shut up and I'll blubber and so will you. We look perfect, so please consider it all said, okay? I love you guys so much. Thank you for...everything."

"We love you too, sweetie." Carrie touched a tissue to the corner of her eye as Sophie sniffed audibly.

Julie cleared her throat loudly. "For God's sake, you saps, cut it out. Listen." She shushed them with one finger to her lips. "Jack's started playing."

Sure enough, when Sarah peeked out, Jack Reilly, Carrie and Liam's son, who was a remarkable musician, was seated at the electric keyboard he'd set up near the fireplace. The strains of "Jésu, Joy of Man's Desiring" soared into the open door of the little office. Second time through was the cue, so Carrie started out the door, followed by Sophie, and then Julie, who paused in the doorway to glance back at Sarah, give her a thumbs-up, and mouth the words *I'm so proud of you.*

Sarah stepped to the end of the aisle between the rows of white folding chairs that Daniel and Libby had set up for guests. A long red runner extended from where she stood to the broad stone hearth where a fire crackled merrily and white lights twinkled on a huge Douglas fir. The air was redolent with pine, the wood of the fire, and the scent of the candles glowing around the room. The white flower petals that Emma had scattered looked like snow against the deep ruby fabric. Her heart ached a bit that Macy wasn't part of the wedding party, but she was convinced her daughter's spirit was present. She'd felt her near more frequently here in Willow Bay than she had in the eight years since her death. Macy would approve; Sarah didn't have a single doubt.

She stopped for the briefest of moments as Jack switched from Bach to the opening notes of the old Etta James song that she'd chosen to walk up the aisle to—"At Last." It was a surprise for Tony, who she had discovered had a passion for old torch singers and music from the forties and fifties. His eyes widened when Skyler Hiatt, the singer whose CD he'd played for her the first night they'd made love, stepped from her seat near Jack's piano and began to sing in her signature sultry voice. Sarah exchanged a quick smile and wink with Carrie, who'd used her influence with the singer to make her appearance possible.

Sarah stood still for the first few bars of the old tune, but when Tony met her eyes, offered that inimitable dimpled grin, and crooked one finger, she stepped forward. His expression of sheer delight drew her to him like steel to a magnet as she walked up the aisle between the rows of guests who had all risen in her honor.

Skyler held the last note as Tony extended one hand to Sarah, meeting her in front of the minister. Her heart pounded as she took his hand, laced her fingers with his, and gazed up at the man who was very nearly her husband. This was right. Anticipation, perfect peace, joy, and hunger for Tony filled her up as the minister began the old words, "Dearly beloved…"

When he got to the part in the service where he asked, "Who gives this woman to be married to this man?" Sarah laughed out loud with pure pleasure. "I give myself," she announced firmly.

Tony didn't hesitate a second. His "And I give myself," brought a rumble of laughter from the guests and warmed Sarah right down to her satin pumps. Before she knew it, the minister was pronouncing them husband and wife together and inviting them to kiss to close the ceremony.

Tony's eyes shimmered with moisture when he gazed down into her face. "Hello, wife." His voice was husky.

Sarah blinked back her own tears and said in a soft voice filled with wonder, "We're married, Deputy."

"You bet your sweet butt we're married, Susannah Elizabeth Boatwright Sarah Everett Bennett Reynard."

And the laughter and applause from the villagers became background music as their lips met and clung.

Once More From the Top

What do you do when the one who got away…comes back?

Carrie Halligan never regretted the choice she made sixteen years ago to raise her son Jack by herself in Willow Bay, Michigan. A successful photographer by day, at night Carrie satisfies her musical passions by playing piano at a hotel bar, maintaining a balance that works for her and Jack. Walking away from Maestro Liam Reilly without telling him she was pregnant with his child may have been the hardest thing she'd ever done, but it was definitely the right thing.

When Liam shows up in town to perform a benefit concert with the local symphony, however, Carrie's carefully crafted life spins out of control. After sending Jack to summer camp, she realizes she can't keep Liam in the dark forever. Telling the truth to the man she once loved more than life itself isn't near as hard as spending time in his presence and realizing that the years haven't diminished his power over her heart. Will her lie be too much to get past, or will the spark of passion between them overcome everything?

Available at: <u>Amazon</u> | <u>Barnes and Noble</u> | <u>Kobo</u> | <u>Smashwords</u>

Sex and the Widow Miles

His life ended. Hers didn't.

Beautiful and aging gracefully, Julie Miles was looking forward to retirement with her husband, Dr. Charlie Miles, in their idyllic Willow Bay, Michigan home. But when Charlie dies of a heart attack, simply getting out of bed becomes a daily struggle. Desperate for a change of scene, she leaves her home to stay in her friend Carrie's unoccupied Chicago apartment.

Her handsome and younger new neighbor, Will Brody, seems to enjoy his assignment to keep an eye on her, and Jules can't help but be flattered. She embraces life—and sex—again, until the discovery of a dark secret shatters her world once more. She knows her feelings for Will are more than casual, and he's made it clear he wants her, but how can she ever trust a man again when her perfect life turned out to be a lie? Determined to get to the bottom of it all, Jules goes in search of the truth and discovers that there's always a second chance to find real love.

Available at <u>Amazon</u> | <u>Barnes and Noble</u> | <u>Kobo</u> | <u>Smashwords</u>

The Summer of Second Chances
It's never too late to start over…

When Sophie Russo inherits two lakeside cottages in Willow Bay, Michigan, she thinks she can start over with a peaceful, quiet summer.

Boy, is she wrong.

First, there's Henry Dugan, the nerdy genius behind the GeekSpeak publishing empire, who has rented Sophie's second cottage so he can write his novel. The instant attraction catches them both off guard. He's fresh off a brutal divorce, and Sophie's still grieving her beloved Papa Leo, so this is no time to start a relationship, but a casual summer fling might be an option…

Then Sophie's long-lost mother barrels onto the scene and opens up a long-buried mystery involving Depression-era mobsters and a missing cache of gold coins worth millions that some present-day hoodlums would like to get their hands on.

Suddenly, Sophie's quiet summer becomes a dangerous dance with her grandfather's dark past. With Henry at her side–and in her bed–Sophie needs to find a way to make peace with the past and look toward the future… assuming she lives that long.

Available at <u>Amazon.com</u> | <u>Barnes and Noble.com</u> |<u>Kobo</u>| <u>Smashwords</u>

ABOUT THE AUTHOR

Nan Reinhardt is a *USA Today* bestselling author of romantic fiction for women in their prime. Yeah, women still fall in love and have sex, even after 45! Imagine! She is also a wife, a mom, a mother-in-law, and a grandmother. She's been an antiques dealer, a bank teller, a stay-at-home mom, a secretary, and for the last 20 years, she's earned her living as a freelance copyeditor and proofreader.

But writing is Nan's first and most enduring passion. She can't remember a time in her life when she wasn't writing—she wrote her first romance novel at the age of ten, a love story between the most sophisticated person she knew at the time, her older sister (who was in high school and had a driver's license!) and a member of Herman's Hermits. If you remember who they are, *you* are Nan's audience! She's still writing romance, but now from the viewpoint of a wiser, slightly rumpled, menopausal woman who believes that love never ages, women only grow more interesting, and everybody needs a little sexy romance.

Visit Nan's website: www.nanreinhardt.com
Facebook: https://www.facebook.com/authornanreinhardt
Twitter: @NanReinhardt
Talk to Nan at: nan@nanreinhardt.com

CPSIA information can be obtained
at www.ICGtesting.com
Printed in the USA
FSHW010950310320
68661FS